TARA SUE ME
THE Master

headline
ETERNAL

Published by arrangement with NAL,
A member of Penguin Group (USA) LLC,
A Penguin Random House Company

First published in Great Britain in 2016
by HEADLINE ETERNAL
An imprint of HEADLINE PUBLISHING GROUP

1

Cataloguing in Publication Data is available from the British Library

ISBN 978 1 4722 2656 3

Offset in Perpetua by Avon DataSet Ltd, Bidford-on-Avon, Warwickshire

Printed and bound by CPI Group (UK) Ltd, Croydon, CR0 4YY

MIX
Paper from
responsible sources
FSC® C104740

Headline's policy is to use papers that are natural, renewable and recyclable
products and made from wood grown in well-managed forests and other
controlled sources. The logging and manufacturing processes are expected to
conform to the environmental regulations of the country of origin.

HEADLINE PUBLISHING GROUP
An Hachette UK Company
Carmelite House
50 Victoria Embankment
London EC4Y 0DZ

www.headlineeternal.com
www.headline.co.uk
www.hachette.co.uk

To Danielle and Elle, who love Cole more than I do.

Acknowledgments

From the day *Seduced By Fire* was published, I've had people asking for Cole's story. It's humbling as an author to have such interest in a character. It's also scary as hell.

The truth is, Cole wouldn't be the character he is without the aid of two people. My eternal thanks to Cyndy, who was kind enough to tell me Cole was flat and boring in an early draft of *Seduced*. And to Danielle, who said, "You should go talk to him again. I think he's a Brit." Truly, you two, this book wouldn't exist without you.

Raechel, you are, as always, invaluable. My humble thanks to you.

Tina, when I read your thoughts after you read the manuscript, I breathed a sigh of relief. Thank you for being in my corner.

Anne Marie and Amy, who share in the Gandy love and my sister, for saying, "Who?"

Claire, Jenn, and the entire Penguin team, who've been as enthusiastic as I am about this book.

Steve, who made it happen.

To those who have pushed, encouraged, and supported me with tweets, texts, e-mails, and messages, when I'm having a particularly difficult day, you keep me going and make me smile.

I think there has to be a special crown in heaven for the spouses of authors. They put up with so much. After all, Mr. Sue Me not only has to deal with me, but all the people who live in my head. He does it all and he never complains.

Finally, for everyone who said, "Yes, but when is Cole's story out?" I hope you find it worthy.

Chapter One

She was going to have to book an extended session with her therapist.

Sasha Blake closed her eyes and tried to take deep cleansing breaths like she'd been told to do when the familiar panic started to take over. But the sharp claws of fear and dread grabbed onto her chest and the simple act of inhaling took more strength than necessary.

"Sasha?" Nathaniel asked. "Are you okay?"

She cracked one eye open. The Dominant in charge of running the meeting looked at her with concern. She focused on him and did her best to ignore everything and everyone else.

"Yes, Master West," she said. "I'm fine."

Fine. Her pat reply to everything. She was fine. Work was fine. Her back was fine. And being told the Partners in Play senior members had decided she could rejoin the BDSM group after a retraining with Cole Johnson?

Abso-freaking-fine.

She was sitting in a small room off to the side of Daniel Covington's playroom where group meetings were held. Only the senior members were present, which meant there were only about ten people sitting around the oval table at the moment.

The side of her face tingled as if someone was staring at her and she slipped her hands under her thighs to keep from rubbing the spot. She used more discipline than what should be necessary to keep her gaze directed on Nathaniel and not to let it wander just a touch to the right, where *he* sat.

Items numbered one through five hundred twelve to discuss with her therapist: Cole Johnson.

Based on conversations she'd had recently—with Nathaniel; his wife, Abby; her own best friend, Julie; and Julie's Dominant, Daniel—she'd expected to be offered a retraining. She'd even looked forward to it: experiencing the thrill of letting someone else take over, rediscovering the peace that came when she knew her Dom would do anything to protect her—and, she wasn't even going to pretend otherwise, having earth-shattering orgasms.

It'd not once crossed her mind, not even in her wildest, craziest, never-gonna-happen-might-as-well-fantasize-about-it dreams, that the group would pick him.

Cole.

She shivered just thinking his name. An alien spaceship must have transported her to an alternate universe because that's how hard it was to believe Cole was going to retrain her. He was an altogether intriguing man, one who had quickly captured her attention. But though he was usually laid-back and easygoing, talk among the group's submissives pointed toward a hard and unyielding Dominant in the playroom.

She didn't have to glance to Nathaniel's right to know who

she'd find watching her. She pictured him all too clearly in her head. Dark tousled hair, devilish blue-green eyes, and a body that seductively hinted at sexual pleasure with every carefully controlled move. And then he'd speak in that oh-so-smooth British accent.

Yes, she'd call her therapist tomorrow.

"Are you okay?"

She jumped at the sound of her friend Dena's whisper.

"I'm fine," she said, repeating the same lie she'd told Nathaniel.

Dena narrowed her eyes in disbelief and rubbed her just-starting-to-show pregnant belly. "Hmm."

But she was stopped from saying anything further by Nathaniel dismissing the meeting. *Perfect.* If she moved quickly enough, she could probably be on her way without having to talk about anything.

Unfortunately, Dena was onto her ploy and grabbed her arm before she could get away. "Not so fast; I want to talk. It's been a long night for you. How do you feel about Master Johnson?"

Her body shook a bit. She had to leave before the panic came back. But Dena looked determined and wouldn't let her leave that easily.

"Conflicted." Sasha took a deep breath. "He's not who I imagined would be suggested." She didn't add that he was the very last person she imagined would be suggested. She narrowed her eyes. "Wait a minute. You're a senior group member. Did you know?"

"No, I excused myself when the topic came up for discussion. I knew I couldn't be objective."

"And Jeff?"

"Yes, I'm sure he knew."

Sasha put her hand on her hip. She found it hard to believe Jeff, Dena's husband, wouldn't have told Dena even if she'd excused herself from the discussion—which made her wonder if Julie knew. After all, she lived with Daniel.

She turned to find the lady in question making a beeline toward her.

"I had a feeling that was going to happen," Julie said. "Are you okay? If you don't want Cole, I'll—"

"Julie. Dena," the smooth British accent she heard in her dreams said.

Sasha spun around and found Cole standing off to her side. "Sasha."

He spoke it like a caress. Soft and gentle and tender, but with an underlying strength that couldn't be denied and with sensual promises woven in every vowel sound. She had an overwhelming desire to hear him say it again.

She opened her mouth, but nothing came out. *Damn it, this is why I should have left right when I stood up.*

"Master Johnson," Julie and Dena said in unison.

"Master West," Cole said to Nathaniel, who stood a few feet away with his arm around Abby. "If I may, I'd like a word in private with Julie and Sasha."

Nathaniel didn't answer right away but eyed Sasha up and down, as if making sure she was okay. He frowned. Hell, did she look that bad?

"Fifteen minutes," Nathaniel said. "You can use the kitchen. Master Covington?"

"I'll come get Julie then," Daniel said from his spot beside Abby.

Cole extended his arm. "After you, ladies."

They made it into the kitchen without speaking. Cole pulled chairs out for both of them and then settled into his own. He smiled, and Sasha found herself questioning the things she'd heard about him.

This was the Badass Brit?

"Anyone care for a drink?" he asked. "I should have asked you before sitting down."

"No, thank you, Sir," Julie said.

"I'm fine, Sir," Sasha quipped.

At her flippant reply, Cole narrowed his eyes and his smile faded away into a frown of displeasure. And in that moment, Sasha knew everything she'd heard about him was true.

Cole Johnson kept his gaze focused on Sasha long enough for her to understand he recognized her answer for what it was. He suspected she'd been fighting back a panic attack and was most likely anything but *fine*. Against his better judgment, he decided not to call her on it. This time.

He wondered what he'd gotten himself into.

When Nathaniel approached him about it, he'd agreed almost at once. In his mind he pictured Sasha as he'd first met her: a scared submissive dealing with the aftermath of a scene gone bad. He remembered catching her the night she almost fell and how she'd been warm and responsive in his arms. That is, until she'd realized where she was and used her safe word to get away from him.

In India weeks later, he was surprised at how often he found his mind wandering back to the troubled woman with the expressive green eyes and a will of steel. And he couldn't deny he'd been secretly pleased when he heard a rumor she was thinking about rejoining the group. He'd been a Dom long enough to understand the strength involved in going through a traumatic scene and returning once more to the community. He respected that strength. He also had a strong desire to control it.

He cleared his throat. "We only have fifteen minutes and I'm positive Daniel is keeping an eye on the time, so let's chivvy this along." He leaned back in the chair so he could watch both women. "It appears as if my reputation precedes me and you're both, no doubt, wondering what the group was thinking with their recommendation."

Humor flashed in Julie's eyes along with something else, but she wasn't saying anything. She hadn't been all that shocked when he'd been named; unlike Sasha, who at this moment stared at him like she'd dash out of the room if he said, "Boo."

He drummed his fingertips on the table. There was a time to push a submissive—this was not one of those times. He needed to draw her to him, to gain her trust, make a connection.

"How's the kitten?" he asked her.

Last weekend Nathaniel and Abby had a party for Jeff and Dena. While everyone was outside, a snake attacked a stray kitten. Cole and Nathaniel had rescued it, but afterward they couldn't calm it down. Cole had held the wiggling mass of fur at a loss about what to do until Sasha simply took the frightened kitten from him and had the creature purring within seconds. It'd been that confidence she showed, the way she pushed aside her fear because her desire to help the kitten was more important, that had made him accept the group's request to retrain her.

As he'd suspected, at the mention of her rescued kitten, Sasha's face lost all traces of worry and fear and a tender smile took their place. "She's doing great, Sir. Plays a lot, eats a lot, and sleeps in front of the refrigerator."

He couldn't hide his smile at her excitement over the little ball of fur. "I'm glad she found you. Sounds like the two of you have hit it off."

She nodded. "I like having her around. I mean, I know she's just a kitten, but it makes the apartment not so lonely."

From the corner of his eye, he saw Julie discreetly check the time. Daniel would be back soon.

Cole cleared his throat. "I can understand your surprise at the group's recommendation, Sasha." She opened her mouth like she was going to say something to the contrary, but he shook his head. "No need to hide your feelings. You were quite gobsmacked when Master West made his announcement."

She pressed her lips together and with that small move, he caught just a glimpse of the feisty submissive he'd heard she was before the Peter incident.

He leaned forward. "The simple truth is, I require a great deal from my sexual partners, and you're not prepared to meet those demands. That's the main reason I was selected for you. Since I know your body is off limits, I'll take my time getting your mind prepared to submit again."

Her jaw dropped. "What?"

"What's the body's most important sex organ?" he asked.

"The mind," Sasha said.

"Right. And we hear it so frequently, the answer is often given without thought." He watched her fingers inch forward on the table slightly. She pulled them back and repeated the motion several times until Julie stopped her with a hand. He continued. "So let's take a moment to think about it. Sex starts in the mind. Submission starts in the mind. As a Dominant, I have to earn my place in your mind before I can earn the right to take you physically. Am I making sense?"

Her voice was calm when she replied, "Fuck the mind before you fuck the body?"

He held her gaze for a long moment until she lowered hers. "Yes, precisely. Which is why I won't be fucking your body. Just your mind, Sasha."

She let out her breath in a half-swallowed sigh and looked at the table. "I understand, Sir."

He bit back his laugh. She might understand, but she wasn't happy about it. "Any questions?"

Sasha shook her head.

"No, Sir," Julie said. "Thank you for explaining."

Daniel walked into the kitchen and stood in the shadows behind Julie.

"When I work with a new submissive," Cole said, "I want to weave myself into her thoughts so that each movement she makes is made with me in mind. I want her to feel my presence when we're apart as strongly as she does when we're together. I'll do it slowly, Sasha." He allowed his gaze to wander over her body. She was a striking woman. "So methodically, you won't notice. And no, I won't fuck your body, but I believe you'll find our mental play nearly as intimate, if not more so, than physical play."

As he'd spoken, she'd leaned slightly toward him, lips parting. He resisted moving closer to her. Yes, he thought, this one would test his own control.

He turned to the other woman sitting at the table. "Julie, what was it you noticed first about Daniel?"

"His eyes."

"Why his eyes?"

"They were so blue and deep and intense." She shivered. "It was almost as if he knew me, though we'd never met."

"And when you're in the middle of a scene, why would he have you meet his gaze?"

"To ground me. Refocus my attention on him. But it's more than that. It's like he's speaking to something deep within me."

Cole kept his voice low and even, drawing out Julie's replies without difficulty. "And when he has to correct you and you look into his eyes, what do you see?"

"Guilt. Remorse. He'll look so sad." She blinked away a few tears. "I don't want him sad. I want him happy and—"

"That's enough, Cole," Daniel interrupted, walking to the table. He stood behind Julie, his hands rubbing her shoulders. "I said you could talk, not play your mind games."

"You know I wouldn't—"

"Your fifteen minutes are up. You two take as long as you need." He pulled the chair back and lifted Julie into his arms. "Let's go upstairs, kitten."

She wrapped her arms around him. "I'm sorry. It just made me remember . . ."

"It's okay." Whatever else he said was too low for Cole to make out.

Sasha's shoulders curled when Julie left with Daniel, almost as if she was protecting herself. Cole didn't like the implication she was afraid to be alone with him. But maybe it had been the implication something had happened recently between Julie and Daniel.

Whatever it was, he wanted to see the fire return to Sasha. It was buried somewhere deep inside her and he needed to entice it back where it belonged.

He was confident that with enough time and patience, he could restore her submissive spirit. Maybe not the same as she was before, but possibly stronger and more knowledgeable. And he was honest enough to admit he'd really like to see her sassy and sharp attitude back. He loved playing with a sub who had spunk.

"Sasha," he said. She looked up from her lap and her eyes held such a cacophony of emotions—longing, regret, hope, trepidation, and anticipation—he wanted nothing more than to whisper encouragement until she believed him. In a way, he realized, this retraining was almost like an extended aftercare session.

His typical preference for aftercare involved hugging his submissive close with her head on his chest. He hadn't been dishonest when he told Sasha he expected much from his sexual partners. After such intense play, he'd found he needed that time as much as his sub did. Time to simply wrap his arms around the woman who'd trusted him with her submission. This, however, was the first time he felt the urge to hold someone *before* they did anything.

He would have to be careful with Sasha. Slowly earn her trust. Keep his hands to himself and limit anything physical. For the moment, though, he needed to know if she was in the right frame of mind to talk more or if he needed to see her home. "How are you feeling?" he asked.

She shrugged and turned her focus back down at her lap. "Fine, Sir."

Hell to the fucking no. He wasn't going to put up with that. "Eyes on me until I tell you otherwise." He leaned forward. Whether she was in the right frame of mind for a discussion or not, there were things she needed to understand about how their time would go. "The most important rule I have, the one that is not negotiable, the one that if you can't agree to, we will end this now, is that there must always be complete honesty between us. I play too intensely for anything less. Think about my requirement and whether you can meet it. If you think you can, give me a verbal response and properly answer the question I asked."

Something flashed in her eyes. If he hadn't been watching her so intently, he might have missed it. But it was there for the briefest of seconds. He wasn't sure, but he thought it was longing.

You're going to have to watch yourself around this one.

A needy submissive, longing to serve. A wounded soul, needing protection. She pushed damn near every button he had. After Kate's rejection after all those years together, something deep inside had broken. And how much more did Sasha need healing after being physically injured in a scene? Perhaps in helping Sasha to heal, he could heal himself.

"I agree with your requirement, Sir," she said so softly he could barely hear.

And that wouldn't do. He wondered why sometimes she was forceful and others she was almost mousey. "Say it again with authority. Own the words you speak. Language is too important to waste with a murmur."

Her eyes flashed, and when she spoke again, there was no doubt she meant it. "I agree with your requirement, Sir."

"Much better, little one. You make me think there's a hellcat buried under that mousey exterior after all."

"I am *not* mousey, Sir."

He cocked an eyebrow and hid his grin. "Good, because mousey submissives have no business kneeling before me. I only dominate women strong enough to know their own minds, those who respect their bodies enough to yield control to a Dominant willing to take it. And make no mistake; what I take, I take completely."

She trembled at his words.

"I'm not feeling fine, Sir," she said in a rush.

He held her gaze for several seconds, making sure she knew how accurately he'd read her. "I didn't think you were. As a result, the word 'fine' has been banished from your vocabulary. You're not to say it, write it, or think it. Understood?"

"Yes, Sir."

He nodded. "Let's try again. How are you feeling?"

She didn't glance at her lap like the first time. Instead, she kept her eyes on him. "I'm tired, and that disappoints me because I know we need to discuss things."

"It would be more of a problem if we tried to discuss or negotiate anything whilst you were spent. There are enough problems in life without knowingly inviting more, wouldn't you agree?"

"Yes, Sir."

This time he let his grin show. "So compliant, little one. It makes me curious as to how you will act when you don't agree with me." Conflicting emotions crossed her face. "We'll worry about it then. For now, we need to get you home. If you're free tomorrow afternoon, we can meet at the coffee shop down from your place for a discussion."

"Thank you, Sir." She moved to push back her chair, but he held out a hand to still her.

"One more thing. Since I've agreed to retrain you, as of tonight you are under my protection. I hold that responsibility in the highest of regards." He waited until her eyes glistened with understanding before adding, "Be it ever so temporary, until further notice, you are mine."

Chapter Two

When the clock beside her bed read four o'clock in the morning, Sasha gave up all pretense of sleeping. She hated insomnia. She'd experienced it frequently following the incident with Peter, but until today it'd been months since she had been unable to sleep all night.

Pulling on the robe she kept at the foot of her bed, she padded into the kitchen to make coffee. It didn't take much thought to figure out why she couldn't sleep. Every time she closed her eyes, she saw Cole Johnson. Her mind wouldn't stop spinning as she tried to make sense of the fact that he was going to be the one who would retrain her.

Why? That was her first question. Why Cole when there were several other Dominants within the group who could do it? Why did Cole agree to the arrangement when he could have any submissive he wanted? Why decide to retrain a submissive so messed up he couldn't even have sex with her?

She hadn't had sex in over nine months, not since Peter. Sometimes she wondered if she'd ever enjoy sex again. Her sexuality was so deeply entwined with her need to submit, it didn't seem possible to have one without the other. She feared she'd never be at the place where she could completely give herself to a Dominant. Cole certainly had his work cut out for him.

She leaned against the counter while the coffeepot gurgled and sputtered. She wished it were a weekday. If it were, Julie would be arriving at their floral shop downstairs in a few hours and they could talk. But it was Sunday and Julie lived with Daniel now. She was collared, bound to him. Sasha no longer felt comfortable dropping by unannounced like she'd done in the past.

"Doesn't really matter," she said to the empty kitchen. "It's not like you would call her at four in the morning anyway."

She poured a cup of coffee and walked over to a window overlooking the historic district. What were the odds Cole was up and looking out his window right now? Was he a light sleeper? Did he hog the covers?

With a shake of her head, she forced herself to stop. He was the Dominant selected to retrain her, and they had no relationship beyond that. She would never know which side of the bed he preferred or if he was a grouch before he had coffee.

Suddenly, she felt very alone.

Everyone else in the group was pairing up lately. Julie had Daniel. Dena had Jeff. And Abby and Nathaniel had been married forever.

As if hearing her thoughts, Pip, the stray kitten, meowed softly and butted her head against her ankles. Sasha reached down and picked her up.

"Thank goodness I'm not totally alone. I have you."

Pip started to purr and Sasha buried her face in the soft white fur. Doing so reminded her of the day Cole and Nathaniel rescued her. Cole didn't quite know how to handle the newly-freed-from-certain-death kitten, especially when the poor animal struggled to get away. But when Sasha had taken her from him, Cole had looked at her strangely. She wasn't sure what it was, maybe surprise? But there was something else she couldn't put her finger on.

She took a long sip of coffee. Was Cole a dog person? No, probably not. He traveled too much. *Jesus.* She tried not to think about him, but the questions just kept coming. Would he be staying in Delaware long? How long would he need to retrain her?

She knew he and his previous submissive, who'd also been his long-term girlfriend, had broken up months ago. She'd never heard exactly what had happened between the two of them. She'd picked up bits and pieces about Cole and Kate from listening to other group members. She knew they had been together for eight years before they split and that Kate had left him.

Maybe Julie would know more, since Daniel and Cole were such close friends. And Dena had been in the group for a long time. It wouldn't hurt to ask her a few questions. But it would probably be best to talk to Abby. After all, Abby was the one Sasha had sat down with first to discuss coming back to the group, after she'd given Nathaniel her paperwork.

Sasha liked Abby. She was easygoing and fun to be around. More so than her husband. Nathaniel was too quiet and intense for Sasha's taste.

But, she pondered, how much did she really want to know about Kate? What would a woman be like who dated a man such as Cole for so long? Not just date, but live with. She tried to imagine what it would be like to live with him: sharing a bathroom and fighting over the toothpaste, sitting on a couch watching a movie, and curling up in bed after a long day.

It all seemed too domestic for how she pictured him.

She set Pip down, poured herself another cup of coffee, and made her way to the living room couch, where she'd left her knitting. After the incident with Peter, she'd discovered knitting kept her mind calm. The meeting with Cole looming before her this afternoon, some time with her knitting needles was just what she needed.

Currently, she was working on baby blankets for the local hospital. On her most recent trip to the craft store, she'd found the softest yarn. It'd been on sale and she'd bought every bit they had. Already she had two blankets completed. Putting her coffee aside, she got comfortable and started on the third.

She was almost late meeting him. He sent a text midmorning asking if two o'clock would be good for their coffee shop discussion. She'd replied back that would work and went to take a shower, only to discover she had no hot water. She found the problem and fixed it, then walked into the living room to be greeted by yarn pulled all over the floor. She cursed Pip under her breath, but knew she could only blame herself. She'd been so frazzled by Cole's phone call, she hadn't put her knitting away. By the time she cleaned the mess up, she was running short on time.

She closed her eyes and took a deep breath as the coffee shop's door closed behind her. Someone had just baked a fresh batch of croissants. The warm yeasty smell greeted her and her stomach rumbled. With everything going on with the water heater and the yarn mess, she hadn't had time to eat lunch.

Food would have to wait a little bit longer, though. She glanced around the shop and started slightly when she found Cole watching her intently from a secluded booth in the far corner. He lifted an eyebrow when their eyes met. She gave what she hoped was a convincing smile and made her way toward him.

"Sasha," he said, standing with a smile and waving her into the booth. "How are you today?"

She slid into the booth across from him. "I'm fi—" she started, but then stopped, remembering his words from the previous night. "If you must know, Sir, I didn't sleep well last night. My water heater went out and I had to fix it so I could take a shower. Then I walked into the living room and Pip had dragged my yarn all over the floor. I didn't have a chance to eat lunch because I ran out of time. I'm tired and hungry, and more than a little apprehensive about the discussion we're about to have."

He gave her an easy smile. "See? Look at everything I would have missed out on hearing about had I not stripped that horrid word from your vocabulary yesterday."

Because she pictured him as a stern Dominant, the jovial, easygoing side of his everyday personality caught her off guard. "I've never thought of it as a horrid word, but I do see your point, Sir."

He leaned forward. "Because of the discussion we're having today, I'm going to ask that you call me 'Cole.' We'll save 'Sir' for when we're more formal."

She nodded. He wasn't pleased she'd called him "Sir," but something about the order he gave her started a fire deep in her belly. Something she hadn't experienced in a very long time. God, she'd missed this so much.

"Also," he continued, "I'm normally not overly strict about diet, but you're much too thin to be skipping meals. I'm going to get you a sandwich and, whilst I'm gone, I'd like for you to think about your goals in being retrained."

It wouldn't take much time for her sandwich to be prepared. In fact, he was gone mere minutes before reappearing with the ham and cheese she requested. But even though he'd told her to be thinking about her goals, he didn't question her about them right away.

She took a bite of the sandwich and hummed in bliss. It was so good. She gulped down two more bites.

"Slowly," he said, and his voice dropped an octave, taking on a slow and seductive quality. "Take your time. People have a tendency to rush through meals. Enjoy it. Savor every bite. The croissant has just come from the oven and the cheese is a sharp cheddar. I've lived in enough remote areas that I've learned to appreciate the joy of fresh food. Allow yourself time to simply enjoy your sense of taste."

Lord help her, he was talking about a sandwich. But more than that, he was giving her orders about eating a sandwich. She would have thought that would turn her off, but instead it further stoked the fire in her belly.

"Now," he said, looking pleased with himself and amused once again. God, he was smug. "I'm not sure what you've heard about me, but judging by your expression last night, I'm guessing the rumor is I break submissives and eat them for breakfast?"

"And pick your teeth with their bones," she said after swallowing a bite, in as much of a deadpan voice as she could manage.

"Right." His left eyebrow quirked up. "But never more than two before lunch."

"Of course not. That would be uncouth."

He laughed. "Uncouth, hmm? I believe, Sasha, that you and I are going to get along famously."

For just a second she wanted to pretend he wasn't just the Dom who was retraining her. That his words meant more than what he intended. But she knew she couldn't, she needed to remember at all times this was not a permanent relationship or one that involved feelings.

"Speaking of which, I thought we should start things out slowly." He leaned back and she was struck by how his every movement seemed methodical, intentional. It wasn't just his voice that drew her in, it was everything about him.

She hadn't expected someone with his reputation to do anything slow. It made her apprehension ease a bit. "Slow would be good."

"I think we should start out by meeting twice a week. And we'll be in touch some way every day." He watched her as if she was the most important thing in the world. He cataloged her reactions, studied her responses. With anyone else, she would have felt self-conscious, but under his scrutiny, she felt protected.

"Isn't that a lot?" she asked. "Every day?"

"Not if I plan to get inside that mind of yours." He said it with a smile, but his tone was serious.

"Okay." She nodded. "You're still staying at Daniel's?"

"For now. I'm actually in the market for a new place."

"In Wilmington?"

"Yes, I like this area and the people. It's one of the perks of my job. I can work remotely from anywhere."

She could only nod, momentarily dazed by the news that he'd be staying in Wilmington for good. Knowing he'd be leaving after her retraining would have helped drive home the fact they weren't in a relationship.

"You wouldn't happen to know any estate agents, Realtors, would you?" he asked.

"I know people from all professions. One of the perks of *my* job." He smiled.

"Let me look over some names," she said. "I'll give you a few next time we talk."

"Thank you."

A waitress came to check on them. Cole assured her they had everything they needed. He looked so normal, so everyday. So very far removed from how she heard he acted in the playroom.

"Will we meet at Daniel's guesthouse?" she asked when the woman walked away.

"I think so. Would you have a problem with that?"

"No, I'm over that way a lot anyway." She waited to see if he would say anything about seeing her there. Since he lived at the guesthouse, it was possible he'd noticed her at Daniel's before. But he just inclined his head slightly.

She remembered the one time she'd run into him at Daniel's. She'd been helping Julie with some planting and suddenly he was standing over them. Her heart had jumped to her chest until she took note of the beautiful woman at his side. The woman he later did a violet-wand demo on. She bet he was some kind of wonderful with that tool.

"I'd like to leave our time together open-ended," he said. "Until we get into it, I won't have an idea of how long we'll potentially need."

"That makes sense."

"We'll discuss it along the way, agree on the timing together."

"Of course."

He reached to his side and picked something up. When he placed it on the table, she saw it was a journal.

"I'm a writer," he said. "As such, I place a lot of weight on the written word. I want you to spend time putting your thoughts down on paper. Every day. I'll read over it, but whatever and however you decide to write is up to you, although sometimes

I'll give you specific assignments. I expect those writings to be both insightful and grammatically correct."

She brushed her fingers over the clothbound book with a frown. Writing was not her favorite thing to do, and she'd always struggled with grammar. "You mean you'll grade it?"

"Something like that." His voice somehow held both humor and warning at the same time. "You don't appear to like the idea of writing. Give it some time before forming an opinion. Many people find writing to be therapeutic. Have you ever written about your BDSM journey?"

Her frown deepened. Her therapist had suggested writing, but she'd never gotten around to actually doing it. Now it looked as if she no longer had a choice. "No," she answered with a sigh. "Never."

"Then you may find out you enjoy it."

Abby journaled, she remembered. Did it so well and for so long, she was actually making it a career now. That would never happen with her.

She shook her head. "I have a feeling it'll only confirm I don't like it." Especially if he was going to grade it. What would he do, break out a red pen? Make her stand in the corner if she made a bad grade? Spank her?

Spank her. Oh . . .

The thought of Cole pushing her over his knee for a spanking made her face feel hot. Her breathing sped up, and a dull ache began to throb between her legs. She shifted in her seat to try and alleviate it.

"Well, now." He sat across from her, eyes fixed on what she was doing. "That must have been a very interesting thought you had. What was it, Sasha?"

She didn't want to tell him. Didn't want to let him know how much the thought of him spanking her turned her on.

She leaned forward over the table. "I could say it's nothing, but if I do, I'm sure you'll see right through me and potentially strip the word 'nothing' from my vocabulary as well. Will you let me just say it was an embarrassing personal revelation I'd rather not share at the moment?"

His forehead wrinkled while he considered her request, and her hands grew sweaty at the thought that he might ask her to share anyway. But right when she'd accepted that she would have to swallow her pride and admit how much the thought of him spanking her turned her on, his expression relaxed.

"Yes, we can leave it at that. I recognize I haven't earned your trust yet. You may keep your secrets. For now."

She shuddered. His *for now* left her with no ambiguity: there would come a time when he would ask for her secrets. She only hoped that when that day came, she was ready to give them.

Cole watched as the meaning of his words became clear to Sasha and he hid a smile at her reaction. He could tell she would be a complex puzzle to solve. There was little evidence of the timid submissive he witnessed last night, probably due to her lack of sleep and the informal protocol he insisted on at the start of their discussion. He liked the fact she seemed slightly more at ease with him and hoped it continued even when she had a full night's sleep.

"I'll allow you that concession," he said. "But there are a few things I will be less than inclined to compromise on."

"I'm willing to take those things under consideration," she said in a tone that left him with no doubt that submissive or not, Sasha knew a thing or two about negotiation. That knowledge pleased him. He meant what he said when he told her a woman had to be strong to submit to him.

He wondered, not for the first time, what had been going through her mind that eventful night with Peter. *Secrets*. He would have hers eventually.

He took the sheet of paper on top of the pile to his right and passed it across the table to her. "My preferences."

"You wrote them down?" she asked, looking over the list.

"I find there's less confusion if everything is clearly spelled out."

"Were you a lawyer in a previous life?"

He laughed. "No, I've probably always been a writer." Before she could read the entire list, he wanted to talk through it. "To begin with, I don't want you to orgasm without my permission."

The paper slipped to the table. "I can't . . . you don't want . . . I'm sorry, what?"

"I believe it's a common requirement."

"Yes, but last night you said you weren't . . . that we . . ."

"Right." He dropped his voice. "I said I wasn't going to fuck you. However, I never said I wouldn't reward you appropriately."

Her cheeks turned the faintest shade of pink, and she replied with a soft, "Oh."

"Likewise, I never said I wouldn't punish you when necessary. There's more information later in the document." He picked the paper up and handed it to her. "Item two."

She quickly scanned the section in question.

"You were injured physically in a scene," he said. "Coming to terms with that, learning to deal with it, takes time and trust in your partner. During our time together, I will never touch you without telling you beforehand, and I'll tell you where I'll touch you."

Her forehead wrinkled as she thought through his words. Quite possibly she understood why he would put something like that in place, but was unsure about how it would work.

He held out his hand. "Place your hand in·mine, little one."

Tentatively, she reached across the table and put her hand on top of his.

"Palm up, please."

She hesitated briefly. Putting her hand palm up made her feel more vulnerable; that's why he had her do it. Her fingers trembled as she flipped her hand over.

"Thank you." He was humbled with the small measure of trust her action showed. "I'm going to trace your palm with a finger from my other hand."

He kept his gaze locked on hers as he brought his other hand to the top of the table. Ever so slowly, he dragged a finger across the base of her thumb. She sucked in a breath and looked over his shoulder to the wall behind him. He was pleased his touch affected her so.

His finger swept the other way. "I need you to understand I will always do what I say I'll do, but nothing more."

She nodded.

"What's your safe word, Sasha?"

She had no trouble finding her tongue when it came to safe words. "Green for more. Yellow to slow down. Red to stop."

"Good, nice and easy." His finger continued stroking her palm. "During your retraining, I will never take away your ability to speak. I know Nathaniel had you fill out a checklist recently, but I'm going to have you complete another one. You should know, even if you don't mark gags as a hard limit, they aren't something I'm going to use on you." He smiled. "Consider it one of my hard limits."

Her head snapped back so she could look at him. Interesting. So she was surprised at that particular hard limit. He wondered why it came as a surprise to her that he wouldn't use a gag. Frankly, he wasn't sure if she'd ever be at the point where she'd be comfortable playing with gags again.

He hoped his honesty in both how and when he would touch her as well as his insistence on not using gags would be a step closer toward gaining her trust. He wanted her to understand that though he might have a reputation as a bastard in the playroom, he wasn't heartless.

"Thank you," she finally whispered to him.

"A Dominant must have hard limits just like a submissive does. I'm not comfortable using a gag on you. What if you panicked, became so scared you forgot your safe signal? Putting a gag on you would serve no purpose and has the potential to harm you further. I won't do it."

She nodded, glanced to the table, and took a deep breath. He waited. He could tell she was struggling with whatever was going on inside her head.

But he was pleased she didn't whisper when she finally spoke. "I know you said you'd have me fill out a checklist, but there's one thing I feel I should bring up now."

"Of course."

He still held her left hand, but she clenched her right one into a fist. "No matter what we do, my shirt stays on. I don't want to be topless."

He continued drawing circles on her palm while thinking over what she'd requested. She felt strongly about keeping her shirt on, and it was difficult for her to bring it up. He tried not to envision the scars that would likely be on her back. He needed to tread carefully. "An odd request. One that will limit breast play, an activity I happen to enjoy."

"I enjoy it, too. My need to keep a shirt on has nothing to do with my breasts."

"Oh?"

"No." She squirmed slightly in her seat. "It's about my back. After Peter, I can't—it's not—I don't go topless. Ever."

She held his gaze while she spoke, as if wanting him to see how serious she was. He had a feeling this wasn't a point she was willing to negotiate.

"I see," he finally said. "Very well, your shirt will remain on at all times. It will be up to you to let me know if you ever change your mind."

She sighed in relief. "Thank you."

"I can tell it's a matter of importance to you." He looked down to where her hand now had a death grip on the finger that had been stroking her palm. "Otherwise, there would be blood flowing to my left fingers."

"Oh," she gasped and released her hold on him. "Sorry."

He shook his head. "That admission wasn't easy for you. I'm pleased you trusted me enough to share." Begrudgingly, he let go of her hand. "Which leads me to the next item. I've arranged for you to meet with Abby West once a week. I think you'll find it beneficial to talk with her."

She nodded. "I like Abby."

"She's a very experienced submissive and she's been working with Nathaniel on improving the group dynamics."

"Do I need to call her and set up a date and time?"

"Yes, I've given her a head's up that you'll be calling. If at all possible, I'd like for you to set something up for this week."

Sasha nodded. "I can do that."

"You went with Abby and Nathaniel to the last play party."

She shifted just a bit at his statement, and he smiled inwardly. He hadn't imagined it then. Not only had she attended her first play party after Peter with Nathaniel and Abby, she'd watched a demo he'd led with a casual play partner. He'd demonstrated how to use a violet wand, and midway through looked up to find Sasha watching with such an intensity that it had thrown him off-guard. Right now, he desperately wanted to question her further, but he knew it would go better for both of them if he waited until she trusted him more.

He stood up. "Let's take a break. I'll go get something sweet and when we finish, we'll go over more details."

Instead of going to the guesthouse when he arrived back at Daniel's, he parked his motorcycle and made his way to the front door of the main house. He wanted to talk to his friend about Sasha. Though he had a house key, he rarely felt comfortable using it. Especially since Julie had moved in.

But when no one answered the doorbell, he let himself in.

"Daniel?" he called, peeking into the kitchen. Both of their cars had been outside. "Julie?"

The house appeared empty. He waited for a few minutes and had just walked to the back entrance to leave when a door downstairs opened and soft voices floated upward.

Ah, the playroom.

He made his way to the top of the stairs leading down to the playroom and, sure enough, Daniel and Julie were holding hands, walking up to the main level. Julie had a robe on.

"Am I interrupting?" Cole asked, crossing his arms.

Julie yelped and stumbled.

"Jesus. Fuck," Daniel cursed, throwing his arms around his frightened sub to keep her from falling. "A bit of a warning next time, Cole?"

Cole was already halfway down the stairs. "Pardon, I didn't mean to scare the wits out of you. Are you all right, Julie?"

"A little shaky." She peeked out of the shelter of Daniel's embrace. "No worries."

Daniel kissed her cheek and they all walked up the stairs. Julie still had the faint glow of a thoroughly satisfied submissive about her, and Cole started to doubt his decision to swing by. He had obviously walked in at the end of a scene and, though it had been a while since he'd observed Daniel play, he didn't get the feeling his friend had finished aftercare yet.

Cole waited in the kitchen while Daniel walked with Julie into the living room. From his seat at the bar, Cole watched as he sat her on the couch and then turned to him.

"Come in here with us," Daniel called, sitting down and pulling Julie into his arms.

He should leave. Daniel wasn't ready to leave Julie alone, and Cole wasn't going to talk about Sasha in front of her. He walked into the living room and stood by the couch. "I'll come back later. I have a few things I want to discuss with you, and this isn't a good time."

Daniel nodded. "I can stop by later this evening."

"I'll be there. Probably going for a run now." Running always helped clear his mind. He had a feeling he would be doing a lot of running for the foreseeable future.

"Give me about an hour," Daniel said. "I'll——" he started, but was interrupted by the doorbell. "Hell, what is this, Grand Central Station?"

"Let me get it." Cole crossed the floor. "I'll send whoever it is away, and then I'll show myself out."

He opened the door, prepared to tell whoever it was that no one was interested, but the words died on his tongue as two surprised green eyes looked up at him.

"Sasha?"

Did she come by to see him? No, not likely with her eyes as wide as saucers. Apparently she was just as shocked to see him.

"I . . . I came by to see Julie."

Of course. If she'd been looking for him, she'd have gone to the guesthouse. He hardened his expression, not wanting her to see any emotion.

"Right." He stepped aside to let her in. "She's in the living room with Daniel. They just left the playroom."

She paled, and sweat beaded on her forehead. "Oh. Then maybe . . . maybe I should come back later. I'll just . . ." She turned back around and ran into his chest.

Instinctively, his hands shot out to steady her. Her arms shook and her lip trembled. He dropped his hands. "Sasha? Are you okay?"

"Yes, Sir," she whispered.

"Look at me." He waited until she lifted her head. "What just happened?" When she hesitated, he added, "Sasha, I can help you, but you have to be honest with me. It was my nonnegotiable condition."

"I'm sorry, Sir." She swallowed in deep breaths. "I just need a minute. Can I sit down?"

"Come in here," he said, leading her into the living room. He wasn't sure what the hell happened in the foyer, but he would get to the bottom of it.

"Hey, Sasha." Daniel looked up from where he was whispering to Julie. "Give me a bit longer, and she's all yours." He glanced over at Cole, then back to Sasha. "Assuming you did come by to see Julie?"

Sasha nodded and sank into the nearest chair.

"You look a bit pale. Are you okay?" Daniel asked. "Cole?"

"We haven't had a chance to talk about it yet." Cole didn't want to discuss anything with Daniel without talking to Sasha first.

Julie studied Sasha with a weary expression on her face. "Sasha, did something happen?"

Her tone was polite and friendly, but Cole could read between the lines. She was asking if something had happened between him and Sasha. Her concern was lovely, the mark of true friendship, but he didn't care for the insinuation he would harm Sasha.

"I'd planned to discuss this with you privately," Cole said, addressing Sasha. "Unfortunately, by bringing you into the living room, I've managed to worry everyone. So we'll have to do this now."

Sasha seemed to curl into herself. He wondered if he should have had the discussion privately, after all. Maybe she didn't feel more comfortable with her friends.

"You had what appeared to be a mild panic attack when I mentioned Daniel and Julie had been in the playroom. What happened?" *Stay with me, little one, let me help.*

Her spine straightened in resolve, but he had a feeling it was all for show. "I'm sorry if I worried anyone. Sometimes I have these little episodes. I never know what's going to bring one on."

"I remember you mentioning them when we talked about you rejoining the group," Daniel said.

Julie cocked her head. "But you said they were rare. I didn't know you were still having them."

"Probably due to lack of sleep and everything that's happened in the last twenty-four hours," Sasha said.

Silence filled the room. *Cole Johnson,* the stillness seemed to whisper. *He's what's happened in the last twenty-four hours.*

"Maybe you need more time," Daniel said. "We may have jumped into the retraining too quickly."

"It's okay if you want to wait, right, Daniel? There's no rush." Julie looked expectantly at her Dom.

What the fuck was she doing asking Daniel?

Sasha seemed to sink further into the seat and in that moment, Cole knew he would have to change his approach. He cleared his throat.

"Excuse me, Master Covington," he said. "But I believe everything pertaining to Sasha and her retraining was placed under my oversight."

"Yes, but——" Daniel started.

Cole held up his hand. "You've known me long enough to know I don't take kindly to anyone second-guessing me. Now, I'm very aware everyone is concerned with Sasha's well-being, but the group has entrusted me with her care. As such, unless Sasha says differently, *I* will be the one to decide how and when she is retrained."

"My apologies," Daniel said. "You're correct."

"Sasha, do you still wish for me to dictate the terms of your retraining?" Cole asked.

Her reply was immediate. She looked . . . *pleased* with the way he stood up for what he wanted. "Yes, Sir."

"I would like for everyone in this room to acknowledge the meaning of Sasha's acquiescence. There will be no more discussion of this." He met Daniel's eyes first, then Julie's. At their nods, he turned to Sasha. "There's been a change to your schedule. I'll

be in the guesthouse sitting room in ten minutes. You'll be waiting for me there, fully clothed, and on your knees."

Oh, shit. Oh, shit. Oh, shit.

The two words repeated themselves in Sasha's head, drowning
out all other thoughts. Realistically, she knew there was nothing
to be worried about. Cole had asked her to fill out a new checklist, and she had fully intended to note the rare panic attacks she
experienced. And though he had told her to kneel and wait for
him, she knew they weren't going to do a scene.

However, all that knowledge paled in comparison to Cole's
calmly spoken, but don't-even-think-about-doing-differently
command. Especially when it was delivered in that smooth-as-
silk accent of his. She didn't know if her body was closer to
panic over kneeling for someone or melting into a puddle of goo
over him issuing the command.

She let herself into the guesthouse. Since Daniel's place was a
popular location for both group meetings and play parties, she'd
been in the house numerous times before. She didn't bother to
look around to see what changes, if any, Cole had made, but went
straight to the sitting room and knelt on the rug.

She'd hoped that somehow her body would calm down once
she made it to her knees. But it wasn't to be. Her arms shook even
after she placed her hands, palms facing up, on top of her knees.
He had discussed positions earlier in the day at the coffee shop.
She'd run through them in her head while driving with the hope
that in doing so, she wouldn't succumb to an episode.

She was close, she felt it threatening to take over. The old
terror and the new uncertainty were too much. Too much and
she'd been wrong, wrong, wrong to come back.

"Sasha."

His voice was calm and gentle. She wanted to cling to it and never let go.

"Close your eyes and focus on my voice."

She squeezed her eyes shut and pictured his voice as a bright light in the darkness.

"Inhale deeply. Then exhale and let all the fear go. No one will hurt you whilst I'm here."

She took a deep breath, concentrating on the rush of air in and out of her body. The terror's grip lessened.

"That's it. Good job. Another one. Just the same."

She inhaled again. She was safe. Exhaled. *Safe.*

"Again."

Safe.

Her heart rate slowed. The terror disappeared.

"Again."

Calm.

"There we go, little one. If you think you're able, stay in that position."

"I can stay here, Sir."

He gave a soft hum of acknowledgment. "Take as much time as you need, and walk me through what happened when you knocked on the door and I answered."

When she took another breath, she smelled his aftershave and knew he'd moved closer. He smelled the way she imagined midnight would: sexy and secret and sinful.

One more deep breath and she was ready. "I came to talk to Julie. I knew I should probably go home and take a nap, but I didn't feel tired. I needed to talk to Julie."

"What were you going to talk to Julie about?"

Her hesitation lasted only a second. "You."

"I'm going to touch your shoulders and rub your back." Two hands gently clasped her shoulders. His thumbs massaged the nape of her neck. The action was both soothing and sensual at the same time. His sure hands soon had her sighing in pleasure.

"Do I scare you?" he asked.

She thought for a minute. "No. I don't think that's it. It's only that I haven't figured you out yet. It keeps me off balance."

His thumbs stopped their massage. "Might I suggest you grow accustomed to being off balance when it comes to me?"

She didn't know how to reply to that, so she remained silent.

His thumbs moved once more. "Is it correct, therefore, to assume I wasn't the trigger today?"

"I don't think it was you, Sir."

"You said you came to speak with Julie, I let you in and mentioned she had just left the playroom with Daniel. It happened soon after that."

The whip cracked in the air and made contact with flesh. She was so cold. Her body shook.

"Sasha." His smooth voice banished the memory. "Stay here with me, little one. Tell me what happened."

Whenever he called her "little one" she felt warm and protected. "I remember."

"What do you remember?"

"Daniel and the playroom. I think that was it."

He was silent for a moment, yet his hands never stopped moving. Somehow his touch grounded her, kept her steady and safe.

"It was Daniel?"

"No, Sir." She paused, just for a second, and then continued. "I was thinking about being in a playroom with you, though."

"I see. So playrooms seem to be a potential trigger."

"I don't know, Sir. Maybe. I'm not feeling panicked right now."

"I don't know, either, but it's something we'll work on." He continued rubbing her upper back and she allowed herself to sink into his touch, relaxing in a way she rarely permitted herself to.

When he'd told her he wasn't going to fuck her, she'd hoped to feel nothing when he touched her. It would be easier to keep the lines clear that way. But now that she had experienced how his hands felt on her body, she knew she'd want to feel them again.

Stupid. He's just being nice because you panicked. Don't get used to it.

"You're tensing up again," he chided. "Whatever you're thinking, stop."

After a few deep breaths, she once more felt relaxed and loose—and mildly surprised it was so easy to obey him.

"There we go," he said softly, and his hands became gentler. "Just so you're aware, I think you're an incredibly brave woman and I'm honored to be the one chosen to help you through this."

Her knees went a little weak. His voice was suddenly so soft, so smooth, and he was so different from how she'd pictured. It wasn't at all how she'd imagined. And he thought she was brave. The thought made her stomach flip-flop. After what seemed forever of feeling so weak, so damaged, so damn afraid, someone saw her as brave. Maybe she could reclaim part of her former self again and *he* would be the one to guide her.

"When was your last attack?"

"Two months ago, I believe, Sir."

He extended the massage to cover her entire back, further soothing her with both words and touch. "Do you know what caused that one?"

"Peter called me."

His hands stopped for a brief moment. "I didn't know he had contacted you."

"I don't like to talk about him," she said. "He called to apologize. Said it was part of his mentorship."

He exhaled heavily. "Peter won't be calling you again."

Her eyes grew teary. This protective side of him was an enduring surprise. "Thank you, Sir."

"Thank me when I show you mercy or when I allow you to climax. There's no need to thank me for protecting or looking after your well-being. That's just who I am."

Once again his words warmed her. She thought she had him figured out, but she was starting to see there was so much more to his character.

"Are there any words, places, or actions aside from what we've talked about that have triggered an attack?"

"Not within the last few months. After—" She swallowed. She could do this. "After it happened, they occurred frequently. I remember the first group meeting I went to . . ."

"Take your time." His voice was soft. Patient. Odd, she thought, since there really wasn't anything soft about him.

"Julie didn't think I should go. We argued. I thought it would be okay since Dena was giving a talk about legal issues. I had a bad attack in the middle of her discussion. I didn't tell anyone. I left after it was over and went to Julie's."

She could picture the way everyone had looked at her, the sideways glances, eyes darting away once she caught them. Even when people approached her to talk, they'd only ask how the shop was doing and once she replied with "fine" the conversation died.

"If you experience another one," he said, his voice no longer soft, "you will contact me immediately. I don't care if it's the middle of the night or I'm out of town or you're working. Understand?"

Once again he made her feel protected. "Yes, Sir."

"How are you feeling now?"

"Much better, Sir." She found the words came naturally. It never crossed her mind to say "fine." "I'm calm and relaxed. I don't feel panicky at all."

"Stand up, little one. Be careful; you've been kneeling for quite some time."

She opened her eyes and moved gingerly to her feet, slightly disappointed he was no longer massaging her back. Even so, he kept a hand on her shoulder to steady her as she stood. The afternoon shadows were growing long in the room, and she wondered exactly how much time had passed. Though she didn't get a lot of sleep the night before, she felt rested.

Cole turned her to face him and then dropped his hands. "A very productive afternoon, I believe."

"I believe so, too, Sir." She followed the path of his hand as he slipped it into his pocket and wondered when he'd touch her again.

His lips curled up a bit at the corners. "Does it bother you when I touch you?"

"I enjoyed you rubbing my back."

"Answer the question, Sasha."

He wasn't going to allow her to get away with anything. Already his expression had changed, all the amusement had fled. "No, Sir, it doesn't bother me when you touch me. I like it."

"There now, you see, that wasn't hard at all." His smile returned. "From here on out, you will always answer the questions I ask. If you don't know the answer, you may reply with 'I don't know, Sir,' and we'll work from there. What you may not do is avoid the question or give me half answers. Are my expectations clear?"

"Yes, Sir."

"Do you have any questions about them?"

"No, Sir."

He studied her intently for long seconds. "I can help you. But I have to have your trust, and that includes your honesty."

Little by little, he was weaving his way into her mind, just like he'd said. It brought her a startling sense of security.

"If you still want to talk to Julie, I'll call the main house and tell them you're on your way."

"Thank you, Sir. I would like that."

"I'll see you tomorrow."

"Yes, Sir. And I'll have the assignment you gave me completed."

"I'm looking forward to it," he said with a faint smile.

Julie waited for her at the side door of Daniel's house. Sasha quickened her step. As Julie welcomed her inside, Sasha looked back over her shoulder toward the guesthouse. Cole was just leaving out the front door. He'd changed into shorts and a T-shirt and he raised his hand in a salute before he took off jogging toward the pond.

Julie led her through the kitchen into the living room, and they sat down on one of the couches.

"I'm not going to ask if you're okay," Julie started. "Daniel said we had to trust Cole, so I'm going to try really hard to do that. Besides"—she gave Sasha a grin—"you seem completely at ease and I haven't seen you look like that in ages."

"Probably the back rub Cole just gave me."

"He took you to the guesthouse to give you a massage?"

"No, we also talked."

Julie wrinkled her eyebrows and curled up so her legs were tucked under her. "Daniel also said Cole was moving to Wilmington."

Sasha picked a loose thread on the couch cushion she held in her lap. "He told me."

"How do you feel about that?"

Sasha shrugged. "Does it matter? This is only a retraining. I don't have any hold on him, and we're not in a relationship."

"But he was the first Dom you showed interest in after Peter, and he *is* retraining you."

"No sex, though."

"You're blushing." Julie smiled. "Something's up."

Sasha glanced around the living room. "Where's Daniel?"

"Are you asking because you want to know or are you changing the subject?"

"A little of both."

"He went to check on something, but he said he'd be back in a few. He wants to talk to you."

"Do you know why?"

"Hey, Sasha."

Sasha looked up as Daniel walked into the room and sat in a chair next to her. He had a concerned expression, but after what Julie had said about trusting Cole, she didn't think he would question her about how she'd spent her time in the guesthouse.

"I didn't know Peter had called you," Daniel said.

"What?" Julie's eyes widened. "You didn't tell me."

"Just a minute, Julie." He held up his hand and turned to Sasha. "Sasha, I wish you would have told me."

"I didn't see the point. It was over and done." But deep inside she knew she should have told someone. If not Daniel, then one of the other senior group members.

"The call triggered a panic attack." His words were simple, but they were true and from the corner of her eyes, she saw Julie cross her arms and press her lips together.

"I told my therapist."

He shook his head. "It's not the same, and you know it. Peter was told he could remain in the group with certain restrictions. But more than that, anytime someone in the group does something to another member that is harmful, I need to know. How am I to keep you safe if I don't know?"

Sasha had to admit that Julie was a fortunate woman. She'd initially had her misgivings about her best friend dating and later wearing the collar of such an experienced Dominant, but Daniel had proven her wrong. He really was a strong protector, and he loved Julie with an intensity and passion that took her breath away.

"I thought I could handle it on my own," she admitted.

"I appreciate that, but we're here to help and support you, and we can't do that if you don't tell us what's going on. Now"— he gave her a knowing smile—"the next time something like this happens, you're to let me or someone else know. But I have a feeling there won't be a next time."

"How can you be so sure?" Julie asked from her corner of the couch.

Daniel chuckled. "Let's just say I wouldn't want to be Peter's mentor right now."

Cole stepped out of the shower and tied a towel around his waist. Walking to the window, he peeked outside to see if Sasha's car was parked at Daniel's. She'd still been there when he returned from his jog. Now, it appeared as if no one was at the main house.

He finished drying off and slipped on a clean pair of jeans and long-sleeve T-shirt. He had a phone call to make, and he'd purposely waited until he'd finished his jog and shower before calling. Over the years he'd found that he rarely reacted out of anger, but for some reason, the thought of Peter calling Sasha made his blood boil.

Master Greene picked up on the third ring. "Hello."

"William, it's Cole Johnson."

"Cole, hello. What's going on?"

"I met with Sasha today. We started on her retraining." There was nothing from the other end of the phone, so he continued, "The retraining that is only needed because of the actions of your mentee."

"I'm acutely aware of the situation." William sounded a little put off. "I would also remind you that he was not my mentee when the incident happened."

"Incident. Such a neat and tidy word. Let's call it what it really was, why don't we? You were not Peter's mentor the night he bound and gagged Sasha, then whipped her until she passed out."

"Master Johnson, is there a reason you called me?"

"Of course. I would like to know if you have any additional plans for your mentee to call or in any other way make contact with Sasha?"

"I'm not sure what you mean by *additional plans*."

"Peter called her to apologize. He said it was part of his mentorship."

Soft curses were the only reply Cole received, and his suspicions concerning Peter were confirmed. "I take from your response that you didn't ask him to call Sasha."

"No, I didn't ask him to call Sasha. I did say that something of the sort might be beneficial to both of them in the future. I made it very clear the timing wasn't right just yet."

"When she told me he'd called, I suspected he went behind your back." Cole felt his anger rise at the thought of Peter's disregard concerning Sasha's well-being. "However, I still hold you partially responsible. You should have better control over your mentee."

"I had no way of knowing he would go against me."

"Be that as it may, I will be spending the foreseeable future trying to undo the damage the phone call created. Make sure Peter is aware that if he contacts her again, he'll be on the receiving end of *my* bullwhip. And I'm nowhere near as nice as Daniel."

"I'll ensure it doesn't come to that. I'll handle it. There's a way to work with fragile submissives."

An image of Sasha kneeling in the sitting room fighting a panic attack flashed before him. He lowered his voice. "Master Greene, have you ever been whipped to the point of unconsciousness by someone you trusted to never hurt you? And then months later, returned to the same environment, willing to give that trust to another?"

"No, but—"

"Then you have no idea what's it's like for her. But let me assure you of one thing: Sasha isn't *fragile.* She's stronger than both of us put together."

William was silent for a long moment before clearing his throat. "If you would allow me, I would like to offer her my apologies at the next meeting on behalf of Peter."

"I'll think about it and let you know."

"Fair enough."

Once he hung up, Cole put the phone on the table beside his chair and looked at the pile of papers he'd printed out to read in preparation for his next article. Somehow he couldn't bring himself to be interested in the Indian caste system at the moment.

He felt listless, the dull ache of nothing looming before him. If he were still in India, he would have found a willing submissive to pass the time with. While he was there for his last assignment, he had never been without female companionship if he didn't want to be.

And before India, there had been Kate. Her absence was probably the cause of his current melancholy, especially since it was a Sunday night. When they'd been together, they had a Sunday night routine. They would sit together in their sunroom and go over schedules for the coming week. If he thought there was something she needed to work on, he'd give her an assignment. It was also a time for her to voice any concerns she had, though she was at liberty to do so during the week as well.

Once they had talked, the evening could proceed in a few different ways. Sometimes they'd go to his playroom, sometimes he'd take her over his knee in the sunroom. Other times, he'd just take her. But she had left, and with her went more of himself than he'd realized the day she walked out the door. What nagged him, though, was he wasn't certain if he missed her or what she symbolized.

He sighed and looked down to the floor, where hours before Sasha knelt.

Sasha.

He closed his eyes and allowed his mind to replace the image of Kate kneeling before him with Sasha at his feet. He imagined calling her name and how she'd look at him with those expressive green eyes.

"What do you want, little one?" he asked, running his fingers through her short dark hair.

"I want to serve you, Sir. However you wish."

"And if I wish for you to sit in the next room and spend the evening by yourself?"

Her expression revealed nothing. "Then I will sit in the next room and spend the evening alone. But you will keep me company in my thoughts."

"Unzip my trousers and take them off."

She quickly had him naked from the waist down. He took his erection in his hand. "And if I tell you to stay on your knees and watch whilst I get myself off?"

"Then I will enjoy the sight of you giving yourself pleasure."

"And if I tell you I want to thrust my cock into your mouth and drive it down your throat?"

"Then I will happily show you how my deep-throating skills have improved."

He grabbed her hair and pushed her head toward his groin. "Suck me down as deep as possible and hold still while I fill that throat first with my cock and then with my come. If I decide you have done a good job, I'll reward you. If you can't take me or if you spill anything, I'll strap your ass."

"With pleasure, Sir," she said and parted her lips to take him inside.

Cole worked his hand up and down his cock, lifting his hips as he imagined using Sasha's mouth. Her fingers would be digging into his skin, holding him as tightly against her as possible. He'd stroke deep, deeper, and she'd take him. He'd press as hard and as far as possible when he felt his release cresting.

With a grunt he spilled into his hand right as his phone rang.

"Fuck," he panted, looking for something to clean his hand with. When was the last time he'd jerked off like a teenaged boy?

The ringer on his phone seemed to grow louder.

"Fucking hell." He hit the speaker button with a finger on his clean hand without checking the caller ID. "Damn it, what?"

"Cole?" a familiar voice asked, all breathy and feminine. "I'm sorry, is this a bad time?"

"Kate?" he croaked. He carried the phone to the bathroom

and placed it on the countertop while he washed his hands and straightened his clothes. "No, this is fine. What's going on?"

He hadn't talked to Kate in months. She might not have been the very last person he thought would call him tonight, but she was pretty damn close to it.

"I spent today unpacking," she said.

She had finally found a permanent place. Before now, she'd been crashing at a girlfriend's. Cole had thought he was beyond feeling anything when it came to Kate, but hearing that she'd moved into a new place proved him wrong. Suddenly, he was acutely aware of how lonely the quiet guesthouse was.

"I'm glad you found a new home." He forced himself to speak through the tightness in his chest. "You'll have to e-mail your address to me so I have it on file."

"That's not why I called."

"Forgive me, then. You don't have to send me your address."

"Would you stop being an ass and listen to me?"

He took a deep breath and hoped his tone sounded more civil to her than it did to him. "Why did you call?"

It was easy to picture her on the other end of the phone. She would be holding it tightly in one hand, anger blazing from her cool blue eyes. He imagined her counting to ten to calm down.

"I unpacked some boxes today," she repeated.

Yes, you said that already, he bit back from saying and instead replied with, "Oh?"

"One of your boxes got mixed up with mine."

"In that case, I'll give you the address where I'm staying for the time being and you can post it to me."

"I know you're staying with Daniel, you told me when we closed on our old house. It's the box containing your mom's jewelry. I don't think it'd be a good idea to mail it."

He cursed under his breath. He thought that particular box had been put in temporary storage. His mother could trace her lineage back to the fifteenth century. Back to some earl who lost his title and estate when he pissed Henry the Eighth off or something. The jewelry had been hidden at the time and passed down through the generations. He never did anything with the pieces. He'd actually thought about giving them to a museum. Regardless, they weren't anything he was going to give to Kate and she was right, she shouldn't mail them.

"I don't have plans to visit New York anytime soon," he said, thinking about his upcoming sessions with Sasha. "And unfortunately I can't make any plans to visit due to previous commitments."

"If it's okay with you then, I'm driving to Mom and Dad's in about a month. I can stop by and give them to you on the way."

Her parents lived in Florida. When they were together, she'd visit them every few months. "That would be fine. Thank you, Kate."

"It's no big deal."

An uncomfortable silence followed. The uncomfortable type of silence that could only be shared by those who had once shared everything and now had nothing to say. The air between them was filled with unspoken history and whispered what-ifs.

"Thank you for calling." They were the only words he discovered he could speak. Four fucking words to the woman he had loved and who had worn his slave collar for years.

"Nice talking with you," she said, but he didn't think she sounded like she meant it.

After he said good-bye, he went back to the living room where he distracted himself with the research he'd been avoiding. It was either that or spend hours thinking about Kate. As it was, he knew she'd be visiting his dreams that night.

But it wasn't a blue-eyed woman with long black hair who filled his head while he slept, rather a wounded submissive with nerves of steel who had admitted she liked it when he touched her.

Sasha rang the doorbell at the Wests' residence on Monday after work. When she'd called Abby the day before, she mentioned that she'd be meeting with Cole on Wednesday, and Abby said she wanted to talk before she met with Cole again.

Abby opened the door with a big smile. "Hey, Sasha. Come on in."

Sasha genuinely liked Abby. She was friendly and down-to-earth, an all-around nice person. And it was becoming harder and harder to find those.

They walked through the house, the sound of childish giggles and shrieks meeting them in the hallway.

"Nathaniel just got home," Abby explained. "He's playing with the kids. We'll go to the office, where it's quieter."

She led her to a large his-and-hers-style office and waved to a love seat.

"This is gorgeous," Sasha said, taking in the large room. Two desks took up most of the space, but the love seat was placed in front of a picture window in a small seating area. It was inviting and warm, just like its owner.

"Thanks. We just had it done. Nathaniel doesn't work from home often, but when he does, we both need our own space."

They sat down and Abby faced her. "Tell me how it went with Cole yesterday."

"He was different than I expected. But in a good way." She thought back to how he'd calmed her down and rubbed her back.

"He's a complex guy, but he has your best interests in mind.

I know he probably wasn't who you thought the group would pick." Abby gave a little chuckle. "I know it surprised me at first, but now I honestly believe he's the best choice."

"You knew he wouldn't have sex with me?" It was a bold question, and Abby seemed to be taken aback for a second—but Sasha wanted to know.

"Yes, in fact, it was that knowledge that finally convinced me to agree for him to do your retraining."

Sasha raised an eyebrow at her.

"You have to be strong mentally before you can submit physically. Once you get the mental down, the physical will follow," Abby explained.

"It makes sense in my head." But damn, she'd like to have sex again. And now, with Cole saying she couldn't orgasm without his permission, it didn't appear like that would be happening anytime soon.

"I've played with Cole before in a mental scene," Abby said, surprising her. "And from that I learned two things: one, he knows what he's doing, and two, he knows what he's doing."

Sasha laughed. "What was it like, submitting to him?"

"He's intense, you know that. So much more so than Nathaniel, and trust me, Nathaniel's intense. But Cole's a good man and he's fair. I don't think you have a thing to worry about."

Sasha had once told Julie that she found Nathaniel too intense. Her stomach flipped over hearing Abby say Cole was even more intense than Nathaniel. Why did the thought of Cole not intimidate her as much as Nathaniel did?

"I trust you," Sasha said. "And I really feel supported by everyone in the group."

"I'm so glad. You said you'll be meeting with Cole on Wednesday. Do you have any idea what you'll be doing?"

"He gave me a writing assignment." Sasha frowned. She'd started on it last night and hadn't gotten very far before she put it down. She hated writing. "I guess we'll go over that."

"You don't seem excited about it."

"I'm not. But everyone talks about how beneficial it is to write my thoughts down, so I'll do it and see how it goes." Those were her words, but Sasha knew exactly how it was going to go. She'd hate every second of it.

Sasha chewed her bottom lip Wednesday while Cole read over the writing assignment he'd given her. She'd spent hours writing down her goals for the retraining on Monday when she got home from Abby's. She'd thought she'd done a good job, but kneeling in the bedroom of the guesthouse he used as an office, with him sitting at his desk, she started to have doubts. He had a red pen in his hand and he was using it far too frequently. Judging by the frown on his face, she guessed he wasn't writing *Terrific insight* or *Excellent work*.

Her suspicion was confirmed when he finally put the pen down and looked at her while taking his glasses off with one hand. Earlier, when he'd opened the door to welcome her inside, she thought he looked ridiculously hot. At the moment, he looked downright frightening.

"Sasha."

She tried to speak, but her mouth was too dry. She licked her lips and managed to sputter out, "Yes, Sir?"

"First of all, stop looking at me like that. We are nowhere near being close enough for me to punish you corporally. You will be very clearly notified when I think that time has come."

"Thank you, Sir."

"That does not, however, mean you will find any punishment comfortable."

"Of course not, Sir." Why was he talking about punishment?

"When I gave you the journal, I indicated written assignments had to be two things. What were those two things?"

"Insightful and grammatically correct, Sir."

"Yes, and while I think these goals are insightful, the horrific grammar keeps me from ascertaining them completely."

She flinched. "Sorry, Sir. Grammar has never been a strength of mine."

He tilted his head. "You didn't tell me this when I gave you my expectations yesterday."

No, she hadn't. "No, Sir."

He held the journal and black pen out to her. "Come get these and flip to a page in the back."

She hurried to do his bidding and stood by his desk, pen in hand and journal opened to a clean page.

"At the coffee shop we went over your position when I'm sitting in your presence," he barked. "Either kneel or sit down."

Fuck. How could she forget so quickly? She sat down cross-legged on the floor and waited.

"Write 'Infractions I Owe Master Johnson For' on the top." Her eyes shot up to meet his. He looked pissed. "You will be given a week's warning before I collect."

She wrote the title at the top with a shaky hand.

He nodded when he saw she'd finished. "Now write 'Number One: Neglecting to inform Master Johnson of difficulties with grammar.'" He gave her time to write and then continued. "'Number Two: Standing before Master Johnson whilst he is sitting.'" When she finished, he held out his hand. "Give me the journal and go back to kneeling in the middle of the floor."

She swore her heart was going to pound its way out of her chest as she made her way back. He stood up and walked toward her, journal in hand.

"Usually when I find errors like yours in writing assignments, I use a ruler on my submissive's upturned palms and then have her rewrite the assignment. I find the combination to be an effective learning method." He lifted an eyebrow. "But you're not ready for such a punishment."

She wanted to look at the floor. She hated that she'd already disappointed him so deeply. Hated that there were already two punishments that would be looming between them. And she really hated that she wasn't at the place where she could take what he thought she deserved for her actions.

"What are you thinking, little one?" he asked in a gentler voice.

His soft tone soothed her. "I don't like disappointing you, and I'm disappointed in myself for not being able to take an appropriate punishment and having it hang between us as a result."

"The fact that you're not ready to be disciplined in a manner I see fit is not entirely your fault. You can't blame yourself for that. And yes, I'm disappointed, but we'll correct your behavior and move on. I'm not one to hold grudges, Sasha, and I believe you'll find I don't dig up past offenses, either."

Sasha could feel a small smile bloom at her lips. One of the things she liked about him so far was he seemed consistent. She always knew where she stood with him.

"I will share with you that one of my concerns in agreeing to this arrangement was the fear that you wouldn't be open and honest with me. Outside of not telling me about your troubles with grammar, you have been delightfully candid."

"Thank you for being honest and candid with me, Sir."

"A Dominant should always be honest and candid with his submissive."

His submissive. Two simple words shouldn't make her stomach a breeding ground for butterflies. "Everyone says that, Sir, and it sounds good and everything. But I've found it's not always the case."

"Then you've been playing with the wrong Doms."

She couldn't help it; she laughed. "I think that much is clear, Sir, or else I wouldn't be here."

He gave her one of his rare smiles. "True enough, little one. And another thing we should add to your list of goals: how to identify a good Dom."

"I would have thought anyone in the group would be a good choice to play with."

"Yes, that would be the assumption. Unfortunately, no program is perfect, not even with the changes Nathaniel and Abby have worked on. And nothing takes the place of personal knowledge."

He didn't push her to talk about the night with Peter. She thought that would be one of the first things he did. But he'd only brought it up casually, leaving her to think either they wouldn't discuss it or he was waiting until later to do so.

He jotted a note in her journal. "Definitely something we can talk about later. Now, let's go over some of these errors. I'm going to go through the list first. Pay attention, because then you'll write them all down on your own."

She was a businesswoman, so she shouldn't have any trouble remembering. But she worried anyway.

"'Its' versus 'it's,'" he started. "When you have the apostrophe, it is always read as 'it is.'"

That one was just a careless mistake.

"'Affect' versus 'effect.' There are exceptions, but 'affect' is almost always used as a verb and 'effect' is almost always used as a noun."

Affect was a verb. A verb was an action. A, affect. A, action. She could remember that.

"Could have, would have, should have," he said. "Never, never, never could of, would of, or should of."

Now she just felt stupid.

"Finally, when you use the word 'literally,' it means exactly what you're writing. For example, 'He *literally* dug his fingers into her skin' means his fingers were digging into her skin, which is probably not what was meant and would be horribly painful. I've said it before, but it needs repeating: words have meanings, you must learn to use them correctly."

"Yes, Sir. I'll do better in the future." She would. Her next assignment would blow him away.

"I'm sure you will. For now, you will make a list of your errors and their corrections. Then you will write the absolutely filthiest sentences you can think of using the words correctly. Finally, you will rewrite this paper making the needed edits."

She hid a half smile. That didn't seem like a difficult punishment at all. She could handle this, no problem.

"I saw that, Sasha," he said. "And just so you're aware, this is only part of your punishment."

She gulped and went to work. The list of errors and corrections was easy, but it was more difficult to come up with the sentences. She finally finished them and went on to rewrite her goals.

Cole was nowhere to be seen when she put her pen down. Not knowing what else to do, she closed the journal and knelt with her head down.

Minutes later, he entered the room. "Did you finish your assignment, little one?"

"Yes, Sir."

"Stand up," he said. "I want your hands behind your back, chest out, and your feet spread."

Even though she was completely clothed, she felt almost as if she was naked as she moved into position. In fact, the way he was looking at her made her feel naked. It was too easy to picture offering her body to him.

He stood by the couch, arms crossed. "Recite your sentences using 'its' and 'it's.'"

He wanted her to say them? Out loud? Her mouth felt like it was filled with cotton. She didn't have a problem talking dirty, but she'd always done so in the middle of a scene. Where actual sex was involved. Not standing in an office with her clothes on. It felt . . . *off* somehow.

"Trying to catch flies, Sasha? What's the problem?"

"Can I ask you to use the ruler on me instead?" That would be quick and not anywhere as embarrassing.

"You may not. I assure you, you are not anywhere near ready to accept pain from me. The sentences. *Now*."

She took a deep breath. She could do this. "I put the vibrator in its place at the back of my nightstand. No apostrophe. It's huge, and that makes it my favorite. With apostrophe."

His jaw tightened. "You've been active as a sexual submissive for how long?"

"Six years, Sir."

"Six years and the filthiest sentence you could come up with using 'its' is, 'I put the vibrator in its place at the back of my nightstand'?"

She didn't say anything. Surely he could tell how embarrassed she was only saying that.

"Completely unacceptable," he said. "Try again."

Jerk. She tried to think of something, but every damn thing had left her brain, making her feel like she was running after words, trying to catch them and arrange them into something resembling a sentence.

"Vibrator is a good item to start with, but try putting it somewhere else." He wasn't going to back down. He would make her do this, she knew.

She closed her eyes. "He slides the vibrator inside me, and its width makes me catch my breath."

"Better. Take that sentence and dirty it up."

She opened her eyes and forced herself not to glare at him. Was he going to do this with every word? "He . . . thrusts . . . the vibrator deep into . . . my pussy." Her face felt hot. "And its width makes me catch my breath."

"Work on the last part. 'He thrusts the vibrator deep into my pussy and its width' . . . What about the width, Sasha?" Even from across the room, she felt the heat from his gaze. He was unrelenting in his quest. "Visualize it if you have to. You're on your back, arms bound above your head. I'm standing by you, holding a vibrator. Your legs are spread for me and your pussy tingles in anticipation, waiting for it, wanting it and yet, at the same time, a little unsure it can accommodate something so hard and thick. And then it doesn't matter because I thrust that massive vibrator deep inside you and its width . . ." He paused to cross the floor and bent down to whisper in her ear, "Finish the sentence. Tell me what the width does to you. How you feel when I fuck you with it."

The words flowed from her mouth without thought. "And it fills me and stretches me and I lift my hips desperate for more."

"Yes." His hot breath brushed across her ear and she couldn't control her shiver. "Yes, you would and I would give you more. I would fucking *delight* in giving you more."

She didn't have to press against him to know how hard he was. His breathing was labored. He was definitely turned on, but whether it was because of her or the wordplay, she couldn't tell. When he pulled away, his eyes were still dark with need.

"Tell me again what your sentence was using *it's* with an apostrophe," he said calmly.

Her body was shaky, but she composed herself enough to repeat, "It's huge and that makes it my favorite."

He grinned. "Oh, Sasha. My shy little sub. It's going to be a long afternoon."

"I think you need a break," Julie told her the next morning as Sasha said good-bye to one of their regular clients.

"Why?" Sasha watched the older lady get inside her car and drive away.

"You just told Mrs. Preston to say hello to her husband."

"And?" Sasha couldn't figure out why Julie was standing there with her hands on her hips. "I was being polite. And Mr. Preston—"

"Is dead," Julie finished and walked to the back room. "We did his funeral last year."

"Oh, shit." No wonder the older lady hadn't turned around or said anything as she walked out the door. Sasha followed Julie to the break room.

"Do you need to get some coffee, take a nap, or something?"

Sasha sat at the table with a sigh. "No coffee, no nap, just the or something."

She'd stayed at Cole's a lot later than either of them had planned. It took that long to go through her sentences. When they finally finished, she'd been so hot and bothered, she feared she'd come simply from Cole looking at her.

And though he still had a faint hint of desire about him, he made no move toward her. He just stated that due to the amount of time her sentences had taken, they were behind the schedule he'd made and could she come back tomorrow?

"Anything I can help with?" Julie asked.

"Nah, I've never had an interest in participating in girl on girl." Julie's mouth dropped open and Sasha laughed. "And it wouldn't matter if I did. Cole won't let me orgasm without his permission."

Julie closed her mouth. "I don't know what to do with any of that information."

"Come on, I bet Daniel doesn't let you climax unless he tells you to."

"Of course not." Julie's fingers brushed her collar and at the sound of the door chime, started walking toward the front. "It's only when you said you needed something, I didn't know you were talking about a screaming orgasm."

"It doesn't have to be screaming. I'll take a quiet one." Sasha grinned. "Heck, I've been so turned on lately, I'll take an orgasm any damn way he wants to give me one."

"I'll be sure to let Master Johnson know that when I see him at the special meeting the Dominants are having later this week."

Sasha and Julie spun around. Kelly Bowman, also known as Mistress K, stood with Abby at the door to the small break room. One of the group's few Dommes, Kelly was a tiny woman with long red hair. Sasha had once heard redheads were either plain or drop-dead gorgeous. Kelly was one of the gorgeous ones. Even with the knowing smile she currently wore.

Abby laughed. "That's mean, Kelly."

"This is why we have the no-kinky-sex-talk-in-the-shop rule," Julie said. "Hey, Abby. Welcome to Petal Pushers, Kelly."

"I always thought that rule sucked." Sasha nodded at the two women. "What's happening?"

"I had an idea," Abby said, dropping her purse on a table and sitting down on a nearby bench. "You're looking good, Sasha."

There was something lurking in her friend's expression, but Sasha couldn't put her finger on it. "Thank you."

"You do look good," Kelly said in agreement. "You have more color than you did at the last group meeting, and you don't look as gaunt. Working with Master Johnson agrees with you. Orgasm denial notwithstanding."

"It's not so much that he's denied me orgasms. He just hasn't allowed them."

"Maybe you should just ask him for one." Julie made her way toward the break room. "Coffee, anyone?"

"Black for me," Kelly called out.

"Black for me, too, thanks," Abby said.

Could she do that? Is that all it took, for her to ask? She wondered if that was part of yesterday's lesson. To help her grow used to being unashamed to ask for what she needed.

But then she tried to imagine standing in front of Cole and asking for an orgasm. What if he agreed, but he made her give herself one while he watched? She had done so for other Doms, but they had been in a relationship. This thing with Cole, this retraining, it left her confused.

They weren't in a real relationship. He was helping her, and though he claimed ownership to her orgasms, it wasn't a forever kind of a thing. He would release her from training and she would be free to carry on the way she had before. She could play with whomever she wanted. Make herself come as often as she wanted.

She looked up to find Julie passing out coffees. "So, Abby, you said it was your idea to pull us all together this morning?" Julie asked.

"Yes, I was going to call everyone, but then I was talking to Kelly and she said she was stopping by." Abby took a sip of coffee. "I think we should have a surprise shower for Dena."

"I love that idea," Julie said. "Just the women, or will we invite the men, too?"

"I vote women only," Kelly said.

"Me, too," Sasha agreed.

"I'm fine with women only." Abby wrote something down in her notebook. "That means we can talk about the men."

"I'm so happy for Jeff and Dena," Kelly said. "They've been through so much. You know, we should set up the shower at a spa. Let Dena get all pampered."

"I like that." Abby nodded and wrote more down.

"Their wedding was so romantic," Julie said with a sigh.

As the other three women started chatting about memories and weddings and babies, Sasha's mind drifted. Cole was expecting her tonight at seven sharp. They were going to be doing whatever activity he'd originally planned for the day before. She was curious.

There was a lull in the conversation, and she noticed all three women watching her. "Sorry," she said. "I'm a little scattered today."

Julie smiled. "Ask him."

God help her. She just might.

Chapter Three

Cole stood, looking over the sitting room setup one last time, when the doorbell rang at five minutes to seven. He opened the door to find Sasha. Her cheeks were flushed and her breathing was a bit labored. Almost as if she'd been running. It seemed as if she often had trouble being punctual, and he was pleased she was making an effort to be on time for him.

"Good evening, Sasha." He stepped to the side to let her pass. "Come in, and let's go to the office."

She wrinkled her nose and then turned away as if hiding her response. But she'd learn soon enough he didn't miss much.

He grinned. "No, I'm not going to make you come up with dirty sentences tonight. I want to talk with you a bit, and you might find the sitting room distracting at the moment."

She led the way down the hall and entered first. She made it to the middle of the room and looked his way for instructions. When he glanced at the floor, she knelt down.

She moved gracefully and looked so delicate kneeling before him. Once again, he despaired she was only his for retraining. He was willing to bet she would be an absolute delight to master. "Very nice, little one. You look quite lovely tonight."

"Thank you, Sir."

He clenched his fist so he wouldn't touch her. He'd told her he wouldn't and it would serve no purpose. It wouldn't lead anywhere because it wasn't in his plan for her to serve him sexually. He would be too rough and she didn't need that. He had to work her back to the submissive frame of mind slowly.

Under her watchful eyes, he sat down at his desk and motioned for her to come to his side. "Kneel here, little one, so we can talk."

She didn't tremble as much as she did previously. As she came closer to him, he couldn't help but wonder what she would look like moving around naked, but he pressed his fist against his upper thigh and hoped his voice came out even.

"Do you know why I had you come up with the sentences yesterday?"

"Because my grammar was horrific and deterred you from understanding my otherwise *insightful* essay on my goals for retraining, Sir."

He choked back the chuckle bubbling in his throat. She seemed to be getting a little of her attitude back. Perfect. "Yes, but it had another purpose—do you want to guess what that was?"

"To help me become comfortable asking for and talking about certain things with a Dom when we're not in a scene."

"Very nice, little one. Tell me how you arrived at that conclusion."

"I'd prefer not to, Sir."

"Your preference has nothing to do with this conversation."

She dipped her head and her shoulders slumped. "It's embarrassing, Sir."

"Then you didn't learn the lesson completely yesterday. Look me in the eyes and recite the sentence you finally came up with using 'should have.'"

Her face grew red, more with anger than shame if he had to guess, but she spoke calmly, "As I straddled his hips, I saw how big his cock was and realized I *should have* used more lube before inviting him to fuck my ass."

He'd selected that particular sentence because it brought up a topic he wanted to discuss. "Have you ever invited anyone to fuck your arse, Sasha?"

"No, Sir."

"But per your checklist, you've had anal sex?"

"Yes, Sir."

"Did you like it?"

"No, Sir."

If she didn't like it, odds were the previous Doms she'd been with had been novices and possibly rushed things. If he was with her, he'd take his time getting her body ready to accept him. He would teach her how to relax and open herself for him. He ached to have her in his bed for one night. Little by little he'd show her mind and body pleasures unknown. He'd make sure she could never claim not to like anal sex again.

He needed to stop thinking like that. But still the image of her on all fours, offering herself to him, wouldn't leave his mind.

"Were you able to orgasm whilst having a cock up your arse?"

"Once, Sir."

"Once." He spoke the word with as much disdain as possible. "What happened the other times?"

"They would finish, pull out, and get me off some other way."

He decided to keep his opinions to himself. After all, he didn't know the entire situation. And since he would never have anal sex with her, it didn't matter.

"Tell me how you arrived at the second purpose for yesterday's lesson."

She steeled her spine, straightened her shoulders, and took a deep breath. "I was talking to Julie about how badly I wanted an orgasm, and she said I should just ask you for one. It occurred to me then, that might have been your purpose with yesterday's exercise."

He schooled his features, ensuring he didn't show anything other than pleasure that she'd shared honestly with him. "See how easy that was?" He didn't wait for her to answer, but continued. "You have a question for me?"

She wanted to deny it, the idea seemed to hold some merit for her, but she looked straight at him and said, "I would like your permission to have an orgasm, Sir."

He was suddenly glad she didn't answer his question the first time, because it gave him an idea. "Of course. In fact, for the next three days, you may come as often as you're able." She opened her mouth, probably to thank him, so he went on. "With conditions. Do you have an anal plug?"

She didn't appear as happy as she had been moments before. "No, Sir."

"Wait here for a moment."

He slipped into his bedroom and took a wrapped package from the nightstand's bottom drawer. Sasha was still frowning when he handed it to her.

"It's a medium-sized one. You're not an anal virgin, so you

don't need a small one, but you haven't had overly positive experiences, so it's smaller than, say, my cock."

She stared at the wrapped plug as if it would bite her.

"My condition is, you may come as often as you're able as long as you're wearing the plug. In fact, I command you to have at least two orgasms a day for the next three days."

She was silent.

"You're forgetting something, Sasha."

"Yes, Sir, I understand your instructions."

He crossed his arms and waited. She shifted her weight.

When it became obvious she wasn't going to say anything else, he spoke.

"You thanked me a few days ago for saying Peter wouldn't be calling you again. What did I say in response?"

She repeated his words flawlessly. "Thank me when I show you mercy or when I allow you to climax."

"Where's your journal?"

She nodded toward the corner where she'd placed her personal items. "In my purse."

He took a black pen from his desk, pulled her journal from her purse, and held them out to her. "Number Three: Failure to thank Master Johnson for his generous allowance of two orgasms a day."

She shook her head. "But I—"

"Hush. You have two choices. One: apologize, thank me, and write it down. After which, we move into the sitting room and continue your retraining. Or two: you talk back or argue and I introduce you to a very, very uncomfortable non-corporal punishment you will hate. After which, you will still apologize, thank me, and write it down. Of course, it'll be too late for your retraining session, so you'll have to come back tomorrow." He gave her a pointed stare. "Decision is yours."

She hesitated, a move he took to mean she gave serious thought to arguing, but then she sighed. "Forgive me, Sir, for my failure to acknowledge your generosity."

"Apology accepted. Your discipline has been deferred to a future date, to be determined by me."

"And thank you for allowing me two orgasms a day for three days."

She didn't seem thankful, but he'd learned early on that if one said the words often enough, the intent and gratitude would follow. "You're welcome. Your second assignment is to document each orgasm. Write it down so you don't forget, then write your third infraction in the back along with the other two. When you're finished, we'll move into the sitting room."

It didn't take her long to write everything down. She finished and placed the journal on the floor.

"Finished?" he asked.

"Yes, Sir."

"I'm going to blindfold you before we go to the sitting room."

He stood up, taking with him the heavy blindfold he put on the edge of the desk earlier. She showed no concern at his statement. Still, he watched her carefully. "I'm going to touch your head," he said before he secured the material over her eyes and around her head. Her breathing remained calm.

"You're totally dependent upon me to be your eyes now." He curled his fingers into a fist so he wouldn't be tempted to touch her again. "You have my assurance I will not misguide you. Place your trust completely in me. Can you do that?"

"Yes, Sir."

"Stand up for me, little one."

She moved slowly to her feet, using her arms to balance herself. "It's a bit scary, Sir."

"That's why you have to rely on me. You've already said I don't scare you."

"That was before you took my sight away, Sir."

"What is the primary foundation for any Dominant/submissive relationship?"

"Trust, Sir."

"Correct. I'm going to push you during our time together. Your mind must learn that I am completely trustworthy, so even when your body balks at what I ask, your mind knows the answer instinctively."

A shiver ran through her. "You ask for a lot, Sir," she whispered.

"And I give so much more. I'm going to take your hand." He touched her hand and her fingers wrapped around his. "Come with me, now. Six steps forward and we'll be at the door."

Step by step, he led her to the sitting room. She knew because he'd told her and it made sense with what she knew about the layout of the guesthouse. Once there, he stopped her at the entrance. Sasha held tightly to his hand, telling herself not to be scared, that she was with Cole and he'd promised he wouldn't hurt her. She had to trust someone at some point, and she wanted to trust him.

"You know where we are?" he asked, his accent so smooth. She could listen to him forever.

"The sitting room."

"Yes, but it's been modified. You wouldn't recognize it." He squeezed her hand. "I'm going to let go now and tell you how to navigate the room. You'll be fine as long as you listen and follow my commands. But if you don't?" He chuckled. "Each bump into a table, chair, or wall carries a penalty. Make it into the sunroom without a penalty and you'll earn a reward."

Nothing too bad was going to happen, she told herself. Even if she bumped into something, the worse he'd probably do was make her write dirty sentences. On the other hand, if she made it?

Hell, yes, she wanted to experience one of Master Johnson's rewards.

"I'm ready, Sir."

"Good job, little one. Two steps forward."

It started out easy enough. Little steps forward. Turn right and two more steps. But as she made her way deeper into the room and farther from him, her nerves and self-doubt tried to get the better of her.

"Don't you trust me?" Peter's voice had been accusatory. Almost as if he was saying she didn't get a say in what they did.

"Of course I trust you, but . . ." How would she safeword?

"No buts. Either you do or you don't."

"Sasha?" Cole's voice didn't sound anything like Peter's. The memory disappeared.

"Yes, Sir?"

"You froze. Are you okay?"

She took a few deep breaths. *I'm safe. I'm with Cole. He'll protect me.* "I had a flashback, Sir, but I feel better."

She heard him walking toward her and then she felt his nearness.

His breath tickled her ear. "I'm going to touch your shoulders."

She only had a chance to nod before his hands were rubbing her shoulders. Her body moved instinctively toward him.

"First of all, breathe, little one. Then tell me what happened."

She took several deep breaths, like he'd told her before. Funny how such a simple act made her feel better. "It was a flashback to that night. Peter. He asked me if I trusted him, but I was afraid. I wouldn't be able to safe out."

"So you knew you shouldn't have moved forward?" His tone was light and non-accusatory. And his hands felt so good.

"Yes, but I didn't say anything. I thought it was sweet we knew each other so well we didn't need safe words anymore."

"I'm not going to give you a lecture on why that was a mistake. I'm sure you've heard it enough. I will tell you that if you're uneasy about anything we're doing, I expect you to yellow. The only thing that will upset me is if you don't use your safe words. Understood?"

"Yes, Sir."

He continued rubbing her shoulders and back. It wasn't long before her tension left completely.

She swayed against him.

"Better?"

"Yes, Sir."

"Do we need to stop?"

"I'd like to finish."

His breath tickled her ear again. "That's my girl," he said with one last squeeze of her shoulder. "You make me proud."

His praise gave her the strength she needed to finish. Though she'd doubted her ability to find a knowledgeable Dom, her instincts told her *he* was a Dom worth submitting to. Unfortunately, he was only hers for this little slice of time. He didn't even think she was submissive enough to have sex with.

But I can show him this. I can prove I can do this.

With a renewed confidence, she focused on his voice and broke out into a huge smile when he told her she'd made it to the sunroom.

"Stay where you are. Keep the blindfold on." His voice moved closer to her.

She was still smiling when he removed the blindfold. Her first sight was his own smile.

"You did it," he said. "Wonderfully and without penalty. I'm so proud of you."

Holy fuck, what that smile did to his face. He was so gorgeous it hurt.

"Thank you, Sir," she managed to get out.

"So, what will it be for your reward? What do you want? If it's within reason, it's yours."

His lips mesmerized her. They were full and so sexy-looking, and when he smiled like he was, her heart skipped a beat.

The words rushed out before she could stop them. "A kiss, Sir. I want a kiss."

He froze. "A kiss?"

She could have kicked herself. He'd been so happy and pleased with her. Now he was looking at her like she'd lost her mind.

She looked at his shoes. "It's okay, I mean, you don't have to. I under—"

"Stop, Sasha."

Silence surrounded them and then he softly said, "I'm going to touch you."

His hand gently cupped her chin and when he lifted her head, she found him staring at her mouth. His thumb traced her bottom lip as if asking a question. He was so silent, she knew he was thinking of a polite way to tell her no. How could she have blurted out something so stupid? She hoped this didn't make things uncomfortable between them.

"Oh, Sasha," he said, his thumb sweeping her bottom lip one last time, and he lowered his head so his lips lightly brushed hers.

She couldn't hold back the low moan that escaped her throat.

He whispered a curse and then his lips were back on hers in a crushing kiss that took her breath away.

His lips were more than full, they were rough and demanding. His arms came around her and he pressed his hips into hers so she felt his sizable erection.

It was more than a kiss. It was a claiming, it was a command, and more than anything, it was an assurance. She could still feel desire and want and need for a man. A Dom, even.

He parted her lips and she tasted mint. She needed more, wanted more of his touch. She wanted to know what he meant when he said he required much from his sexual partners. He was everything she craved and even though he carried about him a hint of danger that should have scared her, it didn't.

One of his hands left her hip and inched up her body, bypassing her breasts and coming to rest behind her head. His fingers dug into her hair, holding her to him while he took what he wanted. He moved half a step closer, eliminating any remaining distance between them.

She had to touch him, had to. She put her arms around his waist and pushed ever so slightly against his ass, hoping to feel more of his cock. She gasped. Damn.

His hips jerked and he pulled back with a groan. She kept her head down and didn't dare look at him. She knew that once she did, she'd only see regret in his eyes and couldn't face that yet. But he spoke her name and when she looked up, she only saw his desire for her.

"I won't apologize," he said in a voice that was several degrees hoarser than before.

"I would hope not, Sir. It's what I asked for."

He didn't smile. "So you did, little one. But I think it's for the best we don't do that again."

She tried her best not to dwell on the kiss. After all, what was one kiss? She'd been kissed hundreds of times. What was it about *his* that should make it so special? Was it because it was the first she'd had after Peter?

Deep down she knew better.

Even if she told herself that and believed it for the shortest moment, twice a day, her body proved her wrong. After she inserted the horrible plug, she'd situate herself on her back, reclining in her bed. Her eyes would close and as she relaxed, she'd let her knees fall apart. And though each time the fantasy was different with regard to what they did, one thing was consistent—when she arched her back and panted with the pleasure of release, the only thought in her mind was Cole Johnson.

She decided to leave that part out of her journal.

On Saturday afternoon, he met her at the shop as she and Julie were closing.

"Afternoon, ladies," he said, looking devilishly handsome in a worn pair of khakis and a blue T-shirt that emphasized his biceps and brought out the blue hues in his eyes.

"Hey, Cole." Julie picked up her purse and dug through it, pulling out her keys. "You two off to somewhere fun?"

He hadn't told her where they were going, only that he would pick her up at closing. Deciding to tease him a bit, Sasha looked up at him. "I don't know, he hasn't told me where we're going. Are you taking me somewhere fun?"

His eyes traveled over her and instead of answering he replied with, "Sasha, you look lovely. I don't think I've seen you in a dress before."

"Thank you." She'd spent an inordinate amount of time trying to find something to wear and had pulled the dress from the back of her closet.

Julie snorted, but thankfully didn't say anything about how rare it was for her to wear a dress. "Bye, guys," she said and headed out.

Cole stood by Sasha's side while she locked up and then led her to his waiting car.

"Today," he said, opening the passenger side door for her, "I'm taking you to do one of my favorite things."

Her mind raced, trying to imagine the possibilities. He didn't say anything else as they drove out of the historic district. She tried to think of possibilities for his favorite things, but she was at a loss and didn't even know where to start.

Now, one of *her* favorite things had to be kissing him, even after just their one kiss. But she doubted they were going to do that. Especially since he made an ordeal about it not happening again.

She watched him from the corner of her eye. He didn't seem affected by the kiss. Even in the shop he acted the same as always. It probably didn't cross his mind after it happened, and she was even happier she hadn't written all the details of her time with the plug.

They pulled into the parking deck of a high-end hotel the Petal Pushers did business with.

"You're taking me to a hotel?" There was only one thing she

could imagine doing in a hotel with Cole, and he'd made it clear earlier in the week that wouldn't happen.

"Yes, but not for the reason you think. Today, we're going to get to know each other by having tea."

"Tea?" She took the arm he offered her and walked with him inside.

"I *am* an Englishman."

"I thought so, considering, you know, the accent and all."

He obviously came by the hotel frequently. Almost every employee they passed greeted him with a "Hello, Mr. Johnson," and he'd reply with a smile and a nod, calling them by name. She didn't say anything until they got to the hostess, a gorgeous woman who looked her up and down before turning her attention to Cole.

"Come here often, do you?" she asked as they were led to a window table.

He flashed his million-dollar smile at the hostess, told her the table was perfect, and held Sasha's chair out for her. "It's so hard to find good tea in the Colonies."

"The Colonies? Seriously, the war's been decided for more than two hundred years. Let it go."

"My dear, when it comes to tea, I'm never content to 'let it go.'"

He was carefree, relaxed, and perfectly in his element as he selected his tea and offered suggestions for hers. They made small talk for a few minutes, stopping only when the waitstaff brought their tea.

She watched as he prepared his tea and copied on her own. Before too long, they were served tiny sandwiches and pastries. The silence and efficiency of the servers caught her attention, and she mentioned it to him.

"This is nothing." He took a sip of tea. "You should see the service exhibited by a full-time slave at high tea. Perfection."

Her hands trembled slightly at the thought. Just as quickly, she had a vision of Cole dressed in a three-piece suit, sitting at a formal table as she served him tea. She had on a short skirt and while she poured him water, his hand slid up her thigh.

"Sasha?" he asked, and she realized she'd spaced out for a moment. "Did you have an attack?"

"No." She squirmed in her seat. At his continued look, she added, "The opposite, actually."

His eyebrow shot up. "Indeed?"

"Yes, Sir."

He didn't say anything else about it, nor did he mention her slip in calling him "Sir." In fact, he changed the subject altogether, asking her where she went to college and how she met Julie.

She went along with the conversation, answering his questions and then asking him about his own education. She knew he'd been at college with Daniel for a while, but knew nothing about his life after.

He spoke of his hometown in England, his days at Oxford, and how, even though he loved the UK, he now considered the U.S. his home.

"When did you first get involved in the lifestyle?" she asked as he prepared her a second cup of tea.

"In Oxford." He leaned back in his seat. "Was doing a bit of research and supplemented with a little hands-on experimenting."

"That sounds quite . . . thorough."

"Never let it be said I cut corners."

"I don't think anyone could ever say that."

He inclined his head in response. "How about you, when did you first enter the lifestyle?"

"In college. One of my boyfriends restrained me . . . during sex."

"And you liked it?"

"Very much." She was reminded of a conversation she had with Julie not too long ago. "But the bondage isn't the main reason I stayed, though I do like that part."

"What kept you coming back?"

"Being able to give control to someone else. Knowing he'll protect me. To just be able to *feel* for the time I'm with him, knowing that in doing so I'll please him."

"Is that what you were doing the night you were with Peter? Giving him control? Trying to please?"

For some reason, she didn't feel the usual tightening in her chest that typically followed talk of that night. Probably because she was in a hotel having tea. Or maybe it was because of who she was talking with.

"I knew we'd have to discuss it eventually," she said.

"Today, we don't have to discuss anything you don't want to. But yes, we will touch on it more eventually. Though I'll remind you, I'm not a therapist. I simply want to help you as you get back into the lifestyle."

She closed her eyes and took a deep breath. Focused on the quiet conversations around them, the faint clinking of china, the aroma of spicy tea.

I can do this. I am safe. He will protect me.

When she opened her eyes, she was ready and, across the table, Cole smiled softly. She swallowed around the lump in her throat.

"Only if you're ready, little one. It can wait."

"He wanted to collar me. No one's ever wanted to do that before." A question filled her mind. "How many submissives have you collared?"

"Only one," he said almost hesitantly.

Kate. And there was something else there. Something he wasn't telling her, but now wasn't the time to ask about it.

"I wanted," she started and then paused. "I wanted to mean that much to someone. I'd been a submissive for six years and never worn anyone's collar. Do you think that's bad?"

"I think it's a big step to wear someone's collar. The fact that you haven't found the right Dom isn't a reflection on you. It just shows you're holding out for the right one."

"And I jumped too quickly when I thought I found him." And she would carry the scars of that poor decision for the rest of her life. Literally, she added with a snort, thinking back to Cole's assignment.

"It's not a mistake to be wanted," he said softly. "And I'm sorry the trust you gave wasn't cared for and cherished the way it should have been. That is a difficult lesson to learn the hard way."

He spoke so tenderly it made her eyes water. Even Daniel, when he'd talked with her about that night, had never touched her so deeply with his words.

"Sasha." He reached across the table to take her hand. "You are a beautiful woman and you have a sweet, sultry, and sassy submissive nature. If someone hasn't claimed you with his collar yet, it is not a reflection upon you."

She sniffled and rolled her eyes. "Please don't say it's because they don't see how special I am."

"I wasn't going to say that."

"Then what were you going to say?"

His grip tightened on her hand. "It's because they know they aren't man enough to master a submissive such as yourself."

She almost laughed at him, but one look told her he was serious. Unfortunately, she had the sinking feeling there was only one man with the ability to master her and he'd already told her he wasn't interested. She tossed her head. "I've been a submissive for six years, I'm willing to bet such a man doesn't exist."

"I wouldn't make that bet if I were you. You'll lose."

When he dropped her back off at her apartment after tea, he'd told her to arrive at the guesthouse on Tuesday after work wearing a conservative dress. She arrived five minutes early and he was pleased to see she'd arranged her hair so it lay flat instead of standing up in spikes like it often did.

"Good evening, little one."

"Good evening, Sir." Her smile seemed to come easier to her lately. The thought made him happy.

He motioned for her to enter the house. "I have something planned tonight I think you'll enjoy. Hand me your journal and go wait for me in the sitting room."

"Thank you, Sir." She gave him her journal and headed down the hall.

He took the journal into his office and read over her entries about the plug. He made it through all of them, then closed the book and leaned back in his chair. She had completed the assignment, and unlike before, she had done exceptionally well.

Many of her entries were completed in pencil and the numerous smudges showed exactly how careful she'd been and how many errors she'd caught. Though he'd enjoyed having her recite the dirty sentences, her dedication to improving and working harder spoke volumes.

He pushed back from his desk and went to find her. She knelt, waiting for him, in the sitting room and he took a minute to watch her. Kneeling appeared to have a calming effect on her. She usually looked so serene as she waited on her knees. What he would like is to have that calm spread to other areas of her life.

"There was a vast improvement in your assignment this week, little one."

"Thank you, Sir."

"Your effort pleases me."

She didn't say anything, but her cheeks flushed a light pink color.

"Stand up and come with me," he said.

She followed him into the dining room and shot him a questioning look when he pulled out a chair from the head of the table and bid her to sit down.

"There was a certain look of excitement you had on Saturday when I mentioned a slave serving high tea. The idea of serving tea appeals to you, doesn't it?"

"Yes, Sir."

"There is something almost primitive about the ritual of serving tea. On the surface, it comes across as nothing more than one person pouring tea and offering food to another. And for some, that's all it is. On the other hand, when done between a slave and Master, it can take on an erotic quality."

She glanced over to his side where a cart stood, filled with silver and china. Once more he was certain he saw a flash of yearning in her expression.

"I would like very much to teach you how to serve tea, little one. Is that something you would like?" He wasn't usually uncertain, but with Sasha having had such a strong reaction to the tea, he wanted to make sure she was comfortable.

"Yes, Sir." She spoke slowly. "I would like that very much."

"Thank you, Sasha."

His hands had an itch to run his fingers through her hair or to graze the nape of her neck, but he restrained himself. There was no reason to touch her at the moment outside of him just wanting to.

"Tonight, I'm going to demonstrate by serving you. You will watch, learn, and serve me at our next session. Do you have any questions?"

She licked her lips and crossed and uncrossed her legs. "It doesn't seem right, Sir. For you to serve me."

"It pleases me to do this."

She looked again to the serving cart. "In that case, Sir, I would be honored."

"Thank you, little one. Now no matter if you are serving only your Master, or a group of twenty, the host is always seated at the head of the table." He motioned to her seat. "After everyone is seated, a slave will wait patiently for her Master to indicate it is time to begin. Your Master will probably have a preference as to how he would like you to serve in a group setting. Either you'll begin with the guest of honor, then the females, followed by the males, and ending with the host or you will start with the guest to the right of the host and then proceed around the table, ending with the host." He raised an eyebrow. "All clear?"

"Yes, Sir. Will you share with me which you prefer?"

He swallowed around the lump in his throat at how she wanted to know his preferences. How long had it been since he'd worked with anyone who had such a sweet serving spirit? She would make some Dom very happy one day.

"I usually request the second option."

"Usually, Sir?"

"I like to keep those serving me on their toes." *Those serving me.* Why had he worded it that way instead of saying *my slave*?

Perhaps because she knew he'd only collared one woman? He may have well said her name.

He wasn't sure if Sasha knew Kate was more than his submissive. That Kate had served him twenty-four/seven as a slave instead of a Dominant/submissive relationship like Daniel and Julie. He was afraid that knowledge might make her more timid or bring on a panic attack.

But he was with Sasha at the moment and didn't want to think about Kate. And Sasha was frowning.

"Tea service is special for me, Sasha. You are only the second person I've done this with."

"Really?" she asked, and he was pleased to see the frown lines ease around her forehead.

"Really." He smiled and continued. "Tea is presented before the food, and you always serve from the right."

She listened attentively as he described how and when to pour and serve. With watchful eyes that missed nothing, she studied the way to position the cup, saucer, and spoon. Though she had been uneasy at the thought of him serving her, he noticed that unease grow as she realized how much there was to remember.

He was going over how a slave was to behave while serving when she stopped him.

"Excuse me, Sir, but can I go get my journal? There's so much to remember, I'd like to write it down so I don't forget."

"No," he said. "You may not. I want to see how much you remember when you serve me in a few days." Her frown lines returned. "It's a learning exercise, little one. There will be no penalty if you forget something." At her smile he added, "The first time, anyway."

He almost added that if she did well, there might be a reward, but before he could form the sentence, he remembered what she requested the last time he rewarded her. He decided not to say anything. After all, though he considered himself very self-disciplined, a man could only take so much.

The next day after closing the shop with Julie, Sasha waited downstairs instead of heading up to her apartment. She went to the break room to turn the light on and had just cleared the table of scattered papers when someone knocked on the door.

She was expecting Abby, but Nathaniel stood at his wife's side, holding a large box. Abby held little Henry, and Elizabeth was spinning around in circles.

"Hey, guys. Come on in." She moved to the side and let the family pass.

"I'm so dizzy." Elizabeth laughed.

Abby shifted Henry and put her hand on her daughter's shoulder. "Come on in, silly."

"Hey, Sasha," Nathaniel said. "Tell me where to put this, and the kids and I will get out of your hair. We have a date at the Children's Museum."

"Dinosaurs." Henry nodded. "*Rawr.*"

"Break room would be great, thanks." Sasha giggled as Henry made dinosaur claws at his sister.

"He's talked nothing but dinosaurs for days," Abby said.

"*Rawr,*" Henry said again.

"Come here, big guy." Nathaniel returned from the break room and reached for Henry. "Let's go hunt dinosaurs."

"You guys have fun," Abby said, lifting up on her toes and kissing Nathaniel.

"Call me when you're ready to go home," he said against her lips.

When he left, Abby turned to her. "Okay, I'm dying to know. Tea service? Is a regular pot not enough?" She spoke with a smile. Obviously, she had some sort of an idea what she needed it for.

"Cole's training me to serve tea, and I want to practice."

They walked into the break room, and Abby started unpacking the china pieces. "I've never done that, so I probably won't be much help."

"That's okay, I just need you to sit at the table."

"That I can do."

For the next fifteen minutes, Sasha practiced serving tea to Abby as best as she could, pulling from memory everything Cole had told her the day before. There were a few times she wasn't sure she was serving correctly, but all in all, she was pleased with what she recalled.

After the second run-through, she plopped down in the chair beside Abby. "Okay, I think I'm good."

"I thought you did great. Of course, I have nothing substantial to base that on."

"That's okay. You helped more than you know simply by being here and bringing the stuff over."

"I'm glad." Abby smiled. "Since this counts as our weekly meeting, why don't you tell me how it's going with Cole? Outside of him teaching you tea service."

"So far, so good," Sasha admitted. "He's different than anyone I've played with. Such a complex combination of easygoing guy and no-nonsense Dominant."

He was such a protector. She remembered at tea how tender and gentle he'd been when she'd confessed her fears about never being collared. There had been a kindness and sincerity she'd rarely experienced when he spoke to her. For a second she let her mind wander and thought about what it would be like to be his for more than a retraining.

"What's the wistful look for?" Abby asked.

Sasha wasn't sure she wanted to admit what she was thinking, but then decided if she couldn't discuss it with someone she trusted, who else was there?

She dropped her gaze to the delicate flower pattern on the teacup sitting on the table. "I was just thinking about what it'd be like to be collared by someone like Cole."

Abby didn't say anything. When the silence grew too lengthy, she looked up at the other woman. Abby's face was unreadable.

Sasha gave her a weak smile. "I know I'm not near ready for anything of the sort, but it doesn't hurt to think, right?"

"When you say 'someone like Cole,' what do you mean, exactly?"

Sasha had a feeling there was more behind Abby's question than what was being asked. "You told me you did some mental play with him. You know what he's like. Or was there more to the question?"

Abby templed her fingers. "How much do you know about his relationship with Kate?"

"I know they were together for a long time, they lived together, and she left him."

"There's more. It's not a secret or anything. Kate was his slave."

Sasha felt her body stiffen at the word. "Slave? As in . . . ?"

"Twenty-four/seven. Yes."

"Wow. That is—" She stopped. She was going to say "completely unexpected" but after only a few seconds of thinking, the statement made sense.

And turned her on.

"Is what?" Abby asked.

"Interesting. That's interesting," Sasha said, trying to hide her curiosity and unexpected arousal. Abby raised an eyebrow, so she continued, "Some of the comments he's made make more sense now."

"And?"

Sasha leaned back in her seat and crossed her arms. "You're as bad as a Dom. You know that, right?"

Abby laughed. "I don't think I've ever been told that, but thanks. Now, tell me what else was going through your head."

"I think the idea of a Master/slave with Cole is hot."

The smile left Abby's face. "Wait. What?"

"When Peter suggested collaring me, he said he wanted to be twenty-four/seven on weekends." Sasha was pleased to discover she only felt a mild uneasiness talking about Peter. Nothing at all like she'd felt in the past. "I didn't like the idea, but somehow thinking about being that way with Cole sounds more attractive."

"Sasha." Abby's voice had grown very serious. "You aren't in a position to serve any Dom like that right now, much less . . ."

She stopped talking and looked down at her lap. Before she could say anything else, Sasha finished her sentence for her.

"Much less one like Cole?"

"I'm sorry, but yes." Abby took a deep breath. "You're only seeing a part of the Dom Cole is. He's holding back a great deal because he's an excellent trainer, but don't be mistaken, he would not be an easy Master to serve."

"I wasn't even thinking of it that way. I was thinking what it'd be to have his care and protection all day, every day."

"And all night, every night. As a slave, you give up control of everything. He wants to fuck at two in the morning, you fuck at two in the morning and you like it."

She knew Abby meant it as a deterrent, but just thinking about it turned her on.

"Sasha, wake up."

His voice is insistent and even though the bed is warm and sleep tempting, she wants to please him more than she wants either the warm bed or sleep. He's been working long into the night lately and while she goes to sleep alone, she knows it won't be too long before he wakes her each night. She loves that he can't sleep without taking her first.

She rolls over to face him. "Yes, Master?"

He is standing naked by the bed, hands on his hips, his erection jutting upward. He crooks a finger at her. "Come here. Arse to the edge of the bed. And make it fast, I'm hard as hell and need to fuck."

He doesn't ask if she's ready. He doesn't have to. It's her place to be ready for his cock at all times. She moves to the edge of the bed and feels the growing wetness between her legs as she does.

He places a hand on each of her knees, keeping her spread for him, and enters her fully with one thrust. "Fuck, yes."

He presses deeper.

"Hell, you didn't hear anything I said."

Sasha snapped back to reality. "I heard the two-in-the-morning-fuck part."

Abby groaned.

"Look at it this way," Sasha said. "I'm safe in my fantasies."

Three days later, she knelt in Cole's office and questioned the intelligence in writing her slave fantasy down for him to read. Though her head was down, she could clearly picture how he looked reading her journal. He would be frowning and there would be worry lines between his eyebrows.

It took him a long time to read.

Finally, *finally,* she heard the chair scrape against the floor. She waited for footsteps, but only more silence followed.

Right when she thought she would be kneeling forever, there was a soft squeak from the seat cushion followed by slow footsteps that came closer and stopped behind her.

His voice was rough. "Interesting reading today, little one."

Glad I could keep you entertained. But she knew better and didn't want to start the discussion out on the wrong foot, so instead she said nothing.

"I was unaware you had an interest in being a slave," he said.

"Before this week, I didn't know I had an interest, Sir."

"What triggered that interest?"

"I had a talk with Abby."

"I see." He gave a coarse laugh. "And Abby told you Kate was my slave."

"Yes, Sir. She said you were twenty-four/seven." She prepared herself for the lecture on how she wasn't ready and why she was foolish to even contemplate such a thing. Damn it, what was she thinking writing it down for him?

"I can see the appeal," he said, surprising her. "There's a certain security involved, at least on some level. And, of course, there's the mutual commitment. But, Sasha, don't romanticize the position of an M/s relationship.

"You are owned by your Master. You are his to tease and torment as he pleases. Serving him is your all-consuming passion and pleasing him your only goal. If he wishes to use only your mouth for a month, you will suck his cock and be thankful for the privilege to taste him. If he tells you to sit naked with your pussy displayed for his viewing pleasure, you will sit with your legs spread so he can enjoy the sight of his cunt. Even if he wants you to stay that way for hours and he spends most of that time in a different room. Do you understand?"

"Yes, Sir," she said, but wasn't sure. She hadn't gone through every possible scenario.

"There are days you'll feel your only worth is tied to your arse, your mouth, your pussy, and how often he decides to fuck them. For instance, I would require you to be naked whenever you were at home, command you to kneel and present yourself for my use when we were in the same room. And make no mistake, Sasha, I would use you and use you often.

"In the morning before you left my bed, you would suck me deep into your mouth. I'd order you home for lunch and spread you out on my table, where I'd take my time feasting on your pussy before I fucked it. And after work, I'd keep you naked and spend hours driving you to the brink of orgasm until finally I'd allow you to come, but only with my cock buried deep in your arse."

He bent down and whispered in her ear, "Is that what you want, Sasha? To be my fuck toy to use when, where, and how I want? You honestly wouldn't mind if, while you were reading a book, I ordered you to your hands and knees on the floor because I decided my cock's need to fuck outweighed your need to read?"

She stiffened at his words. There was more to it than that. And no, she wasn't interested in being used only for sex. It was the whole dynamic of the Master/slave relationship that appealed to her.

"It's more than that, Sir. It's not always like that."

He hadn't moved from behind her. "I'm well aware of the many facets involved in such a relationship. I did have a collared slave for several years. And if asked, I'm sure she would tell you it was like that enough of the time."

"Then there was a part of her that needed to be used like that." She took a deep breath, steadying herself. "The relationship wouldn't have lasted as long as it did if she wasn't being satisfied."

"Think beyond the sexual," he said, not responding to her statement. "You own a business. What if your Master decides he doesn't want you working? Would you be prepared to sell your part of the floral shop?"

"Did Kate work, Sir?"

"I *allowed* her to work. Do you honestly think you could live in a situation like that? To hand over control to every part of your life? From your haircut, to your clothes, to whether or not you could have lunch with your girlfriends when you wanted?"

"I don't know, Sir."

"There are Master/slave couples who don't use safe words."

He spoke it simple and matter-of-factly, but it had the intended impact. She sucked in a breath and swallowed her panic. Her voice gave no hint of fear when she replied, "Everything's still negotiable. I wouldn't enter into any relationship without a safe word. It's a hard limit."

"And I would applaud you for that. However, I won't train you to be my slave. I don't mean to be cruel, but you're not mentally prepared to take on such a role."

She balled her fists so her nails dug into her palms. "I don't want to be your slave, Sir. That's not why I wrote that."

The air behind her moved as he stood. "Then what was your purpose?"

"I want you to give me some training, *just a little taste*, in full-time slave service."

"No."

She took a deep breath, his response exactly what she thought it would be. She knew arguing wouldn't change his mind. In all likelihood, it would only make him angry. "May I propose a compromise, Sir?"

"A compromise?"

"You know, that thing where we both budge a little to reach a mutually satisfying arrangement?"

His voice was terse and unamused. "No, can't say I'm familiar with the concept."

"I agree I'm not ready to serve as a slave right now or even train as one. But can we relook at the idea in a month or so?" There was only silence behind her. "Please, Sir?"

For several seconds, he stood and then he slowly walked away from her. Toward the window, she believed. She heard his sigh from across the room.

"Very well, a month it is. And to give you a *little taste*, you're not allowed to wear knickers for the next month." He smirked at her gasp of shock. "And rest assured, I'll be checking."

Friday afternoon, Cole sat in Daniel's kitchen while his friend prepared steaks to grill.

"You sure you don't want to stay for dinner?" Daniel asked, washing his hands. "I have plenty."

"I'm sure. I have a phone interview with a source in about an hour." And he was starting to feel like a third wheel, staying on Daniel's property. Eating with him and Julie would only make it worse.

"If you change your mind . . ." Daniel let the offer hang in the air.

"Thanks, but I think I'll let you and Julie enjoy your Friday night alone this week." He didn't miss the look of anticipation that crossed Daniel's face. Cole snorted. "Obviously, you have plans for the evening."

"Hell, yes!"

"I guess that means——"

His talk with Daniel was interrupted by the sound of feminine laughter coming from the front door. He recognized Sasha's voice immediately. She sounded carefree and happy and he smiled in response. She needed to laugh more.

"We're in the kitchen," Daniel called out, and Sasha's laughter stopped.

Seconds later, Julie entered the kitchen followed by a now subdued Sasha. Julie made her way to Daniel, who pulled her close and gave her a welcome home kiss. All the while, Sasha stood in the kitchen doorframe, hands behind her back, and her eyes anywhere except on the kissing couple.

"Sasha," Cole said.

She moved her gaze to him. "Sir."

Her voice was breathy and her cheeks slightly flushed. He wondered if she was wearing panties.

"Did you and Julie have a nice afternoon?"

"Yes, Sir."

He locked gazes with her, wanting to ensure she understood his next comment. "How fortunate then you had nothing to take priority over your outing."

She didn't look convinced, her lips pressed together and she stood straighter. "I suppose."

She shifted her weight, which told him she was doing one of two things. Either she was wearing panties and being around him made her feel uncomfortable due to her disobedience or she wasn't wearing panties and she felt the weight of his Dominance just being in his presence.

"Daniel, you and Julie will have to excuse us for a moment. I need a private moment with Sasha."

Julie wrinkled her eyebrows, but Daniel only nodded. "The house is yours."

"Thanks." He turned his attention back to Sasha. "Come with me, little one."

There was a large guest room down the hall from the kitchen. He led her there and into the roomy bathroom attached. Once there, he opened the door and bid her enter first. He closed the door behind them.

"Kneel," he commanded and she went to her knees. "Have you been a good submissive, Sasha?"

"Yes, Sir."

"Thank you, I believe you, but since I told you I'd check, I'm going to check. I want you to stand up and take the shorts off." He let that sink in for a minute. If she had followed his directions, this would be the first time he saw her naked. "If I like what I see, you'll be rewarded."

Ever so slowly, she stood to her feet and unbuttoned her shorts. He held his breath as she inched them down, revealing only bare skin. She was shaved, but the shorts had been on the snug side and left red marks on her skin.

"Good girl." He moved to stand behind her. In that position, he could see them both in the mirror. "Tell me what it was like, being panty-free."

"It made me aroused, Sir. And every time I thought about how turned on I was, you always came to my mind."

"Exactly what I wanted. Are you aroused now? Standing in Daniel's loo, half naked, with your pussy exposed to me?"

She sucked in a breath. "Yes, Sir."

"For being such a good girl, I'd normally bring you to

orgasm. But I don't think you're ready for me to touch you like that, so you'll have to be my hands."

"Sir?"

"You're going to pleasure yourself for me."

She moaned and he met her eyes in the mirror, gave her a smile.

"Spread your legs more," he ordered. When she'd widened her stance, he added, "Start at your waist, brush your skin lightly, tease it, think about where your fingers are going."

She closed her eyes and her fingers drifted to her waist. Her lower lip was sucked into her mouth in concentration.

"Let your fingers brush lower, but don't touch your clit." The color in her cheeks deepened at his words. "Tell me what you're thinking."

It seemed she found it easier to talk with her eyes closed. "I'm thinking of your fingers, Sir. About how they'd feel."

"How would they feel? Tell me whilst you play with your cunt."

She licked her lips. "Good, they'd feel good, Sir. You'd start by seeing how wet I was."

"How wet are you?"

"So fucking wet, Sir."

Her coarse voice turned him on, but he forced himself to ignore his cock. "Your little pussy's so wet and it's aching for me to push my finger along your slit and take care of that ache, isn't it? Desperate for me to fill it. Two fingers, you think, or three?"

"Sir?" she croaked.

"How many fingers do I fuck you with, Sasha? Two or three?"

Her body shook with need. "Oh, God, three, Sir."

He leaned as close as he could without touching her. "Then do it." Her fingers worked themselves between her legs. "Harder. I'd fuck you so damn hard."

He clenched his teeth as she pumped her fingers deep inside. It took almost all of his self-control not to push her hands aside and stroke her to release. He could almost feel her wet heat around his fingers. Her breath grew choppy and her body started to sway.

"I'm going to hold your shoulders to give you support," he whispered. "You keep fucking yourself. If I don't think you're doing a good job, I'm going to make you stop and you won't come for two weeks."

Once his hands were on her shoulders, she leaned into him. The small movement pleased him. Possibly without her even realizing it, her body trusted him to hold her steady while she drove herself to climax.

"How do my fingers feel now?" he asked.

She shook her head and lifted her hips toward her fingers. "Deep . . . so close. . . . I need . . . please . . ."

He thought she grew more and more beautiful as her orgasm approached. "Rub your clit for me, little one. Show me how you like it."

Under his gaze, her fingers worked themselves in and out of her body while her thumb teased her clit. She started to whimper.

"That's it. Good girl. Now let me see you come."

A few more passes of her thumb, and her body stilled as her release swept over her. He kept his hands on her shoulders, keeping her steady and upright, all the while whispering how beautiful her pleasure was, until she stopped shaking.

She slumped against him, breathing heavily. "Thank you, Sir."

Once she had recovered and made herself presentable, Cole took her back into the kitchen and settled her into a chair. Though her checklist indicated playing in public was a turn-on, he had wanted to do her first panty check in private.

Her cheeks still had a hint of darker than normal color to them, and her eyes were filled with contentment. A soft smile tickled the corner of her mouth and every so often, she'd catch his gaze only to quickly glance away.

Julie studied her with frank assessment, but unlike times past, she appeared to be satisfied with what she saw. Daniel, of course, acted as if nothing happened, but Cole knew he didn't miss anything.

"Julie and I are going to start planning next year's melanoma benefit tomorrow. We're going to check out a few venues. Either of you want to come?" Daniel asked.

"Hell, no," Cole said. "Event planning is about on a par with having a tooth pulled. I'd rather stay in the guesthouse and alphabetize canned goods."

Daniel snorted. "You say that like your cans aren't already alphabetized. Sasha?"

If Cole felt like a third wheel around Daniel and Julie, he could only imagine how Sasha felt. She squirmed in her seat.

"Actually," Cole said. "I was going to ask Sasha for help tomorrow."

Sasha laughed softly. "Oh, boy. I either spend the day looking at hotel ballrooms or arranging cans. I don't think I can handle all the excitement. I might have to decline both and wash my hair."

"If you help me, I promise we won't do anything with cans," Cole assured her. She raised an eyebrow at him. "I have an appointment to see a house."

Sasha had given him several names of real estate agents the second time they met for her retraining. Not being in a hurry to move and admittedly not looking forward to the hassle involved with looking for a new place, he'd postponed contacting anybody. He'd finally called one a few days ago, and she wanted to show him a newly listed property.

Sasha tapped her chin in mock thought. "House hunting definitely beats out hotel ballrooms, but I don't know. I really should wash my hair. Give me a second to think."

If he'd known talking her through an orgasm would have brought out this new playful side of her, he'd have done it earlier. He stretched out in his chair and put his arms over his head.

"Either way works for me. But if you're going to be home all day tomorrow, I have a new writing assignment for you."

"I believe that's called blackmail, Sir."

"In that case, you can do the writing assignment no matter what you decide."

Her eyes widened in shock. "You did that on purpose."

"Of course I did." He hid a smug grin, enjoying the playful banter between them. Unfortunately, he had that interview to conduct in about fifteen minutes. He pushed back from the table. "I have a call set up. I'll see everyone later. Sasha, walk out with me, please."

She hopped down and they made their way outside in silence. When they got to the guesthouse drive, he turned to her.

"If you'd like to go tomorrow, I'll pick you up at eight."

He was pleased to see the lighthearted look remained with her even though they were alone. He'd feared she'd feel awkward around him with everyone else gone.

"I'd like to go." She shrugged her shoulders. "I can wash my hair tonight."

He leaned down and whispered, "Wash it tomorrow morning. Tonight you're to write five hundred words on why going without panties made you so wet."

He slept restlessly that night, his thoughts consumed with the way Sasha's body had writhed under his gaze. How she'd followed his commands and brought herself to release at his bidding. She was a wonderfully sexual creature, and he allowed himself a few minutes to wish he hadn't been so insistent they not have sex.

Of course, he'd promised they'd discuss his training her in slave service. Hell, he was a bastard to even consider such a thing. He told himself he was doing it because if he didn't she might find someone else, and he'd be damned if that would happen.

But he knew if they agreed to any type of slave training, they would have to renegotiate their arrangement. In order for her to get the full experience, she'd have to move in with him, he'd have her naked for part of the day, and, if she agreed, he'd drop the restriction on sex.

That he told himself was the real reason he agreed to discuss the potential in a month: having her kneeling, naked and desperate for his cock, at his feet while he worked. Unbidden, his fantasy played out like puzzle pieces:

"You're going to have to wait. I have to finish this article."

He ignores her on purpose, pretending to write, but the entire time he is watching her. Her skin is freshly washed and he can smell just a hint of the lemongrass lotion he bought her. She tries to be still because she knows it pleases him, but he sees the minuscule movements of her body.

Sometime later he bids her to stand and display herself. He fondles her while reading over a draft and slaps her ass when she tries to direct where his hands go.

"Naughty slave, thinking she knows where her Master should touch her."

Next, he has her sit on his desk with her legs spread and finger herself without climaxing. He tells her to get ready, that she better be wet enough. She's dangerously close to losing it. He stands and takes his cock out, telling her if she comes, she doesn't get his cock for three days.

Finally, he allows them both what they want and she comes twice before he pulls back. He takes his still hard dick and tells her to bend over the desk. She knows his plan and she's nervous even as he prepares her with the lube.

But he holds her entirety in his hands and he wants only to bring her pleasure. And though he eventually takes his own release, it is her soft cry of gratification that's his true reward.

He woke up the next morning with an uncomfortable erection. Usually, he would take the matter into his own hand, but he decided to go for a quick run instead. As he'd hoped, the morning air and peaceful surroundings helped clear his mind, though he feared it didn't do much to calm his libido.

His assumption proved correct when he knocked on Sasha's door at five before eight and she answered. Her hair was still slightly damp and she didn't have any makeup on. She looked natural, and the effect was beautiful.

"Good morning, Sir. Would you like to come in?" Her smile indicated she probably slept better than he had. Of course, between the two of them, she'd been the one with the mind-blowing orgasm the day before.

"Thank you." He stepped inside, suddenly curious about the space she called home.

Her apartment was eclectically decorated with sleek contemporary black and white mixed with antique touches of deep red. It wasn't a style to be found on any decorating guide, but somehow it fit her personality perfectly.

Pip, the stray cat he and Nathaniel had rescued, was curled up on one end of the sofa. The kitten opened one eye, decided he wasn't worth her time, and went back to sleep.

"Pip looks good," he said. "I didn't know she was white."

"Hard to tell with all that dirt on her. I'd offer you some

breakfast, but I don't cook." She waved toward the kitchen. "I do have some coffee if you'd like. It's Kona, my favorite."

"I'm good, thanks. Never developed a taste for coffee." As he moved farther into her living room, he was able to look over her small kitchen area. Everything was tidy and neat, right down to the tea service displayed on the countertop. "I'll take some tea if you have it."

"Oh, no. I don't. Sorry."

He raised an eyebrow. "No tea with such an exquisite service? That's a travesty."

"It's Abby's. She brought it over so I could practice."

Her admission made him smile. The tea protocol he'd taught her was so important to her that not only was she practicing, but she'd had a friend bring over the necessary items.

"Have you been practicing, little one?"

"Yes, Sir. Every day."

"Would you like to serve me tea tomorrow?" He'd actually had something else planned, but if she'd been practicing, he felt he should reward her.

She dipped her head, but not before he saw her cheeks flush. "I'd like that, Sir."

"Look at me, little one." He smiled when she lifted her head, and the urge to touch her heated cheek was so strong, he balled his fist. "I'd like that, too."

He let them both stand for a minute in the anticipation-charged air. Excitement lit her features at the thought of serving him. Likewise, he let her see his desire to see how well she'd learned and remembered what he taught her about tea service.

He finally checked his watch, breaking their trance. "We need to head out if we're going to be on time."

She nodded and grabbed her purse and journal. Once they made it outside, he opened the passenger door for her. If he'd been traveling alone he'd have taken his motorcycle, but picked the car since Sasha would be going.

The property was in Southern Pennsylvania, so it took over half an hour to get there. Sasha appeared calm and at ease while they drove. They chatted about nothing in particular.

"I kind of pictured you in a penthouse or something," she said when they pulled onto a quiet road.

"I did think about it," he said. "But I like having my privacy, and that's not always possible in an apartment. I've grown fond of jogging around Daniel's land, as well. A house just made sense."

He turned onto a driveway. The house in the distance momentarily captured Sasha's attention.

"I'm not sure *house* is the right word," she whispered.

He laughed, but had to admit the home appeared larger than what he'd had in mind. The agent waited near the front entrance and greeted them both warmly.

"Mr. Johnson," the petite woman said, holding out her hand. "Pleasure to meet you in person."

Cole shook her hand, noting as he did the glimmer of surprise in her eyes when she saw Sasha.

"Sasha Blake," she said. "I know you gave Mr. Johnson my name, but I didn't know you'd be coming today."

"Yes," Sasha replied. "It's a small world sometimes, isn't it?"

He acted as if he was scratching his chin and instead hid his smile. Sasha was no shrinking violet. He truly admired her for that.

The agent unlocked the front door, but when she started to follow them inside, Cole stopped her.

"If you don't mind, I'd like for Sasha and me to look around first. We'll come find you if we need anything."

Her lips pressed together as if she was keeping herself from saying something, but eventually she nodded. "I'll be out back on the patio if you need me."

When she left, he crooked his finger at Sasha. "Come here, little one. Help me check this place out."

They started downstairs, and Cole was surprised to find he liked both the layout and the design. Looking at the house from outside, he'd feared the interior would be too traditional for his liking. Inside, everything looked modern and contemporary.

"Wow, this is a huge kitchen." Sasha stood near a freestanding island and spun around slowly. "I wouldn't know what to do with all this space. My entire kitchen would fit in one of these cabinets. Do you cook?"

He made his way to the island to stand at her side. "Yes, I taught myself. Comes in handy when I'm in a remote part of the world. Do you really not cook?"

"Never. If I can't nuke it or order it from a take-out menu, it doesn't make it to my kitchen." She ran the fingers of one hand down the island's countertop. He could almost feel the coolness of the stone beneath his fingertips.

"I think granite is my favorite type of countertop," he said. "Do you know why?"

"No, Sir."

He slowly walked around the island. "Let's say you're my slave and I told you to serve dinner at exactly six. Now normally, you're a very obedient slave, but for whatever reason, this time you're very late and I have to come looking for you.

"You're here in the kitchen. You look up, glance at the clock, and groan. You know you are so very late. I slide the belt from my trousers and instruct you lean across the island. You follow my command and press your cheek against the granite. How does it feel?"

Her eyes were locked on the countertop as if picturing herself braced against it. "Cool, Sir."

"Quite a contrast to the heating I'm about to give your backside, wouldn't you say?"

She nodded.

"When I finish, you ask if you can suck my cock in gratitude. I would normally allow it, but instead I hoist you onto the counter so the cool stone presses against the flaming heat of your arse. But you still have to service my cock, so I hold your legs open and take you. Hard. Driving into you, your body awash in the different sensations: hot and cold, pleasure and pain."

Sasha's lips parted slightly and she was breathing a little heavier than before.

"Do you see now why it's my favorite?" he asked, and she replied with a breathy, "Yes, Sir."

"Lean across the island, Sasha."

Chapter Four

His command echoed in her mind. *Lean across the island, Sasha.* She tried to close down the panic, but it was there, scratching the surface. And she knew this time it would win. Because it wasn't an unknown person bent over the island and it wasn't a fantasy. It was her and she was offering her back to a Dominant.

She clenched her fists, squeezed her eyes shut, and choked out a faint, "Yellow."

"Sasha, look at me." His voice was calm and steady. She cracked one eye open, fear still heavy in her throat. "Good girl. Can you open the other one?"

She took a deep breath and opened both eyes. Cole stood in front of her, close but not touching, and watched her with concerned eyes.

"You're safe. You're with me, and I won't let anything or anyone hurt you."

She nodded, but it was an automatic response. He could have said anything.

"Say it," Cole said. "Who are you with?"

"You."

"What's my name?"

"Cole. You're Cole."

"And you're what?"

"Safe." *Safe. Safe. Safe.* She looked into his steady blue-green eyes and knew it to be true. "I'm sorry, Sir."

"No." His voice was still calm, but there was an underlying edge to it. "Don't ever apologize for using a safe word. Understand?"

"Yes, Sir."

"Tell me what happened. You were aroused before I asked you to lean over the island."

She took a deep breath, but needed something more to ground her. "Will you hold my hand?"

"Of course, little one. Nothing would please me more."

He took her hand, and it was warm and comforting and strong enough to chase the fear away.

"Before, when you were talking, it was like it was happening to someone else. Even when you talked like it was me you were with. Because that just made it a fantasy. But when you told me to get into that position, that made it real."

"I see."

"I haven't been in a position like that, presenting my back, since . . . Peter."

He started rubbing his thumb along the top of her hand. "I understand, and I certainly see why you felt the need to yellow. If you feel up to it, I'd like to talk a bit about what might help you in the future."

"Yes, please."

"I was walking you through a scene verbally, and you were aroused. That was my intent, and your response brought me pleasure. Now, at the onset of your training, I told you I'd never do something without telling you. Remember?"

She nodded. "You said you'd never touch me without telling me."

"And have I acted accordingly?"

"Yes, Sir."

"And when you earned your first punishment, what did I tell you?"

"That I wasn't ready and you'd give me a week's notice when you thought I was."

"Right. Very good. So when I told you to lean across the island, what two things could you infer about what would happen next?"

He spoke in a low soothing tone, and his accent was a calming cadence that slowly showed her the path she'd been looking for. "That you wouldn't touch me without telling me and you weren't going to punish me."

"Excellent." His smile warmed the cold places inside her. "Thinking along those lines will help you in the future."

"Thank you, Sir." She felt like she had new weapons to battle the fear with.

"As for the position itself, that's something you'll have to practice. It'll take time."

Standing at the island, with him holding her hand, talking about what happened made her feel strong and brave. "I'd like to try now, Sir."

There was no change in his expression. "You would? Are you sure?"

"I want to try now, when I feel empowered."

He stopped rubbing her hand and gave it a gentle squeeze, then let go. "When you're ready then."

"I'd like for you to tell me to do it, please, Sir."

This time at her request, his expression changed and she saw more than approval, she saw respect. "Lean across the island, Sasha."

By keeping the image of Cole in her mind and reminding herself she was safe with him, she was able to lean across the island without the panic overtaking her.

"Very nice, little one. Take your shorts down."

She felt like slapping herself. Of course. He was checking to make sure she didn't have panties on. She reached behind her and pushed her shorts down, showing him her bare backside.

"You look so damn fuckable, Sasha." He walked closer to her and stopped right beside her head. He leaned over and whispered, "If we had time and there wasn't someone waiting outside, I'd make sure you came as hard as you did yesterday."

He took a step back and from the corner of her eye, she saw him tighten his hand into a fist and release it.

"For being so brave today," he said, "you may come as often as you want tonight. Without the plug."

"Thank you for your generosity, Sir," she said, knowing whose face would take center stage in her fantasies tonight.

"You're welcome, little one. Straighten your clothes now and help me look at the rest of the house."

When she was once more presentable, they explored the second floor. She loved the contemporary feel and thought it matched Cole perfectly. There were four bedrooms other than the master, so together they debated which one would make the best office and which the best playroom.

When they finally made their way outside, the agent was on her phone. She held up a finger to indicate she'd only be a minute longer and walked to the far side of the patio.

"I love what they did with this," Sasha said. "During the summer, I'd live out here." The backyard had been professionally landscaped and boasted a two-level brick patio.

Cole had his hands in his pockets as he looked over the yard. "I like that it's secluded with no neighbors nearby. You could do anything you wanted out here and no one would be the wiser."

She fought back the image of Cole and another woman taking advantage of the solitude to be found outside. She'd had to do the same thing upstairs when he'd picked out which bedroom would make the best playroom.

She pointed to the brick. "Have to watch out for the brick. That would be killer on the knees."

"Trust me." His eyes had darkened. "Her knees would be the least of her concerns. But you bring up an interesting point. If you were a slave and your Master brought you out here, would you kneel if he asked?"

She eyed the rough-looking brick. "Can I ask a question before I answer, Sir?"

"Yes."

"Why would the Master ask his slave to do something that could potentially be painful and uncomfortable?"

"For several reasons. To push her. Because he wants her on her knees. Or maybe to see if she's willing to be uncomfortable in order to please and serve him. For a slave, her Master's wants and needs always come before hers."

There was an intensity in his eyes whenever he spoke of the workings of a Master/slave relationship. What would it be like to be the ongoing focus of that intensity? He would watch his slave with that same stare. Her wants and needs might be second to his, but Sasha knew any slave of Cole's would be protected and cherished.

"And," he continued, "if our time outside became a bit rough, I would care for her body so thoroughly afterward, she wouldn't think twice about doing it again."

Sasha's mouth suddenly felt very dry. It didn't help at all that he moved to stand beside her and seductively whispered in her ear.

"Tell me, Sasha, if I told you to present yourself on the brick, kneeling and naked so I could use you, would you do it?"

She didn't even have to think about it. "Yes, Sir."

"Good girl. You would make your Master very happy, and he would reward you appropriately."

They jumped apart at the sound of the agent's voice.

"Sorry about that. Child drama." The agent approached them with a wide smile. "So what do you think?"

Funny how the house seemed almost secondary to everything else that had just happened.

"I like it," Cole said. "But I'm not sure I'm ready to make an offer just yet."

"Just so you know, it's new to the market and priced to sell."

He waved her comment away as if inconsequential. "I'm not worried, and I won't be rushed into making a decision."

"Do you have any questions, or can I show you another property?"

"No, I think Sasha and I will go to lunch and think this one over. I'll call you by tomorrow afternoon."

They all three walked back to their cars, the agent chatting about the house's location and surrounding areas. Cole didn't ask any questions, just nodded at what she said. He'd probably already researched the area.

Once they got in his car, Cole glanced over to Sasha. "Are you okay to have lunch, or do you need to get back home?"

"I can do lunch."

"I know just the place." He raised an eyebrow. "Ice cream for dessert?"

"Sounds divine."

The drive to the restaurant took just under fifteen minutes. She enjoyed the peaceful-looking scenery, but wondered if Cole wouldn't feel more comfortable in an urban setting. He just seemed like someone who would do better with the heartbeat of a city nearby.

"Here we are," he said, pulling into a long driveway on a property that looked more residential than commercial.

"Friends of yours?" she asked.

"No, I've actually never been here. Daniel told me about it."

Looking through the tree limbs, she saw a two-story building with a wraparound porch. "A bed and breakfast!"

"I take it you have no objections?"

"No, it's perfect." She loved little out-of-the-way places. Few went to the obscure sites, but those who did often returned time and again.

"They make their own ice cream, too."

"I like it even more."

He parked the car and walked around to open her door. The inn's gardens were beautiful, and she pointed out several of her favorite flowers.

"I'll have to get your input on flowers when I move into my new place," he said.

Just thinking about helping him with his landscaping made her excited. She pictured the grounds of the house they'd looked at today and the changes she'd make. "I'm not a landscaper, Sir."

"Maybe not, but I saw the excitement in your eyes when I brought it up just now."

"You Dominants don't miss anything," she huffed.

"If we're good, we don't." They'd made their way to the hostess. "Two for lunch, please."

After they sat down at a table overlooking the gardens, he passed her a menu. "I'd be honored for you to design my new garden."

She watched his eyes carefully, but found no hint of untruth. Of course, she'd already been around him enough to know he didn't lie. So why did she doubt him when it came to her occupation?

"Thank you, Sir." She spoke around the lump in her throat. "Does that mean you're going to make an offer on the house we saw today?"

"I think I will. It had everything I was looking for." He shot her a sexy-as-hell smile. "And those countertops? Perfection."

"Lot of room, for someone single." She bit her lip as soon as the words left her mouth, not believing she said them out loud.

He didn't seem fazed by her outburst. "Probably, but I do like having a lot of space. And it'll be a good spot for play parties. Not only are there plenty of rooms, but you don't have to worry about shocking the neighbors with your party outfits."

She cocked an eyebrow. "I know you aren't buying a house simply because it'd be handy for parties."

"Of course not. I want to bend someone over that island and fuck her senseless."

He said it in all sincerity, though there was still a hint of a smile on his lips.

"You're serious," she finally said.

"I usually am."

She started to read her menu, but he stopped her. "Eyes on me, Sasha."

She put the menu down and looked up.

"Tell me what you'd wear to the party at my house, little one. And don't take your eyes off of mine to see if anyone's listening. That's my job."

Damn, he knew her well. She took a deep breath and forced her eyes to remain on his. "I'd wear whatever my Master wanted me to wear."

"I punish submissives for evasive answers. I asked you the question because I want to know. What would you wear to my play party?"

There was a fantasy she had. It wasn't like her and she didn't think she'd ever do it in real life—but if she ever did act it out, it'd be at Cole's play party.

"I've never done this," she said, "but I've always imagined getting dressed up in black lace lingerie. A bra that gives me cleavage, a thong because when it's worn just right it keeps you aroused, and garters with sheer stockings just because I'd feel sexy as hell."

He very nearly growled. "If you dressed like that, I'd send everyone home except you."

She licked her bottom lip, pleased at the way his eyes followed the path of her tongue. Suddenly, she felt bold. "What would we do all alone in your house, Sir?"

"To start with, I'd give you a tour of the kitchen."

"Oh?" Her pussy throbbed with need.

"Specifically, the island."

"Would I need to look at it really closely?"

"If I did my job properly, your eyes wouldn't be able to focus on much of anything." He cleared his throat and picked up his menu. "Waitress."

Like she could focus on anything *now*. But she picked up the menu and tried her best. She ended up going with a chicken salad. To leave room for ice cream, she explained to Cole.

When the waitress left, Sasha knew she had to change the subject away from Cole and his kitchen island. Besides, she knew so little about his past and this was the perfect opportunity.

"When did you know you wanted to be a journalist?" she asked.

He took a sip of water, keeping his gaze on her while he drank. "I knew when I was eleven."

"Eleven? That young?"

"I discovered it early. Or maybe better stated, it found me." He leaned back and settled into the seat. "My parents didn't have much of a marriage. They only got married in the first place because it was expected of them."

"An arranged marriage?" Did people still do that?

"Very similar, yes. And by the time I was five, my father decided he'd had enough and ran off with his latest mistress. To get back at him, my mother decided to marry her latest boyfriend. Poor decision on her part. The boyfriend was an arse, and my father didn't care one way or the other. To make it worse, he had a son my age who was an even bigger arse, and a bully, too."

"I find it hard to believe anyone would bully you, Sir."

He snorted. "I've changed just a little."

"Sorry to interrupt. Go on."

"At first it was little things he'd blame on me: frogs in the pantry, salt in the sugar bowl. Everyone believed him because he was a bloody brilliant student and practically perfect." He shook his head. "Then one day my mum's jewelry went missing."

"Uh-oh."

"Exactly. And this was no normal jewelry. It was jewelry given to my family in the late fifteenth century. It was almost lost when one of my ancestors pissed off Henry the Eighth—"

"Wait a minute. *The* Henry the Eighth?"

He laughed softly. "There's only one, right?"

"Wow."

"Don't be too impressed. We lost our title as a result of that, but some quick thinker hid the jewelry. So we held on to it."

"At least until Asshole Kid showed up."

"Right, and I decided it was time the world knew his true colors. I did some investigative reporting. Talked to the household help, the neighbors, everyone. A week later I presented my report to my mother."

"Pretty inventive for an eleven-year-old. What happened?"

"He denied it, of course, but the jewelry showed up the next morning." He looked past her to something behind her. "Mum knew the truth, though. And I fell in love with writing."

The waitress delivered their entrees, and they didn't speak until she left.

"Ever think about writing a novel?" Sasha asked, cutting her salad.

"Of course, but why would I want to make stuff up when real life is so interesting?"

"Real life doesn't always have a happy ending."

His smile was gentle. "And you're a happily ever after kind of girl?"

"I have to believe it's out there somewhere."

"I've seen a lot of shit in this world. The truth is, happily ever afters aren't the norm."

"That's just sad."

"It's realistic."

"I'm holding out for the fantasy," she said.

"I wish I had your faith, but I realized the truth a long time ago."

"What's that?"

"I'm not anyone's happily ever after."

Cole was thankful she didn't push him on his statement or try to change his mind. After all, Kate, who had been with him for years, left. He knew he wasn't in a place to be what Sasha needed. Across the table, her face was expressionless as she focused on her salad. For a while they were silent, both trying to enjoy the delicious food. When they started talking again, it was about his recent work in India.

After finishing their entrees, they both agreed they were too full at the moment for ice cream. Sasha suggested walking in the gardens, and he agreed. There had been a certain spark in her eyes earlier when she spoke of the flowers and he wanted to see it again. Though she hadn't seemed as despondent lately, the times she looked truly alive were still fewer than he liked.

She was animated while they walked. She knew just about every flower, plant, and tree they came upon and seemed thrilled to talk about them. He wished his family still owned his childhood home. There had been a maze in the gardens and Sasha would have loved it.

"Have you always enjoyed flowers and gardening?" he asked. He pointed to a stone bench off to the side of the path. "Want to sit?"

She nodded and sat down beside him. "Julie and I were college roommates. She always talked about opening a shop and eventually sucked me into the business."

"You didn't have anything you wanted to do? No big dream?"

She shook her head. "I always sort of just floated from thing to thing. Never really had a big 'when I grow up' vision."

"Are you happy with what you do?"

"Oh, sure. It's fifty percent my business. Besides, Julie and I balance each other out. She's more business and numbers, and I'm more personal relations."

"Where do you see yourself in five years?"

She tilted her head and raised an eyebrow. "Is this a job interview for a position I didn't know I applied for? Next, are you going to ask me if I prefer to work alone or on a team?"

He couldn't help but smile at her sass. "No, I was going to save that for if you made it to the second round."

She laughed softly, a musically feminine sound.

"I like it when you laugh, Sasha," he said.

She smiled and dipped her head. Suddenly, he was acutely aware of how close her body was to him. How easy it would be to gently lift her chin and lower his lips to hers.

"I suppose I haven't had a lot to laugh about the last few months," she said, and her matter-of-factness pained him.

"I'm glad our outing provided you the outlet you needed," he said.

"Me, too," she whispered. "Thank you for that."

The air between them hummed, and he knew if he didn't do something or change the subject, he'd wind up doing something he'd regret.

He cleared his throat and the spell was broken. "Ready for ice cream?"

She opened her mouth to speak, closed it, and looked pensive for several seconds before saying, "Yes, that would be great."

They stood and walked to the creamery portion of the property. The walk was quiet, but not uncomfortably so. Cole had always thought it to be more telling of how well you got along with someone when you could enjoy the silence together. Too many times he found himself trying to fill the silence with words when he was around someone he didn't particularly get along with.

Sasha walked beside him, her hands clasped behind her back. The position thrust her chest out slightly and he wondered if she did it on purpose.

An old yellow Lab slowly made his way toward them as they approached the creamery. He stopped in the middle of the path, midway to them, and waited.

Sasha's step quickened. "Oh, look. He's so pretty."

She stopped in front of him and held out her hand, offering it for the Lab to sniff. When the dog licked her instead, she laughed and rubbed his head. "What a sweetie."

Cole watched from the side, and the sight of her made his heart ache. He knew he was catching a rare glimpse of the happy and lighthearted Sasha who existed before Peter. Her interactions with the dog were natural and easy, almost as if she was a different person. Her smile came effortlessly and her laugh was genuine. It was only when she felt his eyes on her that she stood and brushed off her hands.

"Think we can fit him in your car?" she asked.

"I think he'd be missed."

She gave the Lab a scratch behind the ears. "Probably."

They resumed walking the short distance to the creamery shop. A handful of people milled around outside. They drew to a stop in front of the counter.

"Everything looks so good." Sasha studied the glass case and turned to look at him when he didn't follow suit. "Aren't you going to see what they have?"

"No, I know what I want."

After they ordered and got their cones, they sat at a worn picnic table.

"Why are you looking at me like that?" he asked her.

"You got vanilla."

"And?"

"It's just vanilla. It's plain." She wrinkled her nose.

"It's not plain, it's simple. And it's so simple, it's extraordinarily complex."

"I don't get it."

"Close your eyes and clear your mind." He waited until they were closed and then he held his cone up to her lips. "Taste it like it's your first time."

Her tongue darted out and licked the ice cream. He tried not to think about where he'd really like her tongue.

"Mmm." She licked her lips. "Yum."

"See?" he asked, pleased that she grasped the lesson so quickly.

She opened her eyes and gave him a mischievous smile. "Yes, and I can only imagine how delicious my mint chocolate chip is going to taste when I apply the same thing to it."

"I should have guessed you'd say that."

She licked her own cone. "Yes, you really should have."

They finished the ice cream, making small talk and discussing details of the house they saw earlier. At one point, the yellow Lab wandered over and sat at Sasha's feet. She reached an idle hand down and scratched his head.

During a lull in the conversation, he leaned forward and lowered his voice. "There's a play party next weekend."

She froze and he could see her process his words and their meaning before she relaxed. "Yes."

"Good job, Sasha. You did what I told you to do earlier, didn't you?" She'd remembered he wouldn't touch her without telling her where and how.

"Yes, Sir."

He nodded. "A fast learner. I like that. I would like for you to attend the party with me."

He paused, gauging her reaction. Her cheeks were flushed with excitement. "I would like that," she said.

"Since the party will be held at Master Greene's house and I don't know if he has granite countertops, I won't have you wear the black lingerie."

Her voice was calm when she asked, "What will you have me wear, Sir?"

"I'll have it sent to you this week." Let her think about it for a while.

"I look forward to it."

"We won't formally participate in any scenes, but you will serve as my submissive."

Her lips parted and she nodded. "Yes, Sir."

"Master Greene has asked me if he can apologize for Peter's actions." He watched her carefully, looking for any hint of panic.

"Will Peter be there?" she asked quietly.

"No, in fact I understand that as a result of the phone call, there's to be a meeting to determine if he should be allowed to remain in the group."

Her eyes widened in shock. She hadn't heard that. He was surprised Julie hadn't told her, but then again, Daniel might not have told Julie.

She straightened her shoulders. "In that case, I'm good with Master Greene apologizing."

"That's what I told him, but I also said I wanted to check with you first."

She nodded, but then her gaze grew distant and she looked over his shoulder.

"Everything okay?" he asked. "Are you having second thoughts?"

She slowly returned her focus to him. "No, I'm just thinking about Peter. Now that I can think about him and not risk an episode, I often find myself wondering if I missed something, some sign."

"I understand why you'd do that, but your time would be better spent asking yourself what qualities you're looking for in a Dom." He reached into his pocket and took a twenty-dollar bill out. "Do you know how they train people to recognize counterfeit money?"

Her forehead wrinkled and she frowned in puzzlement. "Sir?"

He passed her the twenty. "They don't give them the counterfeit bills to study. They only touch and hold the real thing. They become so accustomed to the real money that they immediately recognize the fraud."

"I'm not sure I understand what you're trying to say, Sir."

"Focus on what you want from a Dom, how you want him to treat you. Think through the characteristics of a Dom you'd like to play with. That way when you meet someone and you get to know him, you'll recognize if he's a fraud or not."

She nodded.

"To make sure you understand, I want you to make a list of your top ten requirements from a Dom. We'll go over it next time we meet."

Her gaze grew wistful again, but she smiled and replied with a soft, "Yes, Sir."

That Friday night Sasha stood in her bedroom looking at the box that had been delivered earlier in the day. The accompanying note forbade her to peek until she was getting ready for the party. Since Cole would be at her apartment in twenty minutes to pick her up, she decided it was time.

She took a deep breath and lifted the lid. He'd told her it wouldn't be black lingerie, and she was excited to see what he picked out. How did he like to see his submissives dress?

She pushed the white tissue to the side and held up a pair of short black shorts. Judging by the cut, they would fit skintight. Though really, what did it matter? She wouldn't be wearing underwear anyway.

Next she pulled out a sheer pair of black hose with a seam up the leg and nodded her approval. *Nice.* She'd always admired the way they looked on women. The black shirt he'd selected would cover her back completely. Which was more than she could say about the front.

Standing before the mirror, five minutes later, with hose and shorts on, she tried in vain to pull the plunging neckline up. But no matter how she pulled or rearranged, she wasn't able to cover more skin. With a sigh, she dropped her hands to her sides and studied her reflection. Maybe if she moved carefully she could keep a nipple from popping out.

She checked the time and slipped on the heels he'd also picked out seconds before she heard him coming up the stairs. When she opened the door to his knock, she found him standing in her doorway wearing black jeans and a T-shirt. She moved aside to let him enter, but he simply stood and studied her.

"The outfit looks fantastic on you," he said. "I reckon every man at the party is going to picture himself having a go at you. But every man there also knows he isn't allowed to touch you. The combination will drive them crazy."

Funny how a year ago, she'd have delighted in his words.

At the moment, however, all she wanted to know was if *he* wanted her.

He nodded in her direction. "Step just inside the door and kneel for me."

She took a step and dropped to her knees, hoping she didn't tear or put a run in her hose. He followed her inside and closed the door behind him.

"I require higher protocol service at the party," he said, coming to a stop before her. "You will not speak unless I give permission. If I'm sitting, you're to kneel at my feet. You will address me as 'Sir' or 'Master Johnson.' Any questions?"

Her pulse quickened at this side of him—the demanding Dom side of him. She was surprised at how much it turned her on. "I have no questions, Sir."

"I've been known to mark my property before going to a party. Use her mouth for a quick fuck, pull out, and come on her chest. If you were my slave, would you proudly wear such a blatant display of my ownership?"

Part of her wanted to deny it, say it was too crass, too much. But he'd demanded honesty, and the truth was she wanted him to be so intentional about his claim on her that he marked her in such a primitive way.

"Yes, Sir. I would," she confessed. Her head was down, so she couldn't see him, but she heard his sharp intake of breath.

"Bloody hell, Sasha. You have me thinking things I have no right thinking." He took several more deep breaths before continuing. "We need to get in the car before I do something I'll regret."

His frankness caught her off guard even as something inside her delighted she could evoke such a response from him.

"Now, Sasha."

She hurried to her feet.

"Where's your coat?"

She pointed. "In the closet, there, Sir."

He didn't say a word as he opened her closet, took her coat, and held it out for her. She slipped her arms in it, but the entire time she felt his coldness toward her. For a second, she questioned her reply and wondered if she should apologize.

Fuck it, she thought. *He's the one who wanted honesty.*

She held her head up and reached to open the door, but he pushed his hand against it and stopped her.

"I'm not upset with you, Sasha."

"Sir?"

"I'm angry at myself. It's not your fault, and it's nothing you've done." He exhaled loudly. "I'm used to having better control over myself."

"Thank you for being honest with me, Sir." How refreshing it was to be with someone who was so honest and open. With anyone else, she'd have been subjected to an uncomfortable and awkward car ride.

His body relaxed slightly. "You do look incredible in that outfit. If I hadn't—" He shook his head. "But I did, so let's head out so we're not late."

Master Greene lived in an up-and-coming neighborhood not far from her apartment and shop. Several cars already lined the street in front of his house when they pulled up. Her heart pounded a little faster.

Cole turned the engine off, but made no move to get out of the car. Instead, he turned and looked at her. "How are you feeling?"

"Scared, excited, nervous." She took a shaky breath. "Ready to get this over with and willing to sit here all night."

He smiled softly at her. "I know this is a big step for you. Rest assured, I'll be with you every step of the way. And if you get overwhelmed, let me know immediately. Understand?"

"Yes, Sir."

"Once we're inside, we're going to find Master Greene. You are free to talk with him."

"Thank you, Sir."

"Ready?"

She closed her eyes, took one last deep breath, and honestly replied, "As I'll ever be."

He didn't say anything further and didn't ask for additional reassurances, but opened his door and crossed in front of the car to open hers.

She fiddled with her red bracelet as they walked to the house. She could do this. Cole was with her. She didn't feel panic, just a bit of trepidation. Surely, that was normal.

Cole rang the doorbell. As they waited, he glanced down at her. "I'm proud of you, little one."

She was still smiling when the door opened and they stepped inside.

Chapter Five

"Good evening, Master Johnson," a sub she'd known for years said as he welcomed them inside and took her coat.

Cole nodded in reply.

"Good to see you again, Sasha," he said.

She looked over to Cole since he'd told her she had to have permission before speaking to anyone. His expression was blank, though, and offered no acquiescence, so she only smiled and nodded.

They walked farther into the house and she felt oddly at home hearing the familiar buzz of the group. It was a sound unlike anything she heard anywhere else: the hum of conversation, a moan of pleasure here and there, even the occasional smack of skin on skin.

"There's Master Greene," Cole said, walking toward the back of the living room.

Master Greene stood apart from everyone, observing. Once

he saw them approaching, he pushed back from the countertop and held out a hand to Cole.

"Master Johnson," he said. "Let's go into my office."

She followed the two men into the small room and for the first time felt a twinge of anxiety. Which was uncalled for, since, she scolded herself, she'd be with Cole. She would be safe.

Cole remained standing. So she wouldn't have to kneel, she supposed. Master Greene had a calming expression and it only took one look at him for any remaining fear to ease away.

"Thank you for allowing me this opportunity," he said to Cole and then tilted his head her way and raised an eyebrow.

Cole nodded.

Having received permission, Master Greene spoke to her. "Sasha, I can only imagine how difficult this must be for you. I want you to know you have the support of the entire group." He lifted his hand and glanced at Cole. His hand dropped when Cole shook his head.

Sasha breathed a sigh of relief, and since Cole had told her in the car that she was free to speak with him, said, "Thank you, Sir. That means a lot."

"We take a participant's safety extremely seriously. Peter broke that trust once and we gave him the benefit of the doubt. But when he called you, he proved once and for all that he couldn't be trusted."

She'd known she'd never be able to play with him again, but there was a part of her that remembered her joy at the beginning of their relationship. That once joyous person had held out some small hope for him. Maybe one day, if he made it through the mentorship, he'd find someone better suited for him.

Master Greene continued. "Peter is no longer welcome in

this group. Please accept my apology for not being able to ensure your safety where he was concerned."

She swallowed around the lump in her throat. "I appreciate your apology, Sir, but please know I in no way hold you accountable for Peter's actions. It's hard enough to control ourselves, much less someone else."

Master Greene chuckled. "True, but I still feel some responsibility. We all do in fact." He turned to Cole. "Thank you for coming tonight and allowing me to talk to Sasha. If you'll excuse me, I need to get back out to the party. You two enjoy yourselves."

"You're welcome," Cole said and then added with a grin, "And we intend to."

He led her out of the office and through the kitchen. "Let's see if we can find a demo to observe."

At his calmly spoken words, she grew clammy. For a split second she wasn't at Master Greene's, she was at Master Covington's guesthouse getting ready to head up the stairs for her demo with Peter. She had watched a demo a few weeks ago with Abby and Nathaniel, but this felt different. Because she was dressed more like a submissive?

"Please, Sir," she managed to whisper. "Can we wait a few minutes before we do that?"

There was no surprise in his expression when he turned to her, almost as if he'd anticipated her reaction. "Of course, little one. Would you like to find a place to sit for a while?"

At her affirmation, he changed course and went into the living room, where he sat on a couch. With a sigh of relief, she dropped to her knees. The position now felt comfortable. Cole always had her spend time kneeling when they were in a training session.

She closed her eyes and felt her body relax. She took a deep breath and uncurled fingers she didn't know were in a fist. Yes, she could do this.

"How are you feeling?" Cole asked.

"Better, Sir."

"I'm going to touch your head." His voice was soft and gentle and though she knew they were getting some stares from curious group members, she relaxed even more when his hand slid into her hair.

His hand soothed away any remaining nerves. Ever so tenderly he rubbed her scalp in what quickly became an almost erotic massage. She could have easily rubbed herself against him, but she held still, knowing he wanted her obedience.

"You did very well, little one," he said. "You became uncomfortable and you stopped and told me. Though we Doms often act like we know everything, we're well aware we don't. That's why honest communication works both ways."

The crowd around them grew larger, and though no one approached them, they continued to receive more than a few stares. *Odd*, she thought. But then again, maybe it was seeing her again as a submissive. Or that she was Cole's submissive for the party. Probably a combination of both, she decided.

One of the group's Doms, Evan Martin, ran an appreciative eye over her and walked toward them.

"Master Johnson," he said, coming to a stop in front of Cole. "Good to see you tonight. I wanted to get your opinion on something."

The two men started a conversation about an upcoming meeting. Nothing that concerned her. She dropped her gaze to the floor, and that's when she noticed the shirt had shifted and her right nipple was exposed.

Without thinking twice, she lifted a hand to straighten the neckline. No wonder people had been staring.

The hand in her hair tightened painfully. "Leave it alone, sub."

The roughness of his voice caught her off guard and though she didn't move to adjust the shirt, it wasn't until he spoke again that she realized she hadn't dropped her hand either.

"I mean it. You're exposed for my pleasure. Move back into position." His command was spoken softly, but carried enough authority that she immediately placed her hand back on her knee even as she felt desire swell between her legs.

Not missing a beat, he smoothly transitioned back into conversation with Evan. She was relieved to have a few minutes to privately process her reaction to his command. Her response had been instant and visceral. At his demand, some part of her felt at peace. The realization made her happy.

"Excuse me, Master Johnson, may I sit here and wait?"

Sasha snapped to attention at the sound of Julie's voice. A quick look from the corner of her eye indicated Master Evan had left.

"You may," Cole answered.

Sasha waited for him to say something about not speaking to her, but he didn't. Relying, perhaps, on Daniel's training to have covered party etiquette.

"Where is your Master, Julie?" Cole asked her.

"He's teaching bullwhip techniques in the garage, Sir, and told me to wait for him here."

Julie had been present the night Daniel whipped Peter as part of his punishment for the scene with Sasha. Cole's attention had been focused on her, but Julie had almost passed out herself.

"Ah, yes," he said. "I remember you almost fell that night."

"And you'd already caught Sasha. I felt guilty I didn't get to her first."

It was strange listening to them talk about her like she wasn't within hearing distance. She didn't remember much about the night they were talking about. She did remember Cole holding her.

"You're a good friend, Julie. I mean that sincerely."

"Thank you, Sir."

They were silent for several minutes and Sasha's gaze traveled across the room, noting not many people were looking her way anymore. Everyone's attention had been captured by the appearance of a woman Sasha didn't recognize. She had curly brown hair and was glancing around, obviously looking for someone in particular.

Someone breezed past the couch. Master Greene, she noted, making a beeline toward the unknown woman. Whoever she was, she saw him and ran into his arms.

"They're the demo we're going to watch, little one," Cole informed her.

As she watched the embracing couple, his words hit her and she realized he'd never meant for them to watch a demo immediately after the meeting in the kitchen.

"I'm ready now, Sir."

The submissive at his feet grew stronger and more confident every day. And though he was glad she'd come so far, part of him was sad because he knew that meant their time was limited.

Unless he took her up on her request for slave training. That would give him more time.

Already his mind longed to make plans. To have her at his

complete mercy and under his exclusive control. To touch her. Feel her.

Fuck her.

He clenched his fingers into a fist until he got his desire under control. He'd probably scare the hell out of her the first time he took her. He knew damn well it wouldn't be gentle. It would be hard and rough.

Hell, he was a grade-A bastard to even consider it.

"Master," Julie said, sliding from the couch and going to her knees.

Daniel must have finished his teaching. He stood near the couch and held out his hand, helping Julie to her feet. He pulled her into his arms and then looked Cole's way.

"Sorry I can't stay and talk, I told Julie we'd leave after my session." He kissed her forehead. "Been working overtime this week and promised her the weekend would be just the two of us."

Cole chuckled. "I'll make certain to keep my distance from the main house."

"No need," Daniel assured him. "We're going away for the weekend."

They spoke for a few more minutes, but the entire time Cole was thinking about what Daniel had said. *Going away for the weekend.* If he decided to train Sasha as a slave, he should take her away for a weekend. That would be fun and provide new ways to play.

When they left, he stood and said to Sasha, "Stand up and straighten your shirt, little one. It's almost time for the demo."

He'd spoken to Daniel earlier in the week about what the demos would be and who would be doing them. He had a feeling she would enjoy watching Greene and his sub for the evening.

The demo was being held in the garage and, as he expected, a large crowd had gathered. Everyone was standing, so he led her to the corner of the observers where they could watch but also be able to talk without bothering anyone.

"Stand in front of me, little one. I'll be close behind you, but I won't touch you."

He wouldn't touch her, but he was so close he felt her heat and smelled the faint lemongrass scent of her shampoo. If she moved backward at all, she'd push against his erection—but he didn't want to move any farther away from her. He wanted her acutely aware of his proximity.

Before them Greene was speaking in low tones to his submissive, running his hands over her body and eventually bringing her hands above her head to bind. While he worked, she watched him with soft and trusting eyes.

Once he had her secured, Greene whispered to her again and pressed a kiss to her forehead. She nodded and closed her eyes.

Cole dipped his head to Sasha's ear. "You're wondering who she is and what connection they have. They're a long-distance couple. She lives in California and they only see each other every few months."

Sasha leaned forward as if trying to get a closer look.

"He's going to demo a sensual flogging. Nothing too intense, at least for those of us watching. I imagine it'll be quite intense for her. What I want you to do is picture yourself in her place. Let yourself go. Remember the feeling of being pleasured by the one you've turned control over to. And for tonight, I'm the one who decides that pleasure."

His words had the desired effect and he smiled inwardly as she trembled in response. So far he hadn't noticed any sign of panic or distress from her, but he recalled how quickly it'd hit her when they went to look at the house. He believed this was the first flogging scene she'd witnessed since her time with

Peter. And while he felt she was strong enough to watch a sensual flogging, he needed to keep a watchful eye on her.

"Watch," he commanded as Greene began. "You're standing bound before me. Naked and needy. You came to me for one reason: you know I can give you what you need. But now that I've bound you, you realize I'll take what I need from you as well."

They both watched as Greene circled his sub, every so often flicking the flogger toward her, but not striking her with it yet.

"I make you wait for the tails to fall and you try to anticipate it. Try to imagine where they'll first land. You're expecting it to be forceful, so you're surprised when the leather softly sweeps across your back. I'm being so gentle, you don't notice I've picked up a second flogger until you feel it against your backside. I put more power into the stroke and you yelp. I whisper for you to be quiet, telling you that you will take what I give you in silence."

Sasha's gaze was on the couple in front of her, but Cole saw the quick rise and fall of her chest.

"I continue working both floggers, harder against your arse and softer on your back. I ask you if you're getting wet being tied up for my pleasure and receiving a flogging." He wasn't watching the demo scene anymore. His focus was Sasha, and he was pleased she'd shown no unease when he'd mentioned her back.

"Check, sub," he commanded in a low growl. "Slip your hand down the front of those shorts and finger yourself."

She jerked to attention.

"Discreetly. Don't draw attention to yourself." He waited while she checked. "Are you?"

"Yes, Sir."

"Good, because next I'll tell you that you need to be wet because I'm going to slide the handle of the flogger inside you."

She stiffened.

"It's not quite as large as my cock, but it's nothing you want to attempt dry." He leaned so close he almost brushed her ear with his lips. "Look at it as preparing yourself to take me. Rub your clit, but don't come."

This time he didn't have to tell her twice. She obeyed immediately. He let her play with herself while he observed Greene and his sub.

"Rub that needy clit as I work your body with my floggers," he whispered. "At times it feels like a hundred fingers caressing you, almost a kiss. But when I swing it harder, you accept the sweet pain because you know only pleasure follows."

Her voice was strained. "Please, Sir, let me come."

"Not yet. Because whilst you're still floating from the flogging, I'm going to ease the handle between your legs and make you fuck yourself with it."

"Please, please, please," she softly begged.

The silence of the room was broken by Greene commanding his sub to come and her cry of release. His cock grew distractingly hard at the erotic sound, but even so he didn't miss Sasha's spine stiffen, followed by an intense tremble.

Hell, no, she didn't.

"Did you just come without permission, sub?" he asked through clenched teeth.

"Yes, Sir. I'm sorry."

"Apology accepted and punishment deferred. And I hope you enjoyed that orgasm, because it's the last one you'll experience for quite some time."

"I've decided to change my plans for the evening," Cole said. The demo was over and the few remaining people in the garage were talking amongst themselves as they waited for the next one. "We're leaving."

She knew he'd only changed plans because she came without permission. *Fuck*. It'd been too long since she'd had to hold back an orgasm, and listening to his wickedly delicious whispers while watching Master Greene and his sub had been too much.

He was quiet as they made their way to his car. Every so often, she'd look his way and try to gauge his mood. Was he angry? Disappointed? Neutral? He was too damn hard to read.

Silently, he opened the car door for her before getting in himself. They were halfway to Daniel's before he said anything.

"Leaving early was not a punishment. I had planned to do something the next time we met, but I've decided to do it tonight instead."

She continued to stare out the car window. He hadn't given her permission to speak and he hadn't asked her a direct question.

"When we get to the guesthouse, I want you to kneel and wait for me in the office."

Instead of allowing panic a foothold, she did as he'd told her and ran through what she knew would happen: he would give her a week's notice before he punished her, he would not touch her without telling her, and he had this planned before she'd disobeyed him. The panic she feared didn't make an appearance.

They pulled into the driveway, and the absence of Daniel's car signaled he and Julie had already left for the weekend. She wondered if Cole's offer on the house they'd looked at had been accepted and, if so, when he'd be moving. She rather liked looking toward the guesthouse whenever she visited Julie and trying to guess if Cole was inside.

Once inside the quiet house, she made her way to the office.

A small lamp had been left on, so the room wasn't completely dark, but just lit enough for her not to trip over anything.

He entered the room mere minutes after she settled herself on her knees. The soft thud of his bare feet approached the middle of the room, and she saw his toes when he stood before her.

"Before we move on," he said, "I need to know what happened in the garage whilst we watched the demo."

"It's been so long since I've had to delay my orgasm, Sir. I couldn't hold it anymore." She bit the inside of her cheek and hoped he understood.

"Did it once cross your mind to yellow if you thought I was pushing you to do something you didn't think you could do?"

"No, Sir," she said in a small voice. It hadn't. Fuck, she was the worse submissive ever.

"You must learn to use your safe words, little one. Otherwise they are worthless. If you think for a minute I can attempt to slave train you without knowing with absolute certainty that you will use them, you are mistaken. Do you understand?"

"Yes, Sir."

"Your next assignment is to write an essay, no word limit, on submission, its meaning, and how safe words enhance our play. This one will take some time, so you have a week. Do you have any questions?"

While before she dreaded writing assignments, this one actually sounded interesting. It would be insightful to explore her thoughts on safe words.

"No, Sir. I have no questions."

"In that case, we'll move on to your next lesson, which will take place in the garage playroom."

Her chest tightened and her heart thumped wildly. It was almost as if two voices argued in her head. *The playroom. He's taking you to the playroom.* The other one countered, *This is Cole. You are safe.*

"Sasha." His one word banished the voices and grounded her. Tied her to him alone.

"Sir."

"There's nothing to worry about. I'm going to explain everything. Do you trust me?"

She did. One hundred percent. No questions asked. "Yes, Sir."

"I'll keep you safe. Remind yourself of that fact."

"Yes, Sir."

"You will remain in the outfit you currently have on. I will not be attempting to get you into subspace because I need you with me mentally for the entire scene. Any questions so far?"

She'd never played with her clothes on. This would certainly be interesting. But she trusted Cole to know what he was doing. Her job was to simply obey and learn the lesson he was teaching her. "I have no questions, Sir."

"I'm going to be touching you," he said. "All over. And I'm not going to tell you beforehand. This is me giving you notice. If this troubles you in any way, let me know and I won't do the scene."

She took a few minutes to think about his words and their meaning. He was going to be touching her. All over. A few weeks ago, that would have been a hard limit, but now, knowing what she did of Cole, it no longer was. He would keep her safe. And more than that, she liked his hands on her. She *wanted* his hands on her.

"I have no problem with that, Sir."

"I will also be pushing you harder than I have ever before and testing your limits. Again, this is your choice. If you feel uncomfortable, we won't do it."

She almost told him *no,* that it sounded like too much and she didn't want him to push her and test her limits. But deep inside, in that quiet place she hid her secret desires, it was exactly what she wanted. And hadn't she already confirmed she trusted him?

"I want to do it, Sir," she said in a strong voice.

His smile chased away any lingering worries. "Very good, little one. I'm proud of you."

She felt her face heat.

"I don't normally give submissives choices about playroom time, but I'm making an exception here. I can either walk with you, meet you in there, or have you meet me."

He was giving her a choice because he remembered the panic attack she'd had at the mention of Daniel's playroom. She once again realized she had no reason to fear when she was with Cole. He knew her fears and he'd keep her safe.

"I would like for you to walk with me, Sir."

His expression gave away nothing, but his reply was filled with approval. "With pleasure." He held down a hand to her. "Come with me."

She placed her hand in his and rose to her feet. Holding his hand, she felt more confident and she knew she'd made the right decision. They entered the garage and she took comfort in finding it unchanged since her last visit.

He led her to the middle of the garage where cuffs were mounted from the ceiling and adjusted her until her position met his approval. "Look at me," he said. And when she met his eyes, Cole had been replaced by Master Johnson.

He buckled her wrists one at a time to the cuffs above her head. She focused on his face the entire time, breathing deeply and somehow keeping the panic at bay. He finished securing her and took a step back, once more meeting her eyes.

"I'm going to blindfold you, but before I do, tell me what you say if you need me to stop." His gaze was steady and sure and gave her the courage to continue.

"Red, Sir."

"If you're scared, or starting to panic, I don't want you to think twice or second-guess whether you should say it. You say it immediately, understand?"

"Yes, Sir."

"If you're a little uncomfortable and you need a minute to gather your thoughts or you feel like I'm going too fast, what do you say?"

"Yellow, Sir."

"I'm placing an inordinate amount of trust in you. Do you understand the trust I have in you?"

It was the dichotomy of BDSM she'd never fully grasped until that moment. But standing in the playroom, bound by him, and at his mercy, it finally became clear that he had to trust her just as much as she trusted him.

"Your trust is not misplaced, Sir."

"You give me your body for my pleasure, but in exchange, I give you my very soul. In dominating you, I expose a part of myself that is shown to very few. Tonight, I give that part of me to you for your keeping."

The weight of his words caused her heart to tighten, and her eyes prickled with tears. "I will hold it most dear, Sir."

"Thank you." He ran a thumb across her cheekbone and whispered, "Close your eyes, Sasha."

All her lingering doubts had fled and she closed her eyes, feeling nothing but contentment. Even when he fastened the blindfold around her head, there was only security in his touch.

"What color are you at, little one?"

"The greenest of greens, Sir."

He chuckled from behind her. "Good, thank you. And since you can't see for yourself, you'll have to take my word on how fucking hot you look bound and blindfolded."

She loved that she appeared sexy and hot to him. Loved even more that he made her feel that way. He made her feel alive after merely existing for the last few months.

His hands cupped her shoulders and gave them a squeeze. Hell, he made her feel more alive than she ever had before. And his hands were so knowledgeable. Blindfolded and bound for him the way she was didn't make her feel nervous or scared; she felt safe and secure, and when he touched her, she felt need.

He ran his hands down her back, around her hips, and back up the front of her, just barely grazing her breasts. His thumb swirled circles at the nape of her neck and her skin prickled up in gooseflesh at the sensations he created in her body.

"What color?" he whispered while one of his hands swept down her side again.

"Still green, Sir. Your hands feel so good."

"That's what I want. Just relax."

He continued stroking her and she bit the inside of her cheek to keep from groaning, but one escaped.

"Let me hear you, little one. Don't hold back."

He stepped way and the air around her felt colder. She listened for his footsteps but before she could work out in her mind where he was, he was back.

"I want to hear all of your noises, today," he said.

This time it wasn't his hands that were on her; he used something furry that made her laugh as he tickled her.

"It's okay to laugh if the situation calls for it."

He was relentless with the tickler and she kept laughing. She couldn't remember ever doing so before in a playroom and wondered why. By tickling her, Cole was relieving any remaining trepidation. There was a smile in his voice when he spoke again.

"You sound so joyous when you laugh," he said. "And your joy brings me pleasure." He shifted so she felt his erection on her back.

She moaned.

Pressed against her, he spoke into her skin. "Tell me, little one, if you were naked right now, would you be wet? Are you desperate to be filled? Slick at the thought of me pushing inside you?"

"Yes, Sir."

"And that also brings me pleasure."

His hands were on her again, a little rougher this time and more urgent. His touch fanned the flame of arousal she'd feared quenched beyond revival. She didn't want to take the time to examine it, or question it, or wonder if it was only Cole who could make her feel it. She just wanted to experience it.

Thankful for the blindfold, she emptied her mind of anything other than Cole and his touch. She nearly hummed in response to the sensations he created in her body.

The smack of a flogger against her butt made her jump.

"Stay with me, little one." His voice was low and somehow comforting. "This brings me pleasure as well." The flogger landed again. "What color are you?"

She took two deep breaths. "Green, Sir."

"Very good. I'm not taking you to subspace. I want you here with me."

She had always found it took her a long time to reach subspace and it was rare that she did so the first time with a Dom. She hoped she had the chance at some point in the future to play again with Cole. To see if he could get her there.

He worked the flogger over her body in an off-tempo, erratic fashion that wouldn't allow her the ability to get lost in her head. And though he wasn't being gentle, there was no hurting involved.

"What color, little one?"

"Green, Sir."

She relaxed into her bonds. As Cole continued with the flogger, she felt something inside heal. Something she hadn't known how to fix. She smiled and in that moment, she knew everything was going to be okay. She was going to be okay.

She felt like shouting from the roof and probably would have done so, but she knew if she did, he might misinterpret and stop. He continued striking her with the tails, and she welcomed each one, taking, accepting, and acknowledging their meaning. In a way it was as if he was both breaking down her wall and building it up at the same time.

She relaxed even more and she was free. Finally free. She'd never hit subspace so quickly.

"Sasha," Cole said through the haze of pleasure. "Come back to me."

She would go, but only for him. Because he asked and since he was the one who gave her wings.

He chuckled. "So much for my plans. Are you with me, little one?"

"Yes, Sir. Thank you."

"For someone who claimed it was hard for her to reach subspace, that was frighteningly fast."

"Sorry, not sorry, Sir."

He stopped using the flogger and tenderly unbuckled her

wrists. She slumped against him, perfectly content to be held. He carried her to a nearby couch, where he cradled her against his chest.

"It's rather humorous if you think about it," he said, stroking her hair.

"What, Sir?"

"How I once told you I would keep you guessing and off balance and yet"—he kissed her forehead—"you do the same to me."

Chapter Six

The warning she'd been waiting for and dreaded came by text the next Sunday morning: *Saturday at four I will collect what I am due. Further instructions to follow.*

Her hands shook so badly, she almost dropped her phone. With trembling fingers she typed back her reply.

Yes, Sir.

Part of her felt proud that she was now at a place where he thought she'd progressed enough to handle his punishment. But a larger part of her was scared to death. At least, she thought, they'd finally get her punishment out of the way.

She sat down and tried to knit, but the yarn kept getting tangled and her fingers wouldn't work properly. She picked up a novel she was in the middle of, but gave up when she reread the same page for the tenth time. Finally, with a huff, she picked up her journal. He wanted honesty? She'd give it to him.

Flipping to a clean page, she wrote stream of conscious thoughts until she'd filled four pages. Granted, she thought looking back over them, the pages weren't exactly legible. Of course, he'd never said anything about her daily writing having to be legible.

He had said he thought writing would help her and, no surprise, he was right. Her mind felt calmer. She could do this. She'd been punished before. Hell, she'd been whipped until she passed out. No way would anything Cole did ever come close to that.

She slipped her journal back into the drawer she kept it in and decided she wouldn't even think about Saturday until Friday night, at the earliest.

Cole, of course, had other plans.

On Monday, he sent her an e-mail telling her to write the date, time, and location of her punishment under her list of infractions.

On Tuesday, his e-mail informed her that their only meeting for the week would be on Saturday.

On Wednesday, she gave up trying to put it out of her mind and instead thought about what his daily e-mail would say. Typically, he would send something by midmorning, but that day there was nothing before noon.

Sasha and Julie had set up a lunch date that day with Kelly and Abby to discuss Dena's baby shower. Kelly called shortly after eleven and said there'd been a break-in she had to investigate and couldn't make lunch, but to go on without her. Abby arrived right at noon with sandwiches from the local deli, and Sasha slipped her phone into her pocket. Of course, the chime of an incoming e-mail rang out five minutes into their meal. She debated waiting until lunch was over to read it, but her curiosity got the better of her and she pulled out her phone to check.

She nearly choked when she read the subject line.

"Are you okay?" Julie asked, putting down her sandwich and wiping her mouth.

Sasha scrolled through the e-mail. "Holy shit."

"Sasha?" Abby's voice held more than a note of concern.

"I'm okay," she assured her friends. "Just, damn, he's a bastard."

"Must be Cole." Julie shifted in her seat, scooting closer to Sasha and craning her neck. "But now I'm all curious. Just what did he e-mail you?"

"His discipline protocol. It's fucking five hundred pages. Damn writers." She reached the bottom of the e-mail and scrolled back up to the top. She tried reading it, but after the first few sentences decided to wait until there weren't multiple eyes watching her and stuck the phone back in her pocket.

"What? You aren't going to read it?" Julie asked.

"Not yet. I'm hungry right now." Though to be honest, the email had zapped most of her hunger. She looked over to Abby. "What's the smile for?"

Abby shook her head. "He might be a bastard, but he sure as hell knows what he's doing."

"Because he has a five-hundred-page discipline protocol?" Sasha scowled. "I think it just means he has too much time on his hands."

"No, because a few months ago, just the mention of anything pertaining to a physical scene would have sent you into a panic attack." Abby took a sip of her water. "But now, I'm guessing he's going to discipline you finally—and instead of withdrawing into yourself, you're acting a bit bratty. I call that progress."

"I don't know," Julie said. "If Daniel handed me a discipline protocol, I'd probably head for the hills. I think that's a bit much."

"Is it?" Abby asked. "Or does it provide a sense of security knowing exactly what's going to happen, no more and no less? This is what is expected of you, so prepare yourself."

"Well, when you put it that way . . ." Sasha couldn't help but agree it made a bit of sense.

"A Dominant has reasons for everything he does," Abby said. "I doubt Cole wrote his protocol out because he was bored. I'm guessing he wrote it out and sent it as a way to help ease your mind."

Sasha picked her ham and cheese back up. "Nah, I think he sent it as a way to fuck with my mind. Because now I'm going to think about nothing but that e-mail until I have a chance to read it."

"I doubt you'll stop thinking about it after you read it," Julie added.

Abby smiled. "That's why I said reasons. What's better than a mind fuck wrapped up like a security blanket?"

Sasha figured she could come up with at least three hundred twenty things that were better, but kept her thought to herself. What Abby said made a lot of sense. But for the rest of lunch, it felt like her phone was burning a hole in her pocket.

When Julie left for an afternoon appointment and Abby went back home, Sasha pulled out her phone to read the e-mail. She tried to keep what Abby said in the back of her mind while she read. Truthfully, her friend was right. Cole had detailed a lot of what would happen, how he would act, and his expectations of her. There was comfort in that knowledge.

But when he sent her a text before bed that said, "In two and a half days you'll be bent over a chair, bare arse offered for my discipline," she decided he thoroughly enjoyed the mind fuck, too.

It seemed like it took forever for Saturday to arrive, yet when it did, Sasha felt like the week had flown by. She worked in the shop in the morning, breathing a sigh of relief when two o'clock came and she and Julie closed for the day. Julie hadn't asked for details, but she'd watched Sasha with careful eyes.

According to Cole's protocol, she was to wear a dress. She looked through her closet. She didn't want to wear the one she'd worn to tea, so instead she settled on a light green cotton dress someone once said brought out the color of her eyes.

She showered, making certain she shaved everywhere. Another thing she knew was that he would not require her to be naked this time. It wasn't so much that she was nervous about him seeing her naked. She didn't want him to see her back.

As she finished getting ready, the truth of Abby's words hit her again. Sure she was nervous, but he had ensured she knew what to expect. It wasn't until she grabbed her keys, purse, and journal that she realized how much she appreciated that knowledge.

However, even knowing what to expect, the sight of Cole in a three-piece suit took her breath away.

"Good afternoon, Sasha," he said, sounding like a perfect gentleman and not at all like he would soon have her bent over a chair with her naked ass in the air.

"Good afternoon, Sir."

He moved to the side to let her in and with a tilt of his head indicated she was to lead their way to his office. Once inside, she placed her journal on his desk and knelt on the floor.

He followed silently, sat down, and opened her journal to the page in the back. "List out the offenses you're here for."

One by one, she recited them, noting as she did that her voice didn't shake. Surprising, she thought, since every other part of her couldn't stop trembling.

"Thank you." He wrote something in her journal. "To correct your behavior and to reinforce my rules, I am requiring you to take six strokes from my cane. You will not be bound. Firstly, because it will signify your submission to me and secondly, because I don't think it would be in your best interest mentally."

"Thank you, Sir."

"Additionally, I am not requiring you to be naked. I would like to point out that this is not typical for my discipline sessions."

"Thank you for that consideration, Sir."

"You will count each stroke."

"Yes, Sir."

"And lastly, I need to make it clear that as of today any disobedience or defiance will be dealt with fully and swiftly at the time of the offense."

"I understand, Sir."

Nothing he'd said came as a surprise. It had all been listed in the protocol. She'd known to expect a formal setting, but knowing was nothing compared to experiencing. It was so different from anything she'd ever done.

Cole, of course, showed nothing other than his usual control. Was it only because her punishment was so far removed time wise from the offense? Probably not—she couldn't imagine Cole ever acting while angry.

"Everything is set up in the sitting room," he said. "You may go prepare yourself."

"Thank you, Sir."

She stood up, her legs a little more wobbly and her heart beating a little faster than when she'd entered the room. Formal protocol aside, she'd been caned before—she knew it would hurt.

I've experienced worse.

She supposed that was something positive that resulted from the incident with Peter: not much could ever come close to being as painful.

However, stepping into the sitting room and seeing it prepared struck her with another reality: when faced with an imminent punishment, knowing she'd done something more painful really didn't matter. She took deep breaths, told herself she was strong enough for this, and walked toward the waiting chair.

Cole would be in the room in about five minutes. When she first read that, she thought it would be much too long of a wait. Now she thought it wasn't long enough. The absolute worst thing she could do was not be in position when he entered.

She wiped her palms on the dress. "Screw my nerves. I can do this."

Shutting out any thought to the contrary, she bent over the chair, flipped her skirt up, and placed her forearms on the bottom seat cushion. *Fuck, this is embarrassing.*

Then her eyes fell on the cane, displayed so she couldn't miss seeing it, and suddenly she wasn't embarrassed anymore, but acutely aware of what was going to happen. Her fingers gripped the chair's edge, fingernails scratching the wood

He came into the room quietly. Loud enough so she would know he was there, but not loud enough to startle her. Odd, but his presence somehow calmed her down. His footsteps echoed as he walked to stand in her line of sight and then he stripped his jacket off and rolled up his sleeves.

There was nothing said as he took the cane and moved behind her. But she jerked when he placed an unexpected hand on the small of her back.

"You're doing great," he said in a low voice. "You can take the rest."

She felt more like she could when he said it.

His hand slipped to lightly stroke her backside once and then he commanded, "Count."

The first stroke hurt just as bad as she imagined it would, and she had to take several deep breaths before she choked out, "One."

The second landed right above the first and felt just as painful. His protocol required her silence outside of counting as well as her stillness. She bit the inside of her cheek to hold back the yelp desperate to get out, instead saying only, "Two."

His statement that not being bound would reinforce her submissiveness was the absolute truth. It was only the strength of his will and her desire to obey him that kept her from reaching back to block the third stroke.

Her cheeks were wet after the fourth, though she wasn't aware of crying. Her backside felt like it was on fire and she gave serious thought to safewording. The two remaining strokes might as well have been two hundred, as she couldn't imagine them landing on her sensitive flesh.

There was a ragged intake of breath from behind her and she realized Cole was fighting his own battle. She wanted to prove him right about being ready, so she forced herself to relax as much as possible and willed him to continue.

The only thing that kept her from shouting "red" after the fifth stroke was knowing there would only be one more. She panted, sobs clawing frantically to escape from her throat, and hot tears flowed freely down her cheeks.

The last stroke was the hardest, landing diagonally across the first five. She managed to get out, "Six," in what sounded to her like a mixture of a hiccup and a sob, and then she held her breath, squeezing her eyes tight as the pain seeped into her body. But unlike the previous five, this time she was swept up by two strong arms and carried to the couch.

He pressed her against his chest and lightly stroked her hair. "Let it out, Sasha. It's okay. Let it out."

It was as if a dam burst inside her and, at his words, she cried harder than she'd ever cried before. She buried her face against the scratchy wool of his vest and soaked the white shirt underneath. The entire time, he simply held her, stroked her hair, and murmured tenderly.

She cried longer than she thought possible and when she finally calmed down to quiet sniffles, she realized her hands were clutching him in a death grip.

She let go of his shirt. "Sorry, Sir."

"Nothing to apologize for. Do you feel better?" He took a tissue and wiped her eyes and nose.

"Much." She hiccupped. "I needed that."

"When was the last time you cried?"

"Like that?" She shook her head. "Never."

"Even after Peter?"

"I wept a little, but nothing major." Her breathing was coming easier; her heart rate slowed. A feeling of cleansing peace came over her and filled her. She lifted her head to meet his gaze and the reason why she'd wept so little hit her. "Before today, I never felt safe enough to cry."

Her softly spoken words were both his dearest dream and his worst nightmare. For while he wanted her to feel safe with him, he'd never given any thought to how emotionally attached he would be once she got to that point. It shook him how attached he was to the woman in his arms.

"Nothing pleases me more than to hear that." He stroked her cheek and smiled. "I am honored you trust me enough to gift me with your tears."

She felt so soft and inviting in his lap. How easy it would be to lower his head and taste her. But not only could he not afford to kiss her, she'd also been through an emotionally intense scene. He reached behind the couch and took the waiting orange juice.

"Drink for me, little one," he said, holding the straw up to her lips.

When half the juice was gone, he fed her chocolate. Then she finished the juice and snuggled deeper into his embrace. He ground his teeth together, hoping she didn't feel his hardening cock. He'd planned on her being sassy and insolent, but the affectionate side of her surprised him. And the combination drew him in.

He held her for a long time before shifting her a bit. "I need to care for the welts, little one. Can I put you on your stomach here on the couch?

She nodded lazily against his chest and he moved her as gently as possible so she was positioned on her belly with a pillow under her head.

"I'm going to massage you," he said. She already appeared calm and relaxed, but he massaged her back and shoulders, moving slowly toward her waist, skipping over her backside and easing any possible tension from her legs.

Only when he was assured that she was as relaxed as possible did he take ointment and ease it over the marks he'd made. She flinched at the start, so when he finished, he went back to massaging her.

He loved the way she felt under his hands. Soft and pliable, sighing when he touched certain places. He wanted to feel her skin on skin, nothing in between him and her body. But she was so self-conscious about her back, and he'd promised her he would wait for her to tell him when she was ready for him to see. He placed a hand on either side of her waist and started to pull the dress down.

"Please stop," she whispered.

"I'm just pulling your dress down, little one, nothing more." Surely she didn't think he'd take the dress off.

"I know." She took a long breath. "Please take it off instead."

"Sasha . . ." he started, but didn't know how to finish.

"I want you to. I don't want to hide anything from you anymore." Her voice was pained. "Please, Sir. Touch me."

Calling himself every bad name he could think of, he slowly inched the dress up. He shouldn't be doing this. She was too emotional at the moment. But she'd said please and he wanted to see her so badly. And when she'd said, "Touch me," he was done for.

Leaning over, he whispered in her ear, "I've wanted to touch you for so long. Feel you. See you." He took the zipper pull at the top of the dress and lowered it. "Thank you, little one."

She pushed up on her arms, slightly lifting her chest to help and he dragged the zipper completely down and pulled the dress over her head.

He froze when he saw her back. Covering her beautiful skin was a web of scars. His chest constricted and his breath caught in his throat. Thinking of how the scars got there—the force of the whip, the inexperience of the wielder—he shook his head.

"Sasha, I . . . I . . ." He tentatively touched one of the larger lines.

"Don't tell me you're sorry." Her voice was pained. "Everybody says that and I *hate* it. Like they could have done something. Like they could have stopped it."

With both hands he palmed her shoulder blades. "I wasn't going to apologize." He lowered his head to the top of her spine and brushed his lips across the scar there. Against her skin he whispered, "I was going to say, I wish I could have taken it for you."

A soft gasp of surprise shook her shoulders and without giving it further thought, he trailed his lips down one long puckered line. By the time he reached the swell of her hips, her skin was covered in gooseflesh.

"Oh, god," she moaned.

In response, he lifted his head and traced another scar with his finger, softly peppering kisses along the way. Taking his time, he gave each mark the same treatment, lavishing her skin with tender touches and warm kisses. When he finished, she was trembling.

"Please," she whispered in a coarse voice and turned slightly so she could see him. "Cole, please."

"Oh, Sasha." He cupped her cheek and brought his lips down on hers. Her taste was a combination of sweet from the juice and salty from her tears. He couldn't stop himself from pulling her closer so he could have more.

She twisted in his arms, her own attempt to draw them closer, but she winced at the movement and he cursed his disregard of her backside.

"Sorry, I shouldn't have . . ." he started, pulling back.

But her arms stopped him. "Don't stop." She shifted toward him again and he saw her try to cover the pain. "Please?"

Her eyes held the look of longing he so often noticed in her expression. And how could he turn her down, this exquisite beauty who knew so much pain and asked for so little? The truth was, he didn't want to turn her down. He wanted to hold her and bring her so much pleasure, the painful memories slid away, never to be remembered.

He stood beside the couch, his mind decided. "Not on the couch. Let me take you to the bedroom." She moved as if to stand, but he put a hand on her shoulder. "I said, let me take you."

"I can walk."

"And I can whistle 'God Save the Queen,' but that doesn't mean I'm going to do it right this bloody second." Before she could protest further, he gathered her in his arms and lifted her from the couch.

She wrapped her arms around his neck and he carried her down the hall to his room. With her head tucked under his chin, he could smell the lemon mint scent of her hair. He wondered if her skin smelled the same and kissed the top of her head.

He gave a silent prayer of thanks the house was small. Holding a naked Sasha in his arms, impatient to touch her, and curious about her smell was chipping away at his control. He joined her on the bed once he had her reclining on the middle of his mattress.

He put a hand on either side of her head so he was leaning over her, smiling down at her. "Ah, yes, this is much better than the couch. I've dreamed about having you naked and in my bed." His voice fell an octave. "And in my dreams, I always start like this."

He lowered his lips to her neck and started to explore her body. In the last month, he'd learned and observed so much of her. He knew of her reactions and how she responded to certain things, but naked, she was an entirely new person. From the swell of her breasts to the gentle slope of her collarbones, his fingers were hungry for the feel of her and his mouth was thirsty for her shape. Earlier in the day she gave him her tears, but now he craved her moans, her gasps of pleasure, her breathy whispers, and he took and reveled in every one.

He kept her on the edge, not letting her fall over until he once more made his way up her body. Wanting to watch as she finally let go, he trailed his hand down her belly until his finger brushed her clit.

"Give me your pleasure, Sasha. Let me see you come."

"Oh, god." Her back arched while his finger rubbed faster and faster. "Like that."

"Like that or like this?" He shifted his hand so he could push a finger inside her while still working her clit and her hips lifted, trying to draw him deeper.

She gave a loud gasp and her body froze as her internal muscles clenched around his finger. Wanting badly to keep his movements up and push her toward another orgasm, he forced himself to withdraw his fingers instead.

Watching her come had been better than his best wet dream and his cock was uncomfortably hard, but he did his best to ignore it. He rained kisses along her neck and cheek, then turned her to her side and curved himself around her body.

"Rest now, little one." He engulfed her hands in his and brought them to nestle against her breast. "Let me hold you whilst you sleep."

He held her until her deep even breathing signaled her sleep and he realized how uncomfortable he was. He still had his suit on and while his shirt had dried from where Sasha wet it with her tears, the vest had wrinkled under his side and his shirt sleeves had ridden up his arms. Not to mention he was wide awake.

Sasha would probably sleep until morning, so he gently pulled away and got up, covering her with a sheet when he left the bed. He stopped briefly in the bathroom to change before heading to his office to work on his research.

His head shot up when she walked into the office some time later. Then he glanced at the clock and realized two hours had passed. Sasha looked pale and vulnerable wrapped up in the sheet she'd taken from his bed. Fuck, he wanted to rip the sheet off and pleasure her until that lost look of hers was gone forever.

"Am I disturbing you?" she asked.

He slipped his glasses off and put them on his desk. "No, I got caught up working. I'm sorry you woke up alone. I meant to be there."

She shrugged her shoulders and looked to the floor. "It's okay."

"Your body language suggests differently."

"No, I get it. You had to work and you weren't sleepy." She said the words, but she still wouldn't meet his eyes.

"Look at me, Sasha."

She sighed, but lifted her head. Her eyes looked wet.

"There now," he said softly. "Tell me what's wrong. Honestly."

Her spine straightened and she looked as if she was getting ready to tell him to fuck off when her shoulders slumped. "I thought . . . after . . . you would . . . we'd . . ."

Damn, she was sexy when she got all flustered. He raised an eyebrow.

"Ithoughtwe'dhavesex," she said in a rush.

His cock, which had been slowly stirring, shot to full attention. "Ah, I see."

"I mean, why only do half the job? Why stop just getting me off once? Why not"—she paused for a moment—"finish it?"

He drummed his fingers on top of the desk. "For several reasons, actually. One, I'd just caned you and I can't imagine you weren't in some discomfort. Two, you were highly emotional and I didn't want to take advantage of the situation. Three, the expectations I set out from the beginning were very clear about sex." He pushed back from his desk. "Shall I continue?"

"No, makes sense." She looked back to the floor and bit her lip. "I get it."

"Funny." He stood up and made his way toward her. "I don't think you get it at all. Because if you in any way think that I didn't have sex with you because I don't find you desirable, or because I don't want you, you definitely don't *get it*." He took her hand and pressed it against his erection. Dropping his head, he whispered in her ear, "I didn't want to only do half the job. I didn't want to stop at getting you off once. And it's taking all my strength not to rip that sheet off your body so I can, in fact, *finish it*."

Sasha jerked her hand out of his grip, took a step backward, and in a move that left him momentarily stunned, let the sheet drop to the floor.

Hell and damnation, she was gorgeous. She was still too thin and he feared she was still too emotional, but he wouldn't be alive if the sight her standing before him, naked, with her head held high and that *just what are you going to do about it* look in her eyes didn't turn him on.

"Now look what you went and did," he said in a low and even voice when he could speak again. He let a finger trace her collarbone. "You just changed the rules. I certainly hope you're prepared to handle the ramifications."

Chapter Seven

Anticipation electrified her body and every nerve ending she had was hyper aware of the man standing before her. Not just standing, though, he was taunting her, tempting her, and threatening to overtake the space, the very air, she breathed.

"I think," he said as he lazily traced her collarbone from one shoulder to the other, "that you have no idea what you just unleashed. You have no idea how much I've been holding back." He took a step forward, further invading her space, and wrapped his hand lightly around her throat so his thumb rested in the hollow of her neck. "I'll give you five seconds to pick that sheet up and go back to bed. Do that and it'll be like nothing happened. Stay here and I'm finished holding back."

She wasn't about to pick the sheet up. She only hoped he couldn't see how much she trembled. *Please don't be teasing me,* she came close to saying. She didn't want him to hold back anymore.

His lips curved into a lazy smile when her time was up and she

hadn't moved. "You've changed the boundaries of our arrangement. We're going to discuss what that means." He paused for a
second, and she feared he would tell her to go back to bed. But
instead, his smile grew wider. "Tomorrow."

She'd barely processed his words before his hand was in her
hair, pulling her head back so she was forced to meet his hungry
gaze. "Right now, I'm going to show you what happens when a
bratty submissive accuses me of doing a job halfway."

Then she could only process him because his mouth was on
hers, hard and demanding and allowing room for no other
thought. His kiss before had stoked a fire in her body; this one
set that fire free to consume her.

He pulled away only so he had room to nibble his way up her
neck. He bit her earlobe and whispered, "This time I'm not going
to finish until you've been thoroughly fucked and when I do finish, it's going to be with my cock buried as deep as I can get it
inside you."

She whimpered in need. Was it possible to orgasm from words
alone? She didn't put it past him to try. Though she had a feeling
it wouldn't take long, she was already a quivering mess.

"Is that what you wanted when you came into my office and
dropped that sheet?" He snaked his hand between their bodies
and thrust two fingers inside her. "You need my cock here? Fill-
ing you up? Stretching that cunt as I push inside deep and hard?"

Her legs wobbled and she nodded.

"Words, Sasha. Give me words or you get nothing."

"Yes, Sir." She swayed against him, high on lust and need.
"That's what I want."

"Then that's what I'm going to give you and that's what you're
going to take." He gave her neck one last hard nibble and then

stepped back. "And to start with, you're going to take it in your mouth."

She dropped her gaze to his groin and swallowed. *Fucking yes*, she couldn't wait to taste him. He unzipped his pants, pushed them down, and stepped out of them. He didn't have underwear on and, *hot damn*, the size of him made her pussy ache with need. She wanted to have him inside her right then and hoped he didn't wait too long to take her.

"Stop looking at it and suck it."

His voice snapped her back to attention and she scurried to her knees. She moved as quickly as possible, but tried to remember everything about the moment: the hard muscle of his thighs as her hands traveled up the back of his legs, the tight and unyielding way his hands fisted her hair, and his sharp intake of breath when she slid her lips over his tip and flicked her tongue against him before sucking him deep.

"Fucking hell, I knew you'd feel good." His hands held her head steady while he pushed inside. "Take me, Sasha. Take every damn inch of me."

He gave her time to adjust to him, but he wasn't leisurely about it. She had only enough time to feel somewhat comfortable before he pushed deeper.

"There you go," he said, holding still. "A little more." And he went deeper.

She moved her hands to feel how much more of him there was, but he slapped them away.

"Keep your hands on my thighs and concentrate on using your mouth to make my cock feel good." With one last rock of his hips, he hissed, "There. Fuck. There's all of it. Now suck it hard. Suck my cock."

It had been months since she last gave a blow job, but she used everything she knew to get him off and bring him pleasure. He guided her head with his hands and she worked his cock with a combination of sucks and licks that had him moaning.

"Fuck, yes. Your mouth feels so good."

He kept up his movements, using her solely for his pleasure, and she loved it. Loved how she affected him and loved having him in her mouth. She braced herself for his release, but he pulled away with a grunt.

"Bedroom. Now," he commanded, stripping his shirt off.

Her heart raced as she stood to her feet. She meant to head to the bedroom, but was momentarily stunned by the sight of him naked. The man should never wear clothes. Covering up a body like his was a crime against nature.

"You can take your time and look later." He sounded faintly amused. "But right now I want you on all fours in the middle of the bed. Facing the headboard, offering yourself for my use."

His words broke her out of her stupor, but only because the thought of waiting for him that way was such a turn-on.

"Yes, Sir," she said and walked out of the office. She tried to walk as normally as possible, but his gaze was hot on her back and heated her entire body.

She alternated between excitement and *holy shit, what have I done* as she made her way down the hall. No sound came from behind her, but she felt his presence all the same. It took all her willpower not to peek over her shoulder while she got into position.

His words repeated in her head and she was acutely aware of her submission to him. In fact, she wasn't sure she'd ever felt more submissive than she had waiting on the bed for him.

She heard him enter the room only because he wanted her

to. A soft shuffle of feet and a gentle rustle alerted her that he was there. She held as still as possible.

The bed dipped slightly with his weight and his hands brushed her backside. "How are you feeling?"

"Not too sore, Sir."

"In that case, I'll have to adjust my stroke next time."

She gasped as he pressed on a welt. "I meant not too sore to"—she paused, looking for the word—"to continue."

He kissed one cheek. "Good." His hands ran up her body and gently pushed her forward so she rested on her forearms. "This first time will be rather quick. I need to be inside you too badly to go slow. But you're allowed to come whenever you wish."

"Thank you, Sir." She was already so turned on, she knew it wouldn't take much for her to come. For at least this first time she could simply enjoy and not have to worry about holding out.

His hands caressed her backside, careful to avoid her welts. And then, his fingers slid between her legs and dipped into her. "It makes me so hard to feel how wet you are for me. Knowing how much you want me."

"I do, Sir." She moaned as his fingers started pumping in and out of her. "So bad." It had been ten months since she'd been with anyone and until that very moment she hadn't realized how badly she craved the feel of a man inside her. The last time had been with Peter. Her body tensed at the memory.

"Sasha?" Cole's fingers stopped.

"Sorry. Had a small flashback. Please don't stop."

"I need you to be sure."

"I'm sure. Please." She'd never forgive herself if he stopped. "I need this. I need you."

"If you're certain, I want you to ask for it." Ever so slowly his fingers started moving again. "Beg me."

The sensual slide of his fingers ignited her once more. "Please. Fuck me." She gasped as they went deeper. "Oh, god. Yes."

"How many people are in this bed?"

"Two, Sir."

"Whose cock did you just suck?"

She was pretty sure his fingers were moving faster. "Yours, Sir."

"That's right. It's just me and you and what we're doing." He pressed her g-spot and she gasped. "Nothing and no one else is allowed. Understand?"

"Yes, Sir."

He shifted behind her so his cock pressed against her ass. "I can't wait to take you here. I'll get you to the point you're practically begging for it. I'll have you desperate for my cock in your arse." He moved his cock lower. "But tonight I'm going to fuck this cunt."

She spread her legs wider at the feel of his tip against her wetness and almost whined when he didn't press forward.

"Feel that?" he asked. "My dick seconds away from pushing into you? Are you imagining what it's going to feel like when it spreads you open and starts to sink inside?" He teased the tip along her slit. "Can you feel yourself stretching to accommodate my thickness? And you suck in a deep breath because I'm still pushing into you and I whisper you've only taken half."

She wasn't sure she could stand another second without having him inside her. She wanted it so much, she ached. "Please, please, Sir."

He eased the tip into her. "Once I'm inside, I'm not holding back. It's going to be hard and rough and I'm going to fucking own you."

She thought he'd take her then, but instead he withdrew only to tease her again by pushing just the tip in. "Oh, fuck. Please," she begged and rocked her hips back to take him deeper.

He slapped her ass and withdrew. "Not yet."

She bit her lip to hold back further protests. Damn, but if he wasn't trying to kill her with anticipation, she didn't know what he was doing.

"You feel so good." He entered her again and went deeper. "Better than any fantasy." He pulled out. "So fucking hot."

He was playing her now, bouncing the tip of his cock in and out with short shallow thrusts. Never before had she felt so tightly wound, so on edge, so ready to be taken. And still he was just barely entering her. With each withdrawal, she braced for his returning thrust to fill her completely, but it never happened.

She fisted the sheets as his slight strokes continued. "Sir, please, I beg you."

"Think you're ready?" He pulled out and held still.

She nodded into the sheets and he slapped her ass. "Words," he said. "Use them."

"Yes, Sir. I'm ready."

He placed a hand on either side of her waist, holding her steady. "One solid thrust and I don't stop until I'm buried to the hilt."

She held her breath and he pinched her right side. "Breathe."

Obediently, she took a lungful of air, and on her exhale, finally felt him push his way in. He felt larger than what she recalled from when she had him in her mouth and she bit the sheets as he continued his possession of her. *Fuck, the feel of him.* She couldn't remember ever being so completely stretched and filled.

"Oh, my god," she panted when he stopped moving and she felt his groin against her backside.

"Damn, Sasha. The sight of my cock spreading your pussy and the way it took me in." He rocked his hips forward, driving her into the mattress. "I have to fuck you now. Brace yourself."

That was all the warning she got. Before she could take her

next breath, he'd pulled part way out and thrust back into her in what began a relentless pounding rhythm. His seemingly unrestrained use of her drove her to climax almost immediately. Yet he continued to thrust into her, each stroke feeling deeper and harder than the one before.

"More," he said, slipping a hand between her legs and rubbing her clit, while never breaking rhythm. "Fucking give me another one."

Her second climax caught her off guard and when it passed, he pulled out.

"On your back. I want to watch you come this time."

She felt out of breath, but she rolled over and saw him stroking his cock. Damn, he was a sight to behold. "Two times is rare, Sir. Three never happens."

He pushed her legs apart and settled between them. "It's happening tonight." Taking his cock in hand, he lined it up with her entrance and reentered her, the length of him touching her in new ways with the change of position.

"Look at me, Sasha." He started moving within her again. "When I take you like this, your eyes are to be on mine."

Little by little she felt him lifting away the layers of safety she surrounded herself with for so long. He was doing it little by little in small subtle ways: a touch, a word, a look. She met his eyes and was struck by the intensity in them. Instinctively, her body began to move with his, meeting him thrust for thrust, longing to draw him deeper, wanting him to claim her completely.

"That's it, move with me," he said, taking her legs and wrapping them around his waist. "Positioned like this there's nothing allowed to come between us."

He was close, she didn't think he'd be able to hold out much longer. His breathing was coming faster and his muscles were strained. "Come with me, Sasha," he panted. "Let me see you come."

His hand pressed against her clit, different from what he'd done before and somehow the warmth from his skin, combined with the push and pull of his body in her and the desire in his eyes, had her body spiraling toward another climax.

"I can't." It was too much, she couldn't handle it. The pleasure was too much.

"You can." He thrust hard and rocked his hips.

Her body shook as her third orgasm swept over her. "Oh, god. Thank you."

"Fucking beautiful," Cole whispered and then crushed his lips to hers and gave in to his own climax. He held still, gasping in expended effort as he released into the condom. He held her for several long minutes, stroking her hair and pressing kisses to her flushed face.

"I'll be right back," he said, leaving the bed only for as long as it took to dispose of the condom. She meant to crawl under the covers while he was out of bed, but just the thought of moving took more energy than she could manage and when he made it back to her, she hadn't moved.

"Come here, little one." He slid between the sheets and held a corner up for her. Any thought of moving to her side of the bed was banished as he slipped his arms around her and drew her close, so her back pressed against his chest.

Normally, she fell asleep after sex. She should be tired considering the last hour, not to mention the caning. But any thoughts about closing her eyes disappeared with the feel of Cole's arms around her. Especially once his thumb started caressing her arm. Apparently, he wasn't sleepy, either.

Then his lips brushed the back of her neck and the warmth of his breath sent shivers down her spine.

She held still, not sure enough of her place at the moment to know if he'd welcome her turning around or even pressing herself back against him.

Don't stop. Don't stop. Don't stop.

The fantasy of being in his arms didn't come close to the real thing. Real Cole was all hard male muscle mixed with a nearly overwhelming intensity, but with an underlying promise of safety and security. Plus there was the way Real Cole would tease, and that little smile of his . . .

She sighed, knowing she was marching down the road to heartbreak.

"Sasha?" Cole asked. "Is something wrong?"

Not caring about the potential heartbreak involved, she dipped her head and kissed his forearm. "Nothing's wrong, Sir."

As long as I can stay like this forever.

He shifted slightly and, judging by the size of his erection, he wasn't sleepy at all. His lips pressed again against the nape of her neck, but this time, he lingered, nibbling slowly along her shoulder blades.

"I want you again," he said along the top of shoulder. "Are you sore?"

His hand was already sweeping along the side of her body, lightly stroking and arousing the need their earlier joining hadn't quite extinguished. She moaned low in her throat as his fingertips brushed between her legs and teased.

"Never too sore for you." She shifted her legs, giving him better access.

He mumbled something she couldn't make out and she heard

a condom packet open. Then he eased himself inside her, pulling her even closer. "I'll be gentle," he whispered.

He was true to his word and they moved together slowly. The earlier urgency to have each other was gone, replaced by a need to savor their connection. He set the pace and she felt every subtle move, every slight push, and every sharp intake of his breath as he pleasured her and took his own.

"Take my hands," he said, and she entwined their fingers.

She wanted to say something, to somehow let him know how incredible he made her feel, and how being with him was like nothing she'd ever experienced. But they were still too new and the words wouldn't come.

Instead she squeezed his fingers and whispered in her head the thoughts she couldn't voice.

When I'm with you, I'm healed.

Chapter Eight

He woke with her on his chest, his arms wrapped around her, their legs entwined. It had been inevitable, he knew that now. Looking back, he'd known probably as early as that first meeting in the coffee shop.

She stirred against him and frowned. He bit back his smile. Someone was disoriented this morning.

"No frowns allowed in my bed," he whispered in her ear. "Gasps of pleasure, screams of ecstasy, and lusty begging only. No frowns."

Her eyes flew open, and he laughed.

"Good morning," he said.

"Cole, Sir." She rolled away from him and covered her face with her hands. "Oh, man."

"No regrets, either. I mean it, Sasha." He watched as she peeked from between her fingers. "It was going to happen eventually, and we both knew it. Now drop your hands so I can wish you a proper good morning."

She moved her hands. "Good morning."

"There we go. Good morning." Her movements had caused a lower part of his anatomy to stir, but they needed to talk before he took her again. With a groan, he sat up. "I'll start breakfast and put clothes in the bathroom for you. Unless you'd like to wear the sheet to the table?"

"No, Sir."

"Very well, we'll save that for later." He left the bed with her protests following him.

When she joined him at the table half an hour later, she looked a bit sheepish. He nodded to a chair and poured her some juice.

"I don't have any coffee," he explained.

"That's okay, you have pancakes." She didn't look at him, but reached for the butter and syrup.

He let her prepare her food, but when several minutes passed and she still paid him no mind, he cleared his throat.

"You're not acting like yourself," he said. "Is something wrong?"

She put her fork down, took a deep breath, and finally met his eyes. "I don't know how to act around you. This"—she waved her arm around the tabletop—"is confusing. Do I call you Sir or Cole? I don't know what to expect or what you expect from me."

He could have kicked himself. He knew enough about her to know she needed everything defined. In the absence of guidelines she became stressed.

"I'm sorry, Sasha. I should have said something sooner. I'd like for you to call me Cole. And as for any other expectations, we'll discuss those after we eat."

As it turned out, she didn't call him anything for the remainder of breakfast. In fact, she didn't say a word. He finally ended up eating as quickly as possible and getting up to clean the kitchen. He told her to meet him in the living room in fifteen minutes.

She sat in one of the armchairs waiting for him while he finished tidying everything up. Always before, she'd sit on the couch. He supposed she picked the chair so he wouldn't sit next to her. He solved that problem by pulling an ottoman over, putting it in front of her, and taking a seat on it. She took an uneasy breath.

He told himself to remain calm. "Before we discuss anything, I need to know what has you troubled this morning."

"It's stupid."

"You haven't said ten words to me since we woke up. If it's upsetting you, it's not stupid."

She looked at him with weary eyes. "I thought you'd say my training was over."

"I assure you that is not the case. Like everything else, we'll discuss it when the time comes." He tilted his head at her sigh of relief. "All good now?"

She gave him her first genuine smile of the day. "All good."

"Are you ready to talk about the next phase of your training?"

"Yes," she said with an excitement she didn't try to hide.

"I have some thoughts on how we should set everything up, and I'd like your input."

She surprised him by leaning forward and taking his hands in hers. "Tell me what you have in mind."

He looked down at their clasped hands. It was the first time she'd touched him first. His heart felt like it was lodged somewhere in his throat. "Well," he said softly. "After last night, I would like to remove the limit on sex."

She stroked his knuckle with her thumb. "It kills me how you can go from being all down and dirty like last tonight to all prim and proper. *I would like to remove the limit on sex.*" She recited his words in a mock British accent and a sassy smile.

"Look at it this way: last night was the real me, and right now I'm just exercising an inordinate amount of control."

Her smile lost some of its sassiness. "Really?"

"Would I rather be fucking you senseless right now instead of talking? Yes, of course."

"In that case," she said in a sultry voice that made his cock ache, "we'd better finish our talk."

"I like the way you think, Sasha Blake. Perhaps I'll even let you orgasm again today." Pretending to ignore her muffled outrage, he continued. "I'll need you to fill out another checklist. E-mail it to me by Wednesday so I have it in time to plan the weekend."

"I have a blank one saved at home."

"Excellent. Keep in mind if it's not marked as a hard limit, I'll not only test you, I'll push you. And since it won't be a hard limit, I expect you to try your best to take it."

"I understand."

"Using a gag on you is still a hard limit for me."

"Me, too."

A knock on the door interrupted his thoughts.

Sasha looked over his shoulder toward the door. Cole frowned. He wasn't expecting anyone and was slightly irritated his conversation had been brought to a halt.

"I don't know who that could possibly be." He stood up and made his way to the door. "I'll be right back. Let me get rid of whoever it is."

The chair squeaked as Sasha stood up. "Shit. It might be Julie. She probably saw my car stay overnight."

He'd almost reached the door, but at her words turned around. "She *is* aware you're a grown woman?"

"She worries."

"I'm not a monster, Sasha." And he was trying very hard not to be offended, but it was growing harder each time Julie questioned him.

The knock sounded again.

"Just a minute." He shot a look at Sasha and turned to open the door. He was so certain it was Julie, it took a long minute to recognize who it actually was.

"Kate?"

*K*ate?

Sasha craned her head around Cole, but he was too big. He obliterated her view of the front door.

"Hey, Cole," a soft feminine voice said. "Sorry for stopping by so early, but I wanted to make good time on the road."

Cole didn't move or say anything.

"Can I come in and put this down? Is Daniel around? It's been ages. I'd love to say hello. Cole?" she said when he hadn't moved.

He jerked to attention and stepped aside. "Sorry. Come in. Let me get that box."

A dainty woman with long black hair handed him a wooden box and took two steps inside. She stopped cold when she saw Sasha. Kate's gaze traveled over Sasha before looking around the rest of the house. Sasha knew the moment her eyes fell on the out-of-place chair with the cane still propped against it. She was also acutely aware she had on one of Cole's shirts.

"Damn it," Kate said. "This is why I should have called first."

"Yes," Cole agreed. "That certainly would have made this less awkward."

To be fair, Sasha thought, Kate appeared rather distressed at the situation she found herself in.

"I'm so sorry. I never thought." Kate rushed through her apology. "I didn't . . . *interrupt*, did I?"

Cole noticed the cane at Kate's nod to the chair. He sighed. "You did, but not that."

Kate didn't look convinced. "I can just leave."

"You're already here. You should rest for a while." He took a few steps to stand by Sasha's side. "Sasha, Kate. Kate, Sasha."

Sasha shook her hand. "Nice to meet you."

"I'm sorry," Kate whispered.

She couldn't figure out why she kept apologizing.

"Don't worry about it. That was yesterday," Sasha said to try and ease her mind.

"Sasha," Cole warned.

"What?"

"It was?" Kate asked.

Cole cleared his throat and Kate stiffened. "Sasha," he said, handing her the box. "Will you go put this in the bedroom?"

She really didn't want to leave, but since she wanted to argue with Cole less, she took the box and carried it down the hall. It was heavier than it looked and she placed it on the floor beside the bed. She could hear Cole's low voice coming from down the hall, but she couldn't make out his words. By the time she made it back to the living room, Kate was sitting in the chair she'd recently vacated and Cole was sitting on the couch.

Not knowing what else to do, she sat down beside Cole. Because he was toward the middle of the couch, her leg pressed along the length of his. His warmth was somewhat of a comfort, but she couldn't relax, not like she had before. She sat with her spine rigid. Maybe if she didn't touch Cole, it would be better. She tried to subtly shift away from him, but he put an arm around her and, with that sexy smile of his, pulled her close. At his touch, the tension left her body and he squeezed her shoulder when she leaned into him.

She wondered if she should offer Kate something to drink.

"This is cozy," Kate finally said.

Sasha snorted. "Awkward as hell is what it is."

"That, too," Kate agreed.

They were spared from further conversation by a knock on the door.

"*That* will be Julie," Sasha said as Cole stood to answer it.

"Yes, I'm almost certain you're correct." He opened the door. "Julie, come in. We were just talking about you."

"Sorry." Julie stepped into the house. "I only came by because Daniel needs your help down at the west gate."

Cole slipped his hands in his pockets and rocked back on his heels. "That would be why the phone was invented."

"I told him I'd come over. I saw Sasha's car had been here all night." She looked around the room and her face paled when she saw the cane. "I, uh . . ."

"Worry," he finished for her and waved her inside. "I know. Come see that she's very much okay. This is Kate. She stopped by to drop off some of my things."

Sasha thought Julie didn't seem to be impacted by the knowledge that Cole's ex was sitting in his living room. She appeared to stop listening as soon as she saw Sasha wearing Cole's shirt. Julie's lips pressed together tightly.

And Cole looked pissed, but he calmly asked, "Is Daniel already at the gate?"

"Yes."

He nodded. "Kate, you're welcome to stay until I get back. Sasha, we'll take up our discussion later."

Some of the tension left with him, but even though Sasha had wanted to talk to Julie, she wasn't going to do so with Kate in the room.

Julie walked over and shook Kate's hand. "Hey, Kate, I'm Julie."

"Nice to meet you. You must be Daniel's sub."

Julie instinctively ran a finger along her collar and a satisfied smile covered her face. "I am."

"And you're Cole's trainee," Kate said to Sasha.

As perfectly clear by the lack of collar, wearing his shirt, and the cane in the next room? Sasha wanted to say, but refrained. This was Kate and though they were no longer together, she imagined the dark-haired woman was still important to Cole. Yet the fact remained, it was the morning after the best sex of her life and instead of basking in it with Cole, she was spending time with his ex and her own best friend. "Is it that obvious?"

"No. He told me."

Sasha gave her a small smile. "Sorry I'm out of sorts. It's just, this isn't what I pictured my morning would be like."

Julie watched them both. "I probably should have called, but with your car here all night and knowing what was going to happen yesterday, I just had to see you. Are you okay?"

"Yes, I'm fine. We'll talk about it later."

"Don't mind me," Kate said. "I've been on the receiving end of his cane numerous times." Her words were certain, but there was a question of sorts in her expression.

"Canes are still a hard limit for me," Julie said.

Kate nodded in agreement. "Smart woman, keep it that way."

"I don't know," Sasha said. "There's something cathartic about the whole thing."

Though she never would have thought it possible, the crying session she had after the cane had felt cleansing. It was like a burden she didn't even know she'd been carrying had been lifted.

"True," Kate said. "I certainly see that. But when you add in the rules he puts in place, it counteracts the cathartic part."

Sasha assumed Kate meant the protocol he'd sent earlier in the week, but she didn't have a clue as to what she meant by the rules. It didn't seem polite to ask, though. After all, she'd just met the woman and from the look on Kate's face, she regretted saying that much.

"What kind of rules?" Julie asked, obviously having no such qualms about asking. "Is that different from the protocol he sent you, Sasha?"

Kate shook her head. "I can't . . . rather, I shouldn't—"

"It's private, Jules," Sasha said.

Kate threw her a look of thanks, and Sasha gave her a small smile. She didn't blame the woman for not wanting to talk about the details of her relationship with Cole. Not to mention, it wasn't any of Julie's business.

"She's the one who brought it up," Julie argued. "I was just trying to see if he was different with you."

"It's a totally inappropriate thing to ask," Sasha said. "And it's nothing that concerns you."

"I think if he's got certain rules he expects you to follow, he should tell you."

"He does. Always."

"So these are in addition to those. Aren't you the least bit interested?" Julie asked.

She was. She was undeniably curious about the rules Cole had given Kate. But she told herself they'd had a much different relationship.

"If Cole wants me to follow a rule, he'll tell me. Bottom line. Drop it."

"Yes, but—"

"Julie."

All three women turned at the sound of Cole's voice. He stood in the doorway, arms crossed, with fury in his eyes and a look of pure displeasure on his face.

"I have known Daniel for years and am well acquainted with how he expects his submissive to behave," Cole said in a cold voice. "I find it difficult to imagine your Master would be pleased with your current conversation, regardless of how concerned you profess to be."

Julie's face paled as Cole walked toward her.

"You will apologize to Kate and Sasha," he said. Sasha was glad those icy eyes weren't focused on her. "And later today you will inform Daniel of this conversation. Trust me when I tell you it'll go better for you if he hears it from you first instead of me."

"Yes, Sir," Julie mumbled.

Cole turned and made his way to Sasha and slipped behind her. She shivered as he ran his hands down her side and rested his palms along her hipbones. She knew what he was doing—he was staking his claim on her. Letting the two other women know in no uncertain terms who was in charge. And who belonged to him.

"Now," he said. "If there aren't any more inappropriate questions, Daniel's invited everyone to the main house."

It was slow at the shop the next day, and since they were caught up on orders, at two o'clock Sasha told Julie to take the rest of the afternoon off. Julie hadn't mentioned Sasha's overnight stay with Cole—most likely Daniel had told her not to—but that hadn't stopped Julie from watching her just a tad bit too closely all day. Of course, it was very possible the discussion she had with her Dom about Kate also had something to do with it. Sasha couldn't imagine that going over well.

But no matter why Julie was quiet, with her best friend out of the shop, Sasha felt as if she could finally breathe. And think.

She and Cole never had a chance to finish the conversation they'd started yesterday. Everyone made it to Daniel's house to find he had started a huge breakfast. Kate ended up staying long past her originally stated hour and when she did leave, Sasha remembered Pip had been in her apartment, alone, since the day before.

Cole had simply nodded and said they'd talk later. She thought he'd text, but so far she hadn't heard from him. She was still pleasantly sore from her night with him and it made her smile each time an image from their time together came to mind.

With a sigh, she headed toward the break room. There probably wouldn't be any more customers today. She needed to work on inventory, but instead picked up a novel she was reading.

She'd only read a few pages when the door chimed, alerting her that someone had entered.

"Be right there!" she yelled.

In her imagination, it was Cole stopping by to pick up their conversation. She pictured it so clearly: they would chat in the break room and she'd invite him up to her apartment when they'd worked everything out. Once in her apartment, she'd lead him to the bedroom.

The imagery was so vivid in her mind, she dashed into the main room expecting to see Cole, but came to a complete stop when she saw Peter.

Every cell in her body protested and the all too familiar panic threatened to have its way with her. To counteract it, she visualized herself kneeling at Cole's feet while he stroked her hair. In her mind she heard him say, "You're safe, little one."

She heard him so clearly and it felt so real, her body actually relaxed.

"Peter," she said. "What are you doing here?"

He glanced around the shop and rubbed his hands down the front of his pants. His brown hair appeared unwashed and his eyes were ringed with dark circles. "I need some flowers. Are you the only one here?"

"There are five thousand other florists in Wilmington. If you didn't want to see me, maybe you should have picked one of them."

"They kicked me out of the group, you know. Because I called you."

"I think the fact that you lied and said Master Greene told you to call is why you got kicked out."

A surge of rage lit across his face. "William Greene is a pussy."

She wished she hadn't told Julie to go home. She wished it really had been Cole who stopped by. And she really, really wished Peter would leave. "Like they say, takes one to know one. Now what kind of flowers do you need?"

"Did you just call me a pussy?"

"Flowers. What kind?"

"I heard that Cole guy wasn't allowed to fuck you. Why not? Can't handle his dick?"

Cole's comment about knowing what was counterfeit because you knew the real thing so well came back to her. It was true. Peter was no more a Dom than she was. Compared to Cole, he was a wannabe, an impostor.

The most enlightening feeling of power washed over her. Peter was nothing. A fake. A nobody. And she was strong.

She lifted her chin. There was no reason for Peter to be in her shop. She didn't think him capable of violence, but the sad fact was you never knew. "I've decided I don't want you in my shop. Leave and buy your flowers somewhere else."

"Not very wise to mix your personal life with your business. You could be losing out on a big account I have."

"That's a risk I'm willing to take. Leave now, and I won't call the cops." Her fingers inched toward the phone, just to show him she was serious. "And the next time you feel the urge to stop by Petal Pushers, ignore it."

"You're a bitch, Sasha."

"Bye-bye." She wiggled her fingers at him.

Peter had always been more bark than bite. Truthfully, he wasn't a match for her. He knew when he had been bettered. He shot her one last look before heading to the door.

"One more thing," she couldn't stop herself from saying. "Rumors about Cole's dick are seriously minimized. His cock would have you weep with envy."

Peter couldn't make it out the door fast enough.

For a long time, she simply looked at the front door and grinned. She'd done it. She'd faced her nightmare. She hugged herself. Damn, that felt good. She had the overwhelming urge to text Cole.

She patted her pockets. Damn it. She'd left her cell phone in the back room. Seconds later, she found it beside the book she'd been reading. She was scrolling through her contacts when the door chime rang out.

She sighed in exasperation. "I swear, if you brought your

mangy ass back into *my* store, Cole's cock won't be the only thing you'll be weeping over."

There was no sound from the front of the store. *Shit*. She hoped it was Peter and not a customer. She was almost too afraid to go look, but it had to be done. She shoved her phone in her pocket right as the silence was broken by the sinfully sensual accent that made her knees weak.

"Who are you talking to and why are they weeping over my cock?"

Chapter Nine

She stood paralyzed for several seconds.

Shit.

She didn't just yell out in her store about Cole's dick, did she?

"Sasha?" Cole called.

Shit. She had.

His perfectly sculpted face appeared in the doorway. "There you are." At least he was smiling. "I stopped by thinking if you closed up a bit early, we could finish our conversation from yesterday. But now I'm curious as to who you're discussing my cock with."

She was so flustered he was in her shop, just standing there, that she blurted out without thinking, "Peter."

All at once, the smile left Cole's face. "Peter was here? Today?"

"Just now."

He open and closed his fists. "I'll fucking beat the shit out of him."

She moved toward him and held out her hand. "Wait, no. It's okay—"

"It damn well is *not* okay."

"Listen." Something in her tone must have resonated with him, because his expression lost the murderous look and he gave a curt nod. She continued. "I was scared when I first realized who it was, but I did what you'd taught me and I remained calm and didn't panic. Then I told him to leave and never come back. *And* I realized something else."

"What was that?" A hint of a smile touched his lips.

"I finally saw that he was a counterfeit. Just like you said I would."

He nodded. "You've been thinking about what you want from a Dom."

She forced her eyes to remain on his and say the words, "No. I've been thinking about you."

He mumbled something under his breath and moved across the floor with long strides. Before she had a chance to think about what he was doing, he had his arms around her and crushed his lips to hers.

Her mouth opened in surprise and she pulled him closer to deepen the kiss. One of his hands tangled in her hair and the other slid down her back to cup her ass. He jerked his hips against hers, letting her feel his hardness.

"Just as I've been thinking about you," he whispered against her mouth and then kissed her again. Softer this time, but no less intense. Rather, the kiss felt like a slowly communicated promise that he had every intention of showing her exactly what he'd been thinking about. But they had other things to discuss first.

With a guttural groan, he pulled back. "We need to talk before we do anything else."

Sasha nodded and walked to the door to turn the sign to *Closed.* "Easy enough," she said after locking the door. "My apartment or the break room?"

He was already walking to the back of the store. "Break room."

She turned to double-check the door was locked before following him to the back. He was already sitting when she joined him. His fingers drummed on the table and he appeared to be concentrating on the wall across from where he sat.

In fact, he was so deep in thought, she cleared her throat. "Cole?"

He shook himself out of his trance and smiled. "Come and sit down. I was just thinking."

She took a seat next to him, careful not to get too close. Though why it mattered, she wasn't sure. It was obvious they were going to talk about sex.

And being Cole, he got straight to the point.

"Are you still interested in slave training?" he asked.

She blinked. Twice.

"That isn't what I thought we were going to talk about," she finally said.

"To be quite frank, it isn't why I came over. But hearing how you handled Peter made me rethink things."

She didn't think he'd actually consider giving her a taste of the twenty-four/seven lifestyle. Now that it sounded like he was, she was equal parts turned on and scared out of her wits.

"I dropped by so we could discuss adding a more physical element to our time together," Cole said. "But now, I think you might be ready for a, what did you call it? A *taste* of what a Master/slave relationship would be like."

"Why was that the thing that changed your mind?"

He leaned forward. "Because you have to be strong to serve someone twenty-four/seven."

You think I'm strong?

"And after the way you conducted yourself over the weekend as well as what happened today, I think you're ready. Tell me, Sasha, do you still want me to give you a taste?"

He heart pounded so hard, it shook her body. *A taste of Cole. Would it be enough? Just a taste?* She feared she knew the answer, but that wasn't going to stop her.

"Yes," she said in a breathy reply. "That's what I want."

"I need you to realize how hard this is going to be and make sure it's what you want. It'll be intense, and you'll see and experience a different side of me. I've come to value our time together." He shook his head. "I don't want anything to ruin that."

"I can't imagine anything changing my opinion of you."

"You haven't seen all of me."

He said the words to discourage her, but it wasn't working. She wanted to see all of him. Needed to experience all sides of him. And truthfully, the idea of him being stern and forceful didn't scare her near as much as it turned her on.

She pushed back from the table and stood up. His chair wasn't far, she only had to take a few steps to be at his side. Once there, she went to her knees and dropped her head. "Please, Sir. Allow me the honor of seeing and experiencing all sides of you."

He sucked in a breath and buried his fingers in her hair. "Sasha, little one. You disarm me. How am I to argue with that?"

With her head down, but a smile on her face, she simply replied, "You're not."

Cole knew he had no business giving her even a taste of the Master/slave relationship he liked. But when he'd walked into the shop and she off-handedly told him about her conversation with Peter, the thought hit him: *This is the one you're meant to be with.* And it'd struck him in the chest that this woman, this submissive, with all her scars and her past and her emotional hang-ups, might just be his perfect match.

And damn it all to hell, if she wanted to see what it was like to serve twenty-four/seven, he wasn't about to turn that down. Of course, now that she'd agreed, they had to work out the details.

He dug his fingers deeper into her hair. "Very well, then. I propose two weeks of training. It's not optimal, but since it's just to give you a taste, I think it'll do."

"If it's not optimal, why not extend it? Let's do a month."

Her enthusiasm was delightfully refreshing. He hated to see it whither, but knew it would with what he'd say next. "I don't think you'll want to do a month when you hear what I think best for our two weeks." The corners of her mouth dipped low and he continued. "You'll move in with me for those two weeks. No need to bring anything with you, I'll supply everything you need. And you don't work at the shop."

"I don't work? What? But we're completely booked with events for at least the next month. Two weeks . . ." Her arguments died on her lips when she noticed him shaking his head.

"I can only do two weeks and, frankly, it's not worth doing if you spend eight hours a day working. Look at it this way. Remember I told you that you would only work if your Master allowed it? This is me *not* allowing you to work."

"It's not negotiable?"

"It's negotiable in that the other option is not to do it."

She was silent. He could almost see her mind working through the options.

"Julie's going to hate me," she finally said.

"No," he said. "I'm quite positive I'll be the one she hates."

"I'll talk to her tomorrow."

"Don't you think you should hear the rest of what I want?"

She nodded.

"We'll have more discussions before we start anything, but in general, at dinner each night, we'll go over how your day was, talk about any issues or items to work on, and I'll give you my expectations for the following day."

"Will I have any free time? Be able to call and text my friends?"

He nodded. "This is all new to you, and though others might disagree, I think it'd be beneficial for you to have some down time each day. I'll build two to three hours a day into your schedule. During that time, you're free to make calls. Though I do suggest you put my number on your outgoing message. That way, if there's an emergency, I can get that information to you."

"That makes sense." She nodded and her head tilted in that endearing way she had. "How do I address you?"

He'd have to give that issue some thought. Kate had typically used "Sir" or "Master," except when he'd institute lower protocol, which gave her permission to use his first name. While he liked hearing his name spoken by Sasha, he found he liked hearing her use "Sir" a lot more. He didn't think she was ready for "Master." Or maybe he was the one who wasn't ready.

"I think 'Sir' is fine for now," he said.

"I should bring my journal, right? I'm sure you'll have lots of writing for me to do."

"Yes, bring your journal and your purse. Like I said, I'll provide everything else you need."

"Do you need my clothes size?"

Making his voice as dry and deadpan as possible, he asked, "What makes you think you'll be wearing clothes?"

Her eyes grew wide. "I won't be?"

"Sasha, if you have to ask that, I question whether this is really the right thing to do."

She looked down at her hands. "No, I knew I'd be naked some, but I didn't know it'd be all the time." She peeked up at him. "Will it be all the time?"

He swallowed his laugh. "It won't be all the time, but it'll be damn well as often as I want it to be. And I have to say, now that I've seen you naked—"

Her cheeks flushed the loveliest hue of pink. "When should we start?"

"Two weeks?" he suggested. "I'm moving into the new house this week, so that'll give me some time to get settled."

"That works with me."

She looked so beautiful kneeling at his feet, calmly discussing being at his disposal all day, every day for two weeks. Fuck, he was a bastard and a half.

But she wants it.

He couldn't argue with that. The truth was, he wanted it, too. He wanted her in his house, in his bed, and in his chains. He wanted to push her to her knees before him, bend her over his couch, and hold her tight in his arms. He wanted to care for her like no one ever had before and to be the one person she could always count on to keep her safe and protected.

He fucking wanted too much, and wanting always came with a price.

The difference, though, was he just might pay it for her.

Later that evening, he welcomed Daniel and Nathaniel to the guesthouse. He was going about this all backward, but things had happened too quickly at Petal Pushers. He'd called and invited Jeff, but apparently he and Dena were attending a class of some sort at the hospital.

"Come in," he said. "Excuse the boxes."

Daniel looked around the room. "I'm glad you found a place, but I have to admit, I've grown used to having you here. It'll seem so empty without you."

"I don't envy you the boxes," Nathaniel said. "Took us forever to unpack."

"I won't have that much. I let Kate keep most of the furniture and stuff. I'll be buying everything new."

He realized with a start that he couldn't remember the last time he'd thought of Kate—and this time, his chest didn't have that empty feeling like it used to. He was finally moving on.

He waved to the couch, feeling freer than he had in a long time. "Have a seat."

"Are you going to tell us why we're here tonight, or do you want us to guess?" Daniel asked.

"I'm guessing it has something to do with a submissive being retrained." Nathaniel sat down and studied him. "Am I right?"

"You are," Cole said. He felt the need to pace, but he sat down on the ottoman in front of the couch, facing his friends.

"Something wrong?" Daniel asked.

"No, in fact, everything's going well. Better than I expected, actually."

He hated that it felt like he was asking permission. Of course, he really wasn't. He'd already made the plans with Sasha. Was this one of those situations where you ended up asking forgiveness instead of permission?

"Sasha is doing very well," he said.

"I thought so. Especially after she stayed overnight." Daniel had that know-it-all look on his face.

"She what?" Nathaniel obviously hadn't heard the group gossip.

"Sasha spent the night."

"I thought you weren't going to have sex with her." Nathaniel didn't look happy. "That's why you were recommended."

"How many BDSM relationships have you had that didn't involve sex?" Cole asked.

"We aren't discussing my sex life. We're talking about how you explicitly said you weren't going to sleep with Sasha during her retraining."

"I assure you, Sasha suffered nothing. She wanted it. Badly."

"Abby wants a lot, too. That doesn't mean she always gets what she wants in a scene."

"Of course not." Cole felt his blood start to boil. It was only his inner voice reminding him that Nathaniel was simply looking after Sasha's best interests that kept him from saying what he really felt. "I would be a horrible Dominant if I gave my submissive anything she wanted. But I don't do that. And I would hope you know enough about me to recognize that."

"I saw her that next morning," Daniel said. "She looked calmer and happier than she has in a long time."

Nathaniel sighed. "Nothing to do about it now. What's happening? I'm guessing you didn't bring us here so you could tell me you slept with Sasha."

"I'm actually adding a level to her training."

"Oh, no," Daniel said.

Nathaniel frowned. "What? Why do I feel like I'm ten steps behind on everything here?"

"Daniel's known me long enough to see where I'm going with this."

Daniel nodded. "Cole and Kate were twenty-four/seven."

Nathaniel's eye grew wide and then narrowed. "You aren't actually suggesting . . ."

"No, I'm not *suggesting* anything. To either one of you. I'm *informing* you that Sasha has asked me to give her a taste of twenty-four/seven and I've agreed."

Neither man said anything. If they were trying to come up with reasons why he shouldn't, they were wasting brain power. He knew them already. They needed to understand that he felt this was in Sasha's best interest.

"I assure you, I will do nothing to harm Sasha. And you should know I didn't agree to this right away. She made her request some time ago and I turned her down for all the reasons you're probably thinking. But she's progressed well, and she's ready. Frankly, I'd rather be the one she's with than for her to pick some stranger we don't know."

"I guess my thoughts really don't have bearing on this, do they?" Nathaniel asked.

Cole was glad he finally saw that. "I didn't bring you here to ask permission. I'm just letting you know, as a courtesy, how the training has changed."

"We'll need to know how it's going. I'd like for you to check in with either me or Daniel a few times a week while this is happening. And I'd also request that Sasha continue to meet with Abby."

Cole nodded. "Of course, that sounds perfectly reasonable."

Nathaniel chuckled. "I'm not sure *reasonable* is the right word."

Cole smiled and looked at Daniel. "Sasha wanted to tell Julie herself. She's doing it tomorrow, so if you wouldn't mind not saying anything to Julie . . ."

"Not a problem," Daniel assured him. "I don't want to be around for that conversation, anyway."

"You know, Sasha," Julie said first thing the next day. "I was thinking last night, and I believe Nathaniel was right in suggesting Cole for you."

Sasha looked up from the bills she was paying. It had been another restless night, and around five she had gotten out of bed and started working. For a second, she wondered if she'd heard correctly. "Oh?"

"I thought he'd be too much, you know? Too stern and unyielding. But after I thought about it—well, after Daniel made me really think about it—you seem happier and more at ease." Julie buzzed around the main room, straightening things up and pulling out papers needed for the day's deliveries.

Now or never.

Sasha shut her laptop. "I'm so glad you said that. Keep it in mind when I tell you this."

Julie froze. "Uh-oh."

"I'm going to take two weeks off starting the week after next."

"What? Are you serious?" She lifted an eyebrow. "How is Cole involved?"

"I'm completely serious. I'm arranging for a temp to come in and help. She'll be here tomorrow." Sasha stood up and walked to the workbench Julie was standing at. "I've asked Cole to train me at a new level and he agreed, but his condition was I not work for those two weeks."

"That's just crazy. What type of training would require you to . . ." Her eyes grew wide in apparent understanding. "Oh, no. Oh, hell, no. Are you fucking out of your mind?"

Taking a deep breath, Sasha answered as calmly as she could. "I am *not* out of my mind. It's something I want to explore and Cole's been nice enough to agree."

"*Nice enough to agree?* He's going to have a sex slave for two weeks. What man would turn you down?"

"Don't be stupid—you know it's more than that. Or is that not a collar you wear every day?" She took a step closer to her. "Don't tell me if Daniel walked in that door and ordered you to the back room to suck his dick, you wouldn't do it."

Julie crossed her arms. "We don't do twenty-four/seven."

"Well, Cole does and I want to taste it."

"This has 'bad decision' written all over it. I know you. You'll make a horrible slave."

"Thank you so very much for your vote of confidence."

Julie's eyes softened. "You're my best friend. I love you and I want to support you, but you have to be reasonable."

"What about Cole training me as a slave for two weeks is unreasonable?"

"The words that pop out are: Cole, training, slave, and two weeks." She ticked them off with her fingers.

"I could handle your attitude better if you were a random stranger from off the street."

"A random stranger from off the street didn't sit by your side for weeks when you were borderline catatonic!"

Sasha saw the worry and fear in Julie's eyes, but it was time for her friend to face the truth. "I'll never stop being a broken submissive until you stop seeing me as one."

"I don't—" she started, but stopped.

"Cole sees me as strong and sexy. When I'm with him, I feel that way. Don't make me feel broken, Julie. I deserve better."

A lone tear streaked down Julie's cheek. "God, Sasha, I'm sorry. I just, I can't see you like that again."

Sasha pulled her into a hug. "I won't ever be like that again. I'm not even the same person. But I want to do this. I need to do this."

"I hate it and I think it's a rotten idea." Julie squeezed her lightly. "But I love you more than I hate the thought of you and Cole and slave training, so I'm going to support you. Just promise me you'll be careful, and I mean more than the physical."

Sasha muttered a promise to be careful, but she had a sinking feeling it was already too late.

Almost two weeks later, she stood in the foyer of Cole's new house telling herself it was only natural to feel apprehensive about what she was getting ready to do. Arriving to the massive home with only her purse and journal made her feel defenseless. She'd get over it soon.

Cole closed and locked the front door behind her. The sound echoed in the otherwise still foyer. "What are you thinking?"

She took a deep cleansing breath. "How defenseless I feel standing here."

"Good." He walked to stand in front of her and cupped her chin so she had no choice but to meet his eyes. "As of right now, you are defenseless. By agreeing to do this, you have placed yourself under my complete control. I determine everything you do, you say, you wear, and very nearly what you think."

Her heart beat faster. This was a new side of Cole, one she'd only caught glimpses of before.

"Your one goal, your one purpose in life, is to serve me. You will serve me with your obedience, your mind, and your body. You have safe words if you need them, but let's be very clear." He leaned over her and whispered in her ear. "For the next two weeks, I fucking *own* you."

A shiver ran down her spine and her skin broke out in goose-flesh.

He took a step back. "You have an hour to prepare your body to serve me. The master bathroom contains everything you'll need. Once you're finished in the bathroom, you'll find instructions."

Without waiting for her to acknowledge he'd spoken or that she understood, he turned and left her standing alone. Her heart pounded wildly.

Holy hell.

She brought her hand to her chest and closed her eyes. Based on how he'd acted just now, there would be no slow and easy initiation into the next few weeks. Apparently, they were hitting the ground running at full speed.

Her lips slowly curved into smile.

She couldn't wait.

As she climbed the stairs to the second floor, she felt the weight of his stare on her back. She wasn't sure where he was watching her from, but as she walked, she made sure to sway her hips. At the top of the stairs, hoping he still watched, she slipped her shirt over her head, unhooked her bra, and walked topless to the bathroom.

Based on the conversations they'd had over the past week, she knew exactly what would be waiting for her in the bathroom. Placed in a neat row on the countertop were the items she needed: body wash, shampoo, lotion, shaving cream, a razor, toothbrush with toothpaste, tweezers, a hairbrush, and a tube of lube. She purposely ignored the last item for the time being and picked up the body wash, popping it open to smell. Lemongrass.

She grabbed a towel and debated between shower or bathtub. Deciding she was wound too tightly for a bath, she turned on the shower and waited until steam filled the room before hopping in.

As she washed and shaved, she was acutely aware of how vastly different this shower was from every shower she'd ever taken before. This shower was more than a way to get clean. It was preparing her body for Cole in the manner he wanted. She was filled with a desire to be waiting for him smelling, looking, and feeling exactly the way he wanted. She wanted to present herself perfectly to him because that would bring him pleasure.

She dried off and put on the lotion he'd left out. Her hands trembled with excitement while she styled her hair. Her time here would be like nothing she'd ever experienced. There would be nothing to worry or stress over. There would only be Cole.

After glancing at the time, she double-checked with the tweezers to ensure she removed any stray hair missed by the razor. She brushed her teeth and was finally faced with one last item. She eyed the lube before picking it up. When she went to open it, she noticed the writing in black marker:

Bring this with you.

She sighed in relief and placed the tube on top of her clothes. Perhaps he was only reminding her what he planned. It didn't mean he'd do it today.

Waiting for her on the bed were a garter belt, sheer hose, skimpy panties, and a lace bra. All in black. She ran her fingers over the lingerie and smiled.

He remembered.

The conversation about her fantasy party wear. He not only remembered, but he made it happen.

And this was no ordinary lingerie. Though she normally wore nondescript cotton, she recognized the high-end name brand. The Doms she'd played with in the past never really cared what she wore, one way or the other. The one time she'd put on something sexy for Peter, he scoffed and told her it was pointless because she wouldn't be wearing it long. But this?

This was decadent.

She took her time putting on each piece, imagining how she'd look once she had it all on. But when she looked in the mirror, she was unprepared for what she saw reflected.

She'd told Julie that Cole made her feel strong and sexy, but today he'd done more. Today he'd shown her she actually was strong and sexy. She stretched this way and that in front of the mirror. She looked better than she had in her fantasy.

A note had been placed beside the outfit with her name written in Cole's handwriting.

I've been unable to get the picture of you in black silk and lace out of my head. Once you're dressed, meet me in the kitchen. It's time to take responsibility for your actions.

Cole taking her in the kitchen was one of her favorite fantasies. To think he'd had the same one made her want to run down the stairs and beg him to take her. Probably not the best course of action, though.

Doing her best to ignore her pounding heart and trying to appear as if she did this sort of thing daily, she walked calmly down the stairs and into the kitchen. He stood by the island and appraised her as she entered. The look of masculine appreciation and desire made her stomach do cartwheels.

"Very nice, little one. You look fucking fabulous."

She dipped her head. "Thank you, Sir."

"But aren't you missing something?"

Missing something? How was that even possible?

Her eyes widened.

Shit!

"I forgot the lube, Sir."

"Kneel, slave." His voice chilled her.

She dropped to her knees, cursing herself for messing up so soon.

"I gave you a simple instruction, did I not?" he asked in the same frigid tone.

"Yes, Sir. Very simple."

"Are you aware of how painful it would be if I took your arse with no lube?"

Her butt clenched involuntarily. "Yes, Sir."

He walked toward her; each thud of his footstep seemed to vibrate through her body. "There is one thing certain about how this ends. And that's with you bent across the island with my cock up your arse." He roughly took her chin and lifted her face. "The only question is, will I allow you lube or not?"

Holy fuck! He wouldn't try anal sex without lube, would he? She didn't think the Cole she knew would, but that man seemed so different compared to the one currently with her.

She tried not to flinch away from his cool gaze. "I'm sorry, Sir."

His low chuckle sounded downright evil, and she feared what he would say next.

"It's going to take more than *I'm sorry* for you to earn the lube back."

She didn't know what he meant. She didn't move.

"You definitely won't earn it by just sitting there."

Oh.

She thought about asking for permission to suck him off. Based on the way his pants were tented, she could safely say there was one part of his anatomy that wouldn't object. All she would have to do is come up to her knees and unbuckle his belt.

She froze. His belt. Of course.

"If it pleases you, Sir." She stood and moved to stand in front of the island. "I believe you told me once before what happens to disobedient slaves in the kitchen."

He didn't say anything, but appraised her with his unwavering, intense gaze. Watching her—no it was more than that. He was studying her. Weighing her reply. Testing it. She straightened her spine, not wanting him to find her lacking.

"That would go a long way in earning it back," he said in a low, controlled voice.

She was surprised, but pleased he didn't ask if she was sure.

"Once you're prepared, bend over the island."

He was letting her decide how she'd prepare for him, not something he'd ordinarily do. She wouldn't let him regret it. Under his piercing gaze, she reached behind her back and unhooked her bra. She shrugged out of it, one shoulder at a time and didn't miss the hungry way he watched.

Knowing she had his undivided attention, she shimmied the lacy panties down her hips and stepped out of them. Wearing only the garter and hose, she turned away from him and draped herself across the island. Though she expected the granite to be cold, she still gasped when her bare breasts touched the cold stone.

She listened for the telltale sound of a belt being unbuckled, but it never came. Had she somehow missed it? She braced for the first blow and flinched when instead two warm hands cupped her shoulders.

"So jumpy." Both hands ran down her back, squeezed her ass, and stroked back up. "I'm touching you because it pleases me to do so. To know you're here and you're mine for the next two weeks."

He didn't say anything else, but his message was clear, and the weight of his words sunk deep into her mind, even as his hands woke her body to his touch. His massage lulled her into a relaxed state she wouldn't have thought possible moments before.

The first slap of his hand against her backside nearly had her moan in pleasure. Over and over he spanked her, sometimes hard and sometimes light, but always making her need grow. She squirmed in an effort to give her clit some friction.

The crack of the belt on her ass stopped her fidgeting.

"Be still," he said. "You're earning the lube back. Don't even think about coming."

She braced herself for leather, but only the warmth of his skin followed. He'd told her once before he would keep her off balance. He was right and it was useless to try and determine the whys and hows.

She turned her cheek so it rested against the cool granite and closed her eyes. He took his time working her over and though she expected pain, he also gave her pleasure. Between the belt and his hands, both sensations merged together and within minutes, she craved both.

"What color?" he asked bringing the belt across her backside and then followed by circling her clit with two fingers.

"Green, Sir."

The belt landed harder, but so did his teasing of her flesh. She forced herself to be still and accept what he gave her. She wasn't certain how much time passed. For that moment, there was nothing in her world but him and the feelings he drew from her body.

"Last three will be hard and fast. Take them in stillness and silence and I'll allow you to get the lube. Understand?"

Three. She knew she could take three more. She only hoped she could do it quietly and without moving. "Yes, Sir."

She didn't have time to prepare, the belt made contact almost before the words left her mouth.

One.

Two.

Three.

Tears stung her eyes, but she blinked them back.

"Breathe, little one."

She took a large gulp of air. Could she move yet? Should she wait for permission?

The decision was taken from her as he wrapped his arms around her, pulling her up and turning her to face him. She didn't know whether to expect tenderness or harshness, but he showed her both when he crushed his lips to hers in a quick, possessive kiss that left her reeling.

"Nothing makes me harder than knowing I'm about to fuck an arse I just belted." He bit her earlobe. "You have sixty seconds to get the lube and bring it back. You best not fail."

He stepped aside to let her pass and she darted around him and flew up the stairs. She didn't slow down as she grabbed the tube from the bed and hurried back to the kitchen.

He stood by the island, naked, and she only had time to run an appreciative glance over his body before dropping to her knees before him. She held the tube out.

"Three seconds to spare," he said. "Not bad. But I don't want the lube. You use it."

On him?

He fisted his cock. "Better hurry. I've waited about all I'm going to wait. Your arse is mine."

She squeezed some into her hands and coated his cock.

"Make sure you use enough, it'll be tough enough to take me the first time. Don't make it more difficult than it has to be."

She took the tube and squeezed a liberal amount directly on him. He chuckled.

"I think that's enough for now, little one. Hand the rest to me."

The tube nearly slipped out of her hands as she passed it to him. He placed it on the island and her heart pounded faster when he faced her again. Damn, she'd forgotten how huge he was. She doubted his ability to fit, no matter how much lube she'd used.

He, of course, noticed her uncertainty. He crossed his arms. "If you overly worry about it, you'll make yourself tense and it'll hurt. Trust me, and it'll go a lot easier."

"Yes, Sir," she said, but wasn't sure she meant it.

"Of course it doesn't matter to me one way or the other; either way I get off." He nodded toward the island. "I want you over it again, this time with your legs spread more."

She situated herself the way he asked, the temperature of the granite less of a surprise this time. He pressed against her and pushed her head down so it rested on the stone. One of his hands drifted between her legs to toy with her pussy and within seconds, she was fighting the urge to squirm.

"I love the feel of my slave cunt, all wet and hot and desperate for my cock. But today, I'm taking you here." He pushed a lubricated finger inside her ass. "And when I've finished, this hole will be ruined for anyone else's cock." He added another finger. "Because I'm not just going to fuck it, I'm going to Master it."

He worked his fingers deeper while at the same time using his other hand to stroke her clit. And damn it, it had never felt that good before.

"What do you say to that, slave?" His fingers slipped out and she almost whined at the loss.

"Please, Sir, fuck my ass."

He started pumping his fingers in and out of her, still working her clit with his other hand. "Fuck it with what?"

"Oh, god, your cock, Sir."

He kept thrusting with his fingers until she panted with need. Just when she thought she couldn't take it anymore, he stopped. With her next breath she felt the head of his cock against her ass.

"I hope you used enough lube, because you're going to take every last inch of me." His one hand had never left her clit and it continued to tease her. "Relax, little one. Let me in."

She did her best to relax against the insisting intrusion of his cock, but as his tip pressed inside, her eyes grew wide. *Damn.* He was stretching her more than she'd ever been stretched. The plugs were nothing.

"Bear down," he said in a strained voice.

He stilled his body, moving nothing but the fingers that were now easing inside her pussy and starting a slow pump in and out. His thumb rubbed across her clit. As arousal swelled inside her, he began to whisper.

"Bloody hell, you're so fucking hot."

He gave a little push and the tip of him popped inside her. She yelped at the sensation.

"Yes," he hissed. "I want to hear every shout, every sigh, every sound." He pushed slowly inside. "Because hearing you makes me so damn hard and I want to fuck you harder and deeper and never stop."

He moved even slower and she thought her eyes would roll to the back of her head. She couldn't hold back the gasp that escaped her as he entered her body.

"I'm so deep inside, a little more and I'm going to fuck you like you've never been fucked." He gave her ass a slap. "Breathe."

She took a deep breath and when she exhaled, he thrust the rest of the way.

"Bloody hell. Yes." His normally smooth voice sounded like he'd swallowed gravel.

He held still and she panted at the feel of him buried so deep inside her. *Fuck.* Never had she felt so full, so possessed. She was his and he'd just claimed her in the most primal way possible. And now that he'd claimed her, he would use her for his pleasure. Just thinking about it that way turned her on more and she gave her hips a swivel.

The slap to her ass was immediate. "Be still, slave. I said I wanted to hear you, not have you squirming all over the place."

She forced herself to be still, even as he withdrew and thrust forward with greater force than before. His movements rocked her and she grunted when the lower part of her body hit the side of the island.

"Getting ready to really slam into you." The entire time he talked, he gradually increased his pace and intensity. "Time to show this arse who it belongs to."

Her fingers searched frantically for something to hold on to.

"Hands behind your back," he snapped and then continued after she repositioned herself. "Your only job right now is to be still and take what I give you."

Take it she did. With her hands behind her back, she was at his mercy. He didn't voice that thought, though. Rather he proved it with his actions, driving into her over and over. And though he was hard and unyielding, he continued his attentions on her clit and it wasn't too long before she was panting, desperately trying to hold back her orgasm.

"Please let me come, Sir," she begged.

"No," he said without breaking stride.

Her climax swelled within her and she tried everything to keep it at bay. In her mind, she pictured things she hated: spiders, aggressive drivers, litter scattered among flowers, and still she teetered precariously on the edge of orgasm.

"Please, Sir," she tried again, lifting her head to look at him. "I can't—"

"Quiet."

Before she could get the words out, her head was pushed back down onto the granite by the hand that had been stroking her.

"Don't tell me what you can't do. You do anything I say, and right now, you can"—he punctuated each word with a rough thrust into her—"take . . . more."

The feeling of him moving within her, paired with his strength holding her immobile against the island, stirred her desire, pushing her closer to the edge. She began to tremble.

"Not yet," he warned.

She took several deep breaths to calm herself. It only worked for a few seconds; on his next thrust, she was back to trembling.

"Hold out." His voice was a rough command. "Do it because I'm your Master and I wish for you to do it. Do it for me."

"For you, Sir," she whispered. She pictured his approval if she held out until he gave permission and focused on that.

Behind her, his breathing grew short and choppy, while his strokes into her became slow and deep.

"Next time I pull out and come all over your back." His voice was strained and he thrust back inside her with a grunt. "But right now, I'm coming deep inside your hot little slave arse."

She gasped in pleasure and curled her hands into tight fists. He shoved his cock deeper and spoke one word.

"Now."

Chapter Ten

Cole gathered Sasha in his arms. She was weak and trembling with heavy eyelids that she appeared hell bent on keeping open. But she didn't fight him when he carried her out of the kitchen into the downstairs bedroom he'd claimed as his own.

He gently placed her in the middle of the bed and covered her with a thick blanket. "Stay here, little one. I'm going to get you cleaned up and then you're going to rest."

She made a noise low in her throat, but it was impossible to tell if it was in agreement or protest. He brushed her cheek with the back of his hand and when she burrowed into the blanket he decided it'd been in agreement.

He'd set out what he needed before meeting her in the kitchen, but even so, she was asleep after he collected everything, threw on some shorts, and made his way back into the bedroom.

She rested on her side, still covered by the blanket, and her smile of contentment pierced his heart. He'd been rough with her, holding little back, wanting her to grasp just a bit of a Master/slave relationship, and instead of running away, she found contentment in his bed.

He washed her as best as he could without waking her and rubbed ointment on her backside. There was no way for him to guess how long she'd sleep. After he'd caned her, she'd only slept for a handful of hours. This time when she woke up, he wanted to be there.

Decided, he climbed on the bed beside her and curled his body around hers. She wiggled deeper into his embrace and whispered, "Oh, thank you," so softly he almost missed it. He pressed his lips against the back of her neck and wondered if he'd have the strength to let her go at the end of two weeks.

She slept for an hour and woke up delightfully disoriented, twisting in his arms and looking at him for a few seconds as if trying to remember who he was.

He cupped her cheek, fearful she'd had a bad dream. "Are you okay?"

She sighed and rubbed against his hand. "Yes, Sir. You held me."

I always hold submissives after a scene, he almost said, but stopped himself. Though it would be the truth, it wasn't the same holding her as it'd been with other submissives. Even Kate had gotten to the point where she didn't want to be held for very long. For damn sure, she never snuggled close and thanked him in her sleep.

"I wanted to," he stated. "You have a sweet and affectionate nature and I wanted to be sweet and affectionate to you. I know there was very little warmth in the way I took you in the kitchen."

Her hand covered his. "If I may, Sir, there was warmth in the way you took me. Was it a typical warmth? Probably not, but that doesn't devalue it. Being different doesn't make it less."

He arched an eyebrow. "Explain, please."

"You took care to prepare me. You kept me the center of your attention, even while you were taking your own pleasure. You ensured I wasn't pushed past my limits."

"What are you saying, little one?"

She hesitated, backing down a bit and swallowing. "I'm saying, Sir, that maybe you need to redefine how you look at warmth. It's not just hugs and kisses; sometimes warmth can be found in the details. And sometimes it's the details that mean the most."

He let her words sink in. He, who had told her a month or so ago that words had meanings and she needed to recognize that fact, had just learned a much needed lesson. Wanting to catch her off guard, he took her in his arms and rolled them both so she was under him.

"You're full of surprises. Has anyone ever told you that?" he asked.

"Once or twice, Sir. But never while we were both naked."

"I'm not naked. I have shorts on."

She shrugged. "In my dream, you were naked."

She looked so adorable, on his bed, wrapped in his blanket, chatting away about being naked after dropping something so philosophical. He took her hands and brought them above her head.

"Everything about you turns me on. You're such a complex contradiction." He dropped his mouth to her ear. "It's so fucking hot."

He claimed her mouth then, taking her lips in a way that would show her without words just how much she turned him on. There was a time for words, he more than anyone knew that, but there was also a time for action. The woman in his arms had been given words, but too often there had been no follow-through.

He nibbled on her lips and explored them with his tongue, tasting the mint left behind by her recent teeth brushing. She answered back with her own actions and when she bit his bottom lip and sucked on it, he groaned in pleasure. Bloody hell, he hadn't kissed this woman near enough.

He pressed her into the mattress with his hips, making sure she felt every damn inch of him and knew without a doubt just how much he wanted to be inside her. He thrust his cotton-covered erection against her unprotected sex and when she gasped in response, he plundered her mouth.

He kissed her until she trembled in his arms and wiggled in an effort to get closer. It would be easy as hell to ease his shorts down, spread her legs, and give them what they both wanted. Easy, but that wasn't his plan.

Using more control than he thought should be required, he pulled away. She whimpered.

"Hands above your head, slave, and don't move them."

She instantly swallowed her whimper and followed his command.

"Good girl. Now show me my cunt."

Again, there was no hesitation as she spread herself for his scrutiny.

"Very nice." He ran a finger down her freshly shaven flesh. "I meant to inspect you earlier to ensure you prepared yourself properly. Unfortunately, I got carried away with other things, so I'll rectify that now. Do you know, little one, the best way to make sure you didn't miss a hair?"

Her eyebrows crinkled as she thought. "With a magnifying glass?"

"No, with my mouth." He didn't give her time to process his words, he simply shifted slightly, lowered his head, and gave her pussy a lick. She jerked and he bit her gently. "Be still, slave."

Only when he was certain she would remain motionless did he resume. He made sure not to touch her clit, choosing to focus on the surrounding flesh. Only seconds had passed when he noticed her thighs start to shake. Poor Sasha, it'd probably been a long time since she had to work against her natural urges. And right now, it was taking most of her strength not to move.

He decided to help by moving his hands to rest on her upper, inner thighs. That her body stilled under his touch pleased him and he licked her slit from bottom to top, dragging the tip of his tongue so it barely pushed inside.

"So wet already, slave?" he teased. "Did your Master not fuck you enough the first time?"

She didn't budge when she answered, "I can't help it, Sir. What you do to my body."

He gave her another lick. "That pleases me. Firstly, because you have such a strong reaction to me. Secondly, it ensures you're prepared should I decide I want to use you. You're so wet, I wouldn't have any trouble sliding my cock deep inside your hot fuck hole."

Her only reply was a heavy exhale through her nose.

"Right now, though, I just want to eat it."

And with that, he stopped talking and simply enjoyed her. He teased and nibbled and sucked, savoring her taste, but more than that, delighting in the soft noises she made and the obvious effort she spent remaining still. He doubled his actions, sucking her clit and running his tongue over it.

Her legs started shaking again and, just to be evil, he thrust two fingers inside her. "Nope. Wouldn't have any trouble at all. In fact, my cock does need relief. So be a good slave and stay still whilst I shag you and maybe I'll let you come again."

Just about every part of her body below the waist ached. Even after taking two ibuprofens and another soothing massage from Cole, there remained a pleasant awareness of how she'd spent the better part of the afternoon.

Her mind replayed what Julie had said about being his sex slave, but Sasha didn't feel used. Even when he was taking his own pleasure, Cole watched her with such intensity and focus, she felt protected and cared for. And if the earth-shattering orgasms weren't enough, whenever they finished, he would hold her close to his chest for a long time.

He'd brought the black lingerie back up the stairs and told her to put it on. She had twenty minutes before she had to be in his office. Putting the lacy panties on, she told herself it wouldn't always be as good as it'd been today. What she was experiencing now was the honeymoon period of her slave training. She had to think that way, or else she'd never want to leave.

She brushed her teeth again. Cole had made her clean him after he'd taken her in his bed. She'd thought that after coming in both the kitchen and the bedroom, he'd need time to recover. He'd laughed at her surprise when he grew hard again in her mouth. He didn't finish, though. Instead he'd told her to clean up and meet him in his office.

He was sitting at his desk when she entered, minutes later. His glasses were perched haphazardly on his nose and he frowned at something on his laptop. Not wanting to disturb him, she knelt in the middle of the room.

"By my side, Sasha," he said, without looking up.

Unexpectedly pleased at his request, she started to stand.

"Crawl." He still hadn't looked up from his computer.

She froze, slightly caught off guard by his request. She'd crawled in play before, but they weren't currently in a scene.

Except she was in a scene all day, every day, for the next two weeks.

She crawled as quickly as possible to his side and knelt beside his chair with her head bowed. As soon as she stilled herself, his hand fisted her hair.

"You hesitated."

Denial danced on her lips. Or an excuse. If she thought really fast, she could probably come up with several good ones. But her heart raced as she realized the truth and knew there was only one thing to do.

"I did, Sir." The fingers in her hair tightened and she added, "I'm sorry."

"I had planned for us to spend the evening relaxing, perhaps watching a movie. Now, however, I feel your time would be better spent writing one thousand words on crawling, its symbolism, and its meaning."

She dug her nails into her upper thighs. *No!* she wanted to yell. She wanted to spend the evening with him, watching a movie, not working on a stupid writing assignment. But the hand on her head reminded her of her purpose in being in his house and she replied with, "Yes, Sir."

"In the last sentence I spoke, did the word *its* have an apostrophe or not?"

What the fuck? Where did that come from?

"No apostrophe, Sir."

"Very nice, little one. I expect no improper word usage to-night, but you should know that this time, I won't have you recite dirty sentences." She didn't have time to be relieved before he added, "I'll be the one coming up with the sentences, and you'll have to act them out."

And his sentences would be evil and wicked. While she thoroughly enjoyed that side of him, she had a feeling she probably shouldn't goad him. "I understand, Sir."

His hand left her head and she assumed he went back to work. Why then had he requested her to come to the office if he wasn't going to say or do anything? She thought about all the other things she could be doing, but then stopped short. Here at Cole's house, there wasn't much for her to do.

She reminded herself, once again, that she was getting a taste of what it was like to be a slave. She should be thinking about how to please her Master—something she'd messed up on minutes before.

Maybe if she thought through what she was going to write on crawling, it wouldn't take her that long to complete and they could still spend the evening together. Although, he might be working. He certainly seemed engrossed at the moment.

The room had grown noticeably darker before he pushed back in his chair. "Sometimes the simple presence of another person makes all the difference. I enjoyed having you in the room with me as I caught up on a few items, little one. So much so, I think we'll make this a regular occurrence."

She tried to cover her shock at his revelation and felt a little prideful that she'd made a difference. "Of course, Sir."

"Come sit in my lap."

He held out a hand and helped her to straddle his lap, facing him. He ran a finger down her cheek. "You look beautiful in black lace, but I think tomorrow I want you naked all day."

She swallowed. She'd expected to spend time naked, but hadn't planned on spending the entire day naked. Not on the second day.

"Yes," he mused. "I think I'll display you like a fine piece of art. Perhaps on a table. I can appreciate your beauty as I work, all the while imagining all the sordid things I want to do to your body. And then, when I finish for the day, I'll write them all down and have you pick one."

She was going to sit on a table? All day?

"Is that a frown?" he asked.

"Just trying to understand how it'll work, Sir, with me being on a table."

"It will work how I say it will work. It's not your place to understand. The only thing you need to understand is that I have everything under control."

"My brain has a hard time shutting off, Sir."

"Yes, I know. Do you see now why it's best you not work at the shop for these two weeks?"

"Yes, Sir."

"I know it's a difficult state of mind to get to, but once you do, you'll stop analyzing everything so much."

"Thank you for understanding my struggles, Sir."

He traced her lips with his finger. "I think I have something that might help."

"It's not an anal plug, is it?" *Please don't let it be an anal plug.*

He snorted in surprise, took a deep breath, and shook his head. "No, nothing quite as awful as a plug. In fact, I think you'll like this. Go kneel in the middle of the room."

As she moved off his lap, her mind raced trying to imagine what it could be, but she came up with nothing. The sound of a drawer opening led her to believe he had it stored in his office, and that just confused her more. The only thing she would think he'd have in desk drawers were office supplies.

"Look at me, Sasha," he said from a few feet before her.

His voice sounded a bit hoarse, which made no sense. He'd been talking all day and even up to a few minutes ago sounded normal. She lifted her head and her breath caught.

He was holding a collar.

Excitement surged through her veins and her heart pounded like she'd just finished a five-mile run. She blinked to make certain she looked at it right.

"It's a training collar," he explained. "Just for these two weeks."

She kept her eyes on the collar as he stepped closer. It looked like a thin band of black leather.

"If I were collaring a slave, the collar would be locked around her neck and I alone would hold the key. This collar has a clasp, making it easily removable. Though we agreed on two weeks, there is nothing stopping you from walking out my door."

Even as shocked and happy as she was to be offered a simple training collar from Cole, she didn't miss the trace of emotion he'd been unable to hide while speaking. Having his collar locked around her neck hadn't stopped Kate from walking out of his door.

"I know you're aware of the meaning behind a collar," he said. "And though this one is only temporary, I think wearing it for these two weeks will be beneficial."

He probably had a point. With a reminder of who she belonged to for this time, always there around her neck, she imagined it would be easier not to let her mind lead her into hesitation.

He reached down and cupped her cheek, so gently his thumb stroked her skin. "Will you wear my training collar, little one?"

Tears prickled her eyes over a *training* collar. She mentally scolded herself. It wasn't even a real collar; it was temporary. But she'd never been collared before, even in a training sense, and she couldn't keep the fears tamped down that this might be the only time anyone would ever offer her his collar.

"Yes, Sir. I will gladly wear your training collar," she said, surprised by how husky her voice sounded.

He reached behind her and buckled the collar into place, dragging his fingertips along the leather's edge and making her skin rise in goose bumps. She closed her eyes. Cole had just collared her and for that moment in time, she pretended it wasn't only for two weeks.

"Your neck was made to display a Master's collar," he whispered. "Just as your body was made for his dominance. My collar looks good on you, slave."

My collar. It felt good, too. "Thank you, Sir."

"I want you to stay in here in that position. Meditate on how wearing my training collar will help keep you in the proper mindset. When you're finished, you may put your clothes on for an hour of free time before dinner. I'll allow you clothes at dinner tonight, too."

"One question, Sir."

"Yes?"

"May I start on my writing assignment during my free time?"

He raised an eyebrow. "You may, but your free time is limited and it'll probably be tomorrow night before you get more time to yourself."

"I know. It's just——" She paused for a second, then told herself to be bold. "I'd like to spend the evening with you instead of writing."

"I'd much rather you spend the evening with me, too. So if you finish your assignment and I have a chance to look over it, maybe there'll be some time to be together."

"Thank you, Sir."

The woman who joined him at the dinner table a few hours later appeared calm and content and nothing at all like the wounded submissive he'd first taken notice of. Sasha was strong now, physically and mentally, yes, but even more so because she believed in herself. While he was pleased with the transformation, he knew at the end of her training he'd need to let her go. She needed to see that she could be strong and confident with other Dominants, not just him.

She sat across from him with a smile. Fuck, she looked so good wearing a collar.

But not just any collar. His collar. Even if it was only for training.

She'd handed him her journal while he waited for dinner to be ready. Though he hadn't had a chance to look over it, he had the feeling there would be no errors or grammatical mistakes tonight. So far Sasha didn't seem to be one who had to be taught something more than once.

He'd selected a shirt with a plunging neckline for her to wear tonight. He remembered how much fun it'd been to shop for her. How he imagined her in the clothes he bought. The shirt she currently had on gave him a nice view of her breasts, but even better, it showed off his collar. He loved the way the black leather wrapped around her throat. *Taken*, it said. *Claimed. Unavailable to you.*

And yet to him it whispered something more. *Yours. Take me. Use me.*

He needed to keep that whispering voice in check. Technically, she was only his for the next thirteen days. Thirteen days.

And twelve nights.

"Dinner smells wonderful, Sir," she said, shifting his focus away from his plans for the night.

"When you're wearing clothes, you may call me Cole."

"If it's okay with you, I'm more comfortable using Sir all the time."

She'd applied light makeup while dressing for dinner and her lips were full and red. It was rather hard to think about anything other than her mouth when she wore lipstick that color. Or if it wasn't her mouth, it was whether or not her lipstick would stain his cock if she deep throated him.

She tilted her head as if waiting for a response.

"I'm sorry, what?"

Her laugh was musical. "I said, if it's okay with you, I'm more comfortable using Sir all the time."

"When we're observing lower protocol, I don't want you to feel inhibited. I've found that it's easier to remember if you're able to use my given name."

She leaned forward and he did the same instinctively. In a low voice, she explained, "I only have these two weeks to call you Sir. After that, you'll just be Cole unless we're with the group. Please let me call you Sir. I promise I won't let it make me feel inhibited when I'm wearing clothes."

It had "Bad Idea" written all over it. He should tell her no and insist she call him Cole. But it was such a little thing. She rarely asked for anything. Surely, he could give her this.

He reached across the table and took her hand. "All right, little one, if you want to use Sir, I won't make you do otherwise."

Her smile transformed her entire face and she beamed at him, like he'd just bought her the damn moon. Bloody hell. Was he that much of a jerk that allowing her to call him Sir could elicit such a response?

He tightened his grip on his fork. Time to change the subject. "How do you feel after your first few hours of slave training?"

"My mind's fighting me more than I thought it would. I thought it'd be easy to stand down and let you take over, but it's hard."

"You've worked your entire life to be strong and self-sufficient. Of course it's hard. And not everyone is cut out to be a full-time slave."

A small smile danced on her lips. "I think it's a bit early to make that call, don't you?"

"Perhaps. Perhaps not. If you really hated it . . ."

She shook her head. "If I really hated it, I wouldn't have accepted your training collar earlier."

"Point taken."

"I think I'll give it another day, at least. I'd hate to make a decision without experiencing a complete night with you."

The words left him. He opened his mouth, but nothing came out. Something flashed in her eyes, but she dropped her head to her plate before he could tell what.

Changing the subject, he brought her phone out of his pocket. "No one's called or sent a text today. Do you need to get in touch with anyone?"

"No." She scooped up rice on her fork. "I told my parents I was going to a work conference out of town and I'd call them when I could, but it probably wouldn't be often."

He raised an eyebrow. "You lied to your parents?"

"The other option was to tell them I was living with a man I've known less than a year so he could train me to be a slave and I probably wouldn't be able to call very often seeing as how I'd have his dick in my mouth a good portion of the time."

Her matter-of-fact statement was spoken so off-handedly, he choked on his wine. "Yes, I can see why you went with the first option."

She shrugged. "I'm more than happy to tell them the truth, but they probably wouldn't take it so well."

"Are you close to your parents?"

"Not overly. They retired to Florida, so I usually only see them at Thanksgiving or Christmas."

"Brothers or sisters?"

She took a bite of rice before replying. "Suddenly interested in my family?"

"I'm interested in how you became the woman you are today."

Her gaze dropped to her plate, but he thought he saw the beginnings of a smile. He was certain of it when she looked up and he saw the delight in her eyes at his statement.

"I have an older brother," she said.

"Uh-oh, should I be afraid?"

She laughed. "I won't tell him if you don't. He's a car sales-man in Dover. We aren't all that close, but I see him more fre-quently than I do my parents. I had a very average and normal childhood. Graduated high school and went to college, where I met Julie."

"College was where you also discovered your submissive ten-dencies."

"Yes."

"What made you stay in the lifestyle? As one of the group members, I mean. Why not just be a dabbler?"

She took her time thinking through his question. "I didn't see the point in doing it halfway. I knew almost immediately that I was submissive, so it only made sense to seek out likeminded people."

"You told me a few weeks ago that one of the things you liked about being a submissive was turning over control so you could just feel while knowing that you would be protected."

She nodded.

"What makes you feel the most protected?"

"During a scene or outside of one?"

"Either."

"Earlier today, after the kitchen island, when you took me to your bedroom. That made me feel safe and protected. I mean, I know it's aftercare and you have to do it, but I felt so secure with you holding me. It was as if nothing else and no one else could touch me."

"It may be aftercare and I may do it regardless of the scene, but rest assured I got just as much out of holding you as you did."

"I never understood that part of being a Dominant."

"I can't speak for every Dominant, but after a scene, I need to hold you. I need to feel you in my arms, so soft and satisfied and know that you're okay. Know that we're okay. When I hold you after a scene, it's a way to reconnect and ensure our relationship grows. Plus, I've always found it's easier to talk when you're cuddled together."

"You don't strike me as the cuddling type."

"Perhaps *cuddle* is the wrong word."

"I didn't think you ever picked the wrong word," she teased, watching him carefully over the rim of her wineglass.

"All writers have editors." He leaned back in his chair, enjoying the lighthearted conversation. "Let's see. If I had to replace cuddle with another word, I'd say, 'I've always found it's easier to talk when you're wrapped together skin-on-skin and so close your bodies speak in ways your mouth can't.'"

The wineglass she'd been drinking from was now suspended halfway between the table and her lips.

"Sasha?" he asked.

"Uh, what?" She put the glass down. "I got lost somewhere between skin-on-skin and mouth."

He laughed. It seemed it was always easier to laugh when Sasha was around. "I'll help you clean up the kitchen and then we'll see if we can find a movie to watch."

She woke the next morning, not surprised to find the bed empty. He'd told her he was an early riser. What was surprising was that they hadn't done anything the night before. When they made it to bed, he'd simply pulled her to him and whispered that they had plenty of time.

She stretched, still feeling the slight aches and pains of the day before. He'd told her what her morning routine was to be, so she scurried out of bed, made it, and freshened up in the bathroom.

Naked, she walked to the large picture window in the bedroom that overlooked the backyard. She took only a second to glance outside and in doing so, noticed Cole on the patio. Without looking to see if he was watching, she knelt down and started her new morning ritual of meditation.

She'd never meditated before, but Cole had told her all he expected was for her to spend time in quiet reflection and he'd let her know when her time was up. That she could do.

But on her knees, she discovered it was hard to still her mind. Numerous questions popped up, one after another: what were they going to do today, what was he doing outside, did she over-sleep, what about breakfast?

Switching tactics, she focused on her breathing and took a deep breath in and slowly let it out. In her mind, she heard Cole's voice praising her, "Good girl." After a few cycles, her body set-tled into the quiet peacefulness she'd anticipated. She focused on Cole and how excited she was to be with him for the next few weeks.

The shuffle of footsteps worked their way into her conscious-ness. Cole was back; her time must be up. She waited in stillness for him to say something.

But he continued moving silently and he came to a stop in front of her. His feet were bare. That was the only part of him she saw with her head down. And still he didn't say anything.

Finally, he moved. He shifted his feet so they were farther apart. In the next second, his jeans slid down around his ankles.

That probably meant what she thought it meant, but would he want her to assume or wait for instructions? She clenched her fists in exasperation. She didn't know because he didn't tell her.

He cupped her chin and lifted her head slightly so she was eye level with his erection. "Did you enjoy your quiet time this morning, little one?" he asked in a whisper.

"Yes, Sir." She licked her lips, hungry for the taste of him.

"Elaborate."

"I first focused on my breathing and it was almost as if I heard you giving me instructions. Once my mind settled down, I was able to think about this week and seeing you. Serving you."

"And you still want to continue?"

"Very much, Sir."

"Thank you, little one. I'm glad to hear that." He shook first one leg and then the other, removing his pants completely. He grabbed a handful of hair and moved her head closer to his groin. "Show me."

She didn't want to just give him a blow job, she wanted to lavish his cock with everything she felt at that moment. Tentatively, she placed her hands on his upper thighs and engulfed his length in her mouth. First taking him as deep as possible, then pulling away and swirling her tongue around his tip. With both hands, she worked the base.

His fingers tightened, giving her hair a slight pulling. "Mmm, little one. That's right. Worship that cock. Show me how much you love it. What it does to you."

His words of praise filled her with warmth. She took him down her throat and didn't move, allowing him to enjoy the feeling of being inside her that way. With her whole being she paid homage to his cock using her lips, her tongue, her hands, and, most importantly, her mind.

It had the desired effect on him. His breathing grew raspy and his fingers held an almost painful grip on her hair. He was close and she was ready. She wanted to taste the evidence of how much she'd turned him on.

But right when she thought he was going to come, he stopped completely, and jerked out of her mouth. She dropped back so her butt rested on her heels and looked at his feet.

"Eyes on me, little one. I do enjoy watching you swallow, but right now I'm going to come all over you. Lift your head higher. I'm not going to come on your face yet."

Damn. That meant he would eventually, right?

She didn't want to admit how much that thought turned her on.

Once she'd lifted her head, he worked his erection and within seconds, he painted her chest and shoulders with his come. It felt feral kneeling before him as his release slid down her skin. She shouldn't like it. She should be disgusted. But she wasn't. She loved it. Loved that it was like he'd marked her. That he gave that part of him to her.

He offered her a hand and helped her to her feet. "I'm going to enjoy eating breakfast with you wearing nothing but my collar and my spunk."

It was an unusual breakfast to say the least. Cole didn't have her sit across from him at the table, the way she thought he would. He told her he wanted her in his lap and proceeded to feed her from his plate.

"You really can't cook?" he asked.

She swallowed the bite of omelet she had in her mouth. "I really can't."

"Nothing?"

"Nothing."

"It's not that big of a deal for me, but if you do want to enter into a Master/slave relationship at some point, there are Masters who require domestic service."

"I make a mean pot of coffee."

"You're not that bad with tea, either."

"Thank you, Sir."

He held the glass of orange juice up to her lips and she took several sips.

"Speaking of cooking," Sasha said, "I'm having a package delivered here today. It's perishable. If you let me know when it gets here, I'll take care of it."

He lifted an eyebrow. "Is it food?"

"Kinda. Julie told me about this site where they send you the ingredients and give you the recipe and supposedly it's easy to fix."

"Really?"

"I know it's an area I need to work on. I totally forgot until you said something. I ordered it last week."

Before she could get her next sentence out, his lips were on hers and he was giving her a kiss that curled her toes and made her very aware she was naked in his lap.

"You never stop surprising me," he said. "How do you do that?"

"I don't know, but if I do it again, will I get another kiss?"

"I'll give you more than a kiss."

She decided she needed to work out different ways to surprise him.

The package was delivered shortly after lunch while Sasha was working on a writing assignment Cole had given her. He carried the box into the kitchen and then went to get her.

He knocked on the door to the sunroom, where she sat writing. "Your package arrived, little one. If you need to go take care of it, you may finish the assignment later."

She glanced at the clock on the wall and then stood and walked to him, where she knelt. "Thank you, Sir. Is it okay with you if I start dinner?"

"Of course. I look forward to whatever it is you're making."

"It might be wiser to wait until you actually taste it, Sir."

He stroked her hair. "You took the initiative to work on an area you wanted to improve on. It wasn't anything I requested or anything I would have required. You did it because you wanted to. No matter how it tastes, it's going to be wonderful."

Did she have any idea how rare that was? For anyone to have that drive impressed him. For it to be a submissive woman he had feelings for? It blew his mind.

He ran his thumb over her lips. "You may go to the kitchen, little one. And you may slip some clothes on."

She rose to her feet and kissed his cheek. "Thank you, Sir."

Yup. Mind blown.

He waited until she made it to the kitchen before sitting down at a small desk he had in the living room. Doing so gave the illusion he was working, but in reality, it afforded him the opportunity to watch her.

She carefully opened the box and unpacked the contents, placing everything on the countertop. By the time she finished, vegetables, meat, and spices covered an entire side of the kitchen. She stepped back and looked over it. "Shit."

He wondered about Julie's definition of "easy to fix."

With a resolute sigh, she pulled out the recipe card and read it, lining up the items as she went. From where he sat, it looked like some sort of rice or pasta dish. She took out a pot and several bowls from the cabinet and started working.

It looked like things were progressing well until she got to the carrots. Apparently, she had to peel and slice them and from what he could tell, Sasha had done neither before. He hoped she didn't lose a finger the way she worked the knife.

By the time she made it to the second carrot, the water she'd put on to boil was bubbling over the top of the pot. Once she had that under control, she went back to the carrots and managed to get through the second one. Her shoulders slumped as she saw how many were left.

She threw two in the trash can, took another glance at the pile left and threw away another.

"Who the hell needs so many carrots?" she asked the empty kitchen. "Seriously."

She drummed her fingers on the countertop and without

warning, turned and walked his way. He dropped his eyes and pretended to work.

"Sorry to interrupt, Sir," she said. "But I have a quick question."

"Yes, little one?"

"Are there rabbits in your yard?"

He tried to hide his smile. "Rabbits?"

"Yes, Sir. I have some carrots left over and I was wondering if I could put them outside?"

"I've never seen any rabbits. Why don't you just use them in whatever you're cooking? I love carrots."

"Really?"

He nodded. "Yes, and Sasha?"

"Mmmm."

"I smell something burning."

"Fuck!" she yelled and ran back to the kitchen.

He kept his laughter to himself. Poor Sasha, trying to cook and getting sidetracked by carrots. He debated going to help her, but stayed where he was. Odds were, she wouldn't welcome his being in the kitchen. She wanted to do this dinner by herself, so he would let her.

"Damn, damn, damn," she cursed from the kitchen, doing her best to salvage whatever she'd been boiling.

When she had everything under control, she took a step back and wiped her nose with her sleeve. Her sigh was audible from where he sat. But she didn't stop, she went back to peeling carrots and preparing the other vegetables.

She'd told him the Web site said you could cook a meal from start to finish in thirty minutes. So far, she'd spent all her time with carrots and boiling water.

"Thirty minutes, my *ass*," she said, echoing his thoughts.

She finished dinner an hour later. The kitchen looked like a disaster area, with nearly every bowl, pot, and pan he had piled in the sink. Carrot peels littered the countertop. An unknown liquid had been spilled on the floor and the air was still heavy with the tinge of burned food.

But in the middle of it all, Sasha stood beaming and handed him a bowl. "Taste it, Sir. See if it's good."

He took it and headed to the table. "Bring yourself a bowl and sit with me."

"I don't know, Sir." She spooned some pasta into a bowl and poured sauce on it. "What if it sucks?"

"It smells divine and my kitchen looks like someone catered a meal for twenty. There's no way it sucks."

She didn't look convinced. "Sorry about the kitchen. I'll clean it up."

"Don't worry about it now. Let's eat."

He took a tentative bite and hummed in pleasure at the taste. "Sasha, this is incredible."

She looked as if he'd just told her she'd won a million dollars. "Really?"

"Taste for yourself." He held his fork up to her mouth.

She took a bite. "Wow."

"You did very well," he said.

"Thank you, but as I was cooking, I made up my mind about something."

"What was that?"

"I'll never serve a Master who expects me to cook. Once was enough. I mean, hell, the carrots alone were enough to drive me up the wall." She shook her head. "And to think I'd have to do that two or three times a day? Hell, no."

They finished eating and she took their empty bowls to the sink.

"Oh, man, I forgot I had all this left to clean up."

"I'll help," he said. "We'll both clean up the countertops, and then you wash and I'll dry."

"You'd really think someone like you would have someone come in to do this sort of thing."

"Nah, I like my privacy too much."

They worked quickly together clearing the countertops and Sasha was soon up to her wrists in sudsy water. "They have dishwashers for this, you know."

"I don't like putting dirty dishes in there."

"It defeats the purpose of a dishwasher if you wash them first."

"Perhaps, but at least this way I don't have a bunch of dirty dishes in my kitchen."

"But they're in the *dishwasher*. Oh, fly!" She waved her hand to shoo the insect away, but in doing so splashed him.

"Sasha." He wiped the water from his face.

"Sorry, Sir, it was buzzing in my ear."

He pretended to be stern. "And that makes it okay to get me wet?"

She studied him as if weighing his words and expression to determine if he was serious. "Frankly, the only thing that would be more okay is if you were wet all over." She shook her hand again, getting more water on him this time.

He looked at her in shock. "You're going to pay for that."

"Not if you don't catch me." And before he could reply, she spun and ran out of the kitchen, through the living room and out the back door, giggling.

Game on.

He let her have a few seconds of a head start and then followed. She waited on the patio behind his new table. "Splashing me and running away?" He shook his head. "Someone's been a very bad girl."

"It was a mistake," she said with a grin.

"It was a mistake the first time. The second was on purpose."

"It's not my fault you look hot when you're wet."

"Is that right?"

"I don't want you getting a big head or anything, but yeah. You are."

He walked out onto the patio, keeping an eye on her. She moved back away from the table, still giggling, onto the grass, her hands up in a keep-your-distance signal.

In his mind, he mapped where she was standing in relation to his sprinkler system. Her left foot was almost at one of the heads. He pretended his phone buzzed and pulled it out of his pocket.

"Talk about rotten timing." He looked at the display as if reading a text, but in reality he scrolled through his apps until he found the one he was looking for.

There it was, the new app that allowed him to control his sprinklers from his smartphone. "Hold on, I just need to take care of this really quick."

Her hands fell to the sides of her body and she relaxed, appearing to be waiting patiently for him to play again.

"Here's what I was looking for." He looked up at the same second he pressed the button for the sprinklers to cut on.

Sasha shrieked as the cold water hit her and brought her hands up to her face. "You cheated."

"How can I cheat when I'm the one who makes the rules?"

"Then I guess I'm the one who breaks them." And with that, she proceeded to take her clothes off.

"Are you trying to distract me?"

"Of course not, Sir. I just don't like wet clothes."

He wasn't sure he believed her. She was quite the distraction standing in his yard, naked and wet. "You look pretty hot wet, yourself," he told her.

"You could come join me." She ran her hands down her body. "I'm getting lonely standing here all by myself."

As the idea of what to do next came to his mind, he drew the shirt over his head and tossed it on the brick patio floor. "We can't have that," he agreed. "You might get lonely."

"And when I'm lonely, I do bad things."

"We definitely can't have that."

He started walking toward her, holding her gaze as he crossed the patio. Making sure he kept his expression neutral and moving slowly, she didn't suspect anything when he made it to her side.

"See?" she said. "You look hot with your shirt off. Now we just need to get you wet."

She took a step to the sprinkler, but before she could put her foot down, he yanked her up in his arms and threw her over his shoulder.

"Hey!" She pounded on his back. "What are you doing?"

"Enforcing the rules," he said with a smile.

"How did I break rules?"

"Oh, I don't know. Maybe splashing your Dom, running away from him, and trying to distract him with your nakedness for starters."

"Oh, *those* rules."

"Indeed." He was pleased she picked up that they were made-up fun rules and she wasn't really in trouble. He was even more pleased he'd had the foresight to set up his backyard for playing a few days before she arrived. "Though I would suggest you stop hitting my back."

Her hands stilled and he carried her across the yard to a far corner where the lot was wooded. He found a fallen log and sat, placing Sasha over his knee.

"Now this is a lovely sight." He ran his hand over her backside. "I've never had you in this position before, but I think I like it. In fact, I may turn you over my knee every night before we go to bed."

She just groaned.

"Tell me, slave. Have you fantasized about being facedown across my lap?" He slapped her butt cheek when she didn't say anything. "Tell me."

"Yes, Sir."

He rubbed the spot he'd just slapped. "Good girl. Now tell me what I did in your fantasy."

"You spanked me."

"With my hand?"

"Sometimes."

"Sometimes?" He reached behind the log and picked up the switch he'd found days ago. "That means more than one fantasy?"

She didn't reply as quickly as he wanted. He tapped her backside with the switch. "Answer."

"Yes, Sir. More than one."

"Tell me about your favorite."

"It's not really what you do that makes one fantasy stand out, Sir."

"Oh?"

"It's what you say and how you say it."

"Very interesting. Give me an example." He brought the switch down harder and at the same time, teased the sensitive flesh between her legs.

"In one, you'll tell me to take my panties down and bend over your lap. In another, you tell me to prepare for the spanking I'm about to receive. You make me get what I want you to spank me with and then ask you to work over my ass."

While she talked, he continued his teasing with one hand and marking her arse with the switch with the other.

"Look at this bum, already turning pink under my hands. Show me how much you want me to continue. Lift it up for me."

She moaned, but did it anyway.

"You've been a naughty slave, haven't you? Teasing your Master and then fantasizing about him spanking you." He pushed two fingers into her—*fuck*, she was so wet. "Look how turned on you are. I'm going to spank you and then I'm going to fuck you against a tree. How does that sound?"

"Like my new favorite fantasy, Sir."

"I'm already living my fantasy. And that's you on your knees, offering yourself for me to take however I damn well want." He brought the switch down hard and at the same time thrust two fingers inside her. "Pleasure and pain. After a while, they start to feel the same, don't they?"

"Yes, Sir."

"Lift that arse back up. And stop wiggling on my lap. You'll come when I say you can and not a minute sooner." He spanked her again. "Hungry for my cock, aren't you?"

"Always, Sir."

"Good. Because I'm ready to give it to you." He dropped the switch. "Go stand against the tree to my right. You'll know the one when you see it."

She crawled off his lap and walked toward the trees. He knew when she found the one he'd told her to stand against because she stilled momentarily. He imagined it looked a bit scary at first glance. He'd set it up with rope and chains.

"Put your back against the tree and reach up and grab the ropes." He waited while she got into position and then walked to stand in front of her. He unzipped his pants. "How does the tree feel?"

"Rough, Sir."

"It's going to be rough on your back and you'll have scratches. Are you okay with that?"

"Yes, Sir," she said with no hesitation.

He pushed his pants down and stepped out of them. "Still wet for me?"

"Yes, Sir."

He lifted her legs and wrapped them around his waist. "Keep them here. I'm going to pound you into that tree."

She whimpered.

"Here we go. Going to slip inside." He pushed into her. "Ah, yes. So good like this."

She tightened her legs around him as he started moving deeper. He didn't know what it was about Sasha. She told him that he made her strong, but the real truth was, she allowed him to be strong. When he was with her, he felt like he could be himself.

He moved his hands to her face. "Look at me."

Her green eyes were hazy with lust. He continued moving inside her as he held her gaze. The intensity of their union struck him in the center of his chest. This woman who had come to him hurt and yearning for healing had somehow healed him.

"Too much," she said, echoing his thoughts. "It's too much."

"No, little one." His voice was far gentler than he felt. "It will never be enough."

"I know. I know." She pushed her head against the tree, but kept her eyes locked on his.

Suddenly, it wasn't enough to be inside her. He needed more. "Touch me. I'll hold you," he panted. "I want your arms around me."

It was precarious, but she let go of the ropes. And he had no choice but to be strong. After all, he had to secure her. She was held by only his arms and the tree. Her nails dug into his shoulders, and it was the most welcome pain he'd ever experienced because it was she who gave it to him.

He wondered if that's what a submissive felt when under a Dom's control.

The thought made him more forceful and he wasn't going to be able to hold out much longer.

"Are you close?" He didn't wait for a response and because he couldn't risk moving his hand to help if she needed it, added, "Get there."

"Harder. Mark my back." Her lips parted and for a few precious seconds, they shared the same air.

He felt her start to tighten around him and her eyes beseeched him. He wanted to hold out a little longer. She felt too good. But her whispered request unleashed him and he gave her what she wanted, slamming her against the tree.

"Almost. Please," she whispered.

"Yes," he replied, feeling dangerously close himself.

Her release followed with her breath hitching in the most sensual way and the moan that came from her throat pushed him over the edge of his control. He pushed into her one last time and covered her lips with his in a kiss that came nowhere near expressing what he felt at that moment.

But his sadness at not being able to show or tell his feelings was overshadowed by one crushing thought.

This was only temporary. She wasn't really his.

Sasha moaned as Cole gently helped her to her feet. For the moment, she ached all over. Not that she was complaining. Emotionally, she felt better than she had in a long time. Something about Cole set her at ease, even when he was being so commanding he drove her mad.

"Are you okay?" he asked.

"Just pleasantly sore, Sir."

He nodded. "Let's get you inside so I can take proper care of those pleasantly sore spots. You remember what I said about the brick patio?"

"Yes, Sir. You said by the time you finished, your submissive wouldn't remember her knees."

"Let's see if I'm right." He lifted her into his arms, ignoring her squeal of protest.

He carried her across the yard and into the house, not stopping until he'd placed her on the bed. He was still naked, but he pulled on a pair of shorts as soon as he put her down.

"On your stomach, little one. I need to take care of your back first."

She rolled over, slightly miffed that she couldn't watch him, especially when she heard him walk away. Where did he go? She thought about lifting her head, but she was suddenly so tired after the intensity of their sex, the way he'd looked at her and made her look at him. Her eyelids grew heavy. It seemed so surreal.

"You have some scratches." Cole's voice woke her. "Nothing that really broke the surface. Hold still, I'm going to wash your back."

Ever so gently, he pressed a warm, wet cloth to the nape of her neck and slowly slid it downward, pressing and patting.

"Does that feel okay?" he asked.

"Wonderful, Sir." She was tired before, but now with him touching her in addition to the warm washcloth, there was no way she could keep her eyes open. Still, it didn't seem right to just fall asleep on him.

She was supposed to be serving him. She couldn't just take a nap. Could she? He'd made his way to the lower part of her back and took a warm towel and laid it across her shoulders.

"Still okay?" he asked.

"So sleepy." It took a lot of effort to get the words out.

"Close your eyes and rest."

"Feel bad."

His lips brushed her lower back. "No need to feel bad. I need a slave who's well rested. Take all the time you want."

Satisfied, she allowed her eyes to drift closed and when she dreamed, she dreamed of Cole. Though it really seemed lifelike when he climbed in bed with her and put his arms around her.

She woke to find her head on his chest. She stretched as her eyes blinked open, but the movement hurt her back. "Ow."

His hand stroked her shoulder. "Back hurt?"

"Yes, Sir. But not too much. I just wasn't expecting it," she said. He didn't say anything. She hoped he wasn't second-guessing the scene. "In a way, I like it."

"How is that?"

"It's like you obliterated my scars. Or at least covered them with your own marks."

His laugh made her feel warm inside. "I like the way you think, Sasha."

"Maybe we should do that every day. Have you cover my skin."

"It's a tempting thought."

"Now, my legs are a different story." She wanted to tease him, to draw out the playful man she knew he kept hidden. He was so complex and the realization struck her, she liked each facet of his personality. Each one so different and yet so perfectly *Cole*.

His fingers skimmed her upper thigh. "What's wrong with your legs?"

"They're a bit sore, too. I doubt I could do that every day."

"I bet I could convince you otherwise."

"I bet you could." She propped up on an elbow and looked down at him. The words she'd planned to say left her when she saw him looking at her. In fact, she had the strongest urge to pinch herself. Was she really in Cole's bed?

For the next week and a half.

This was temporary. She was only in his bed because she'd asked to be trained like this. It wasn't as if he'd asked her or that they were permanent.

His forefinger traced her lips. "Why the frown, little one?"

"Nothing."

He raised an eyebrow, but damned if she was going to tell him what she was really thinking. She almost told him she was thinking they'd left their clothes outside and she thought it was going to rain later. But she couldn't lie to him like that. Besides, he'd know and they'd had such a great day, she didn't want to ruin it.

"If you must know," she said. "I was thinking how I wished your marks were permanent."

He traced her collarbone and brushed the training collar. His mouth opened like he was going to say something, but he closed it.

Damn, now she'd made him uncomfortable. She swirled her finger on his chest. "I mean, in place of Peter's. You know?"

"Look at me, Sasha." His voice was rougher than normal and

his eye held a strange expression. "I know exactly what you're talking about."

She was straightening up the bed the next afternoon when she heard his footsteps coming down the hall. Her body froze and she tried to tell if he was walking her way or not. He'd received a phone call earlier in the day and though she didn't listen in, she'd been able to tell he was agitated.

"Sasha?" he asked, peeking into the room. "Oh, there you are."

He didn't look aggravated; maybe she'd misread something. She walked up to him and knelt at his feet. "Do you need me, Sir?"

It was a requirement he'd added today. She rather liked it, though she could see how it could be an issue if she was in the middle of doing something.

"I wanted to let you know we're having company for dinner tonight," he said. "A good friend of mine who happens to be working temporarily in New York is stopping by."

"I look forward to meeting them, Sir."

She said the words, but truthfully, she was disappointed she had to share Cole. Their time was limited enough and now this friend was coming over and cutting in on it?

"It's been a while since we've gotten together. I'm looking forward to it as well."

"What type of work is your friend doing in New York, Sir?"

What if his friend was female? What if it was the woman he'd done the demo with months ago?

She really, really, really hoped it wasn't her.

"He's a contractor. Right now he's working on a project for someone Nathaniel and Jeff know."

She almost missed the part about the job because she was too busy rejoicing it was a man.

"I'll warn you ahead of time. He's a very large guy. He's intense, and he's a Dominant."

No big deal. If she could handle Cole, she could handle Mr. Large and Intense Dominant.

"How do I address him, Sir?" she asked.

"He prefers submissives address him as Herr Brose."

"What?"

"He's German. Still lives there when he's not working in the States."

"How do you know him, Sir? If you don't mind me asking."

He reached a hand down. "Stand up and come with me to the kitchen."

They made their way down the hall and she'd finally accepted that it obviously wasn't any of her business how they met when he spoke.

"Fritz Brose and I met about ten years ago. He was my mentor." He flashed her a smile. "You could say everything I learned about BDSM, I learned from him."

"I thought you said you researched it while at university."

"I did. He was my main source of information and when I decided to take a more hands-on approach, he said he'd make sure I learned the right way." He came to a stop outside of the kitchen. "You've heard people say there's no one true way?"

She nodded.

"Fritz doesn't believe that. There's his way and there's the wrong way."

Those words still echoed in her head when the doorbell rang a few hours later.

Cole instructed her to wait in the living room and though he didn't specifically tell her, she knelt by the couch. She wore a green dress that came to her knees when she stood. She thought it brought out the green in her eyes, and that the plunging neckline showed off the collar.

Funny, she didn't own a lot of dresses, but they were Cole's number-one item for her to wear and she'd grown to like them. She could only imagine the look Julie would give her if she started wearing dresses to work. At the moment, work and Julie seemed so far away, like they belonged in a different world.

From the hallway came the sound of male laughter. She double-checked her posture in her mind to make sure she was perfectly positioned and took a deep breath.

Cole's voice seemed to be filled with pride when he spoke from the doorway. "Come on in. There's someone waiting to see you."

"Ah, the lovely Kate," a gruff voice replied and then just as suddenly added, "That's not Kate."

Tears sprang to her eyes unbidden, but even worse, the familiar unrelenting clawing of a panic attack filled her throat. Her body shook. She tried to say something, but all that came out was a squeak.

"Bloody hell, Fritz." Pride no longer filled Cole's voice and suddenly he was on the floor, by her side. "I'm going to touch your back," he said, reverting back to how he'd talked to her weeks ago.

She couldn't even nod, but his hand felt good and his whispered, "Breathe in, little one," helped ground her. She took a shaky breath in.

"Good girl," he said. "Exhale for me."

Her body obeyed without effort.

"There we go. Again."

Deep breath in. Let it out.

His hand rubbed her back in comforting circles. "Again for me. You're safe. Nothing will hurt you while I'm here."

Safe.

The panic receded.

"Excellent. One more time." His hand moved up her back and brushed the training collar. "Who am I?"

"Cole," she whispered. "You're Cole."

"That's right and what are you?"

"Safe."

"You are, Sasha. You are safe and nothing's going to touch you or hurt you." He continued rubbing her back while he talked. "And you looked so gorgeous kneeling here waiting for us. I'd never seen a more beautiful sight."

"I'm sorry." She didn't know why she was apologizing. Maybe because she'd messed up the meeting with his friend or maybe because she wasn't Kate.

"There's nothing to apologize for, little one. It's my fault."

Actually, now that her mind was clearing up, she really thought it was Fritz's fault. Fritz, who hadn't said a word during the entire exchange.

"Can you come sit with me on the couch?" Cole asked.

She nodded, not sure she was ready to meet Fritz, but she had to try. She took a hasty glance around the room as she stood. It was empty.

Cole led her to the couch and pulled her into his lap. "He's waiting in the kitchen."

His arms felt so good around her. She didn't ever want to leave their shelter.

"I'm sorry," he said. "It was my fault. I didn't tell Fritz about Kate and I breaking up, so he assumed it was her waiting in the living room. To be honest, it's been almost nine months. She's so far out of mind lately, it didn't even occur to me to tell him."

She snuggled deeper into his embrace.

"I'm fairly certain Fritz is beating himself up in the kitchen. I know you don't know him, but that's not a common occurrence. When you're up to it, I know he'd like to apologize to you."

"Can I sit here just a little bit longer, Sir?"

"For as long as you like." And she didn't think she imagined his arms tightening around her. "God, Sasha. You have to know there isn't a thing in this world I'd do to hurt you."

She inhaled deeply, drawing in the scent of him. "I know."

"When I saw you start to shake . . ."

"You always know what to say to make me feel better and to stop it."

"Before today, it'd been quite some time since your last attack, right?"

"Yes, Sir."

"Good. I'll be thrilled when you don't have them anymore."

"You and me both."

He kissed her head and stroked her arm and in that moment, she closed her eyes and let herself get lost in his embrace. Pretended, just for a second, that she was his and he would always be at her side to keep the panic from taking over.

But as comforting as his arms were and as much as she enjoyed being in his lap, they couldn't stay like that forever. She pulled back. "I'm ready to meet him, Sir."

"Are you sure? If you're not up to it, I'll send him away and tell him to come back later."

Though she would never ask him to do that, just him saying it endeared him to her even more. "I'm positive."

He helped her to her feet and then put his arm around her as they walked to the kitchen. Fritz had been sitting at the table, but he stood when they made it inside.

He was devilishly handsome with sharp, angular features that spoke of his German heritage. His hair was dark and cut above his collar. His eyes traveled over her in frank assessment and then he looked to Cole. For permission, she supposed. Everything about the way Cole was touching her said, "Mine." She looked up at him, and he nodded.

"Sasha," Fritz said. "I made a horribly incorrect assumption, and I'm deeply sorry if it caused you any pain. That was not my intent."

"Apology accepted, Herr Brose. I can understand how shocking it must have been."

"Are you feeling better?"

"Yes. Master Johnson helped me."

"I see that." His look at Cole was filled with questions she knew he was anxious to ask. She felt like a third wheel. It was obvious the men wanted to talk, but were uncomfortable doing so in her presence.

She tilted her head up. "May I be excused, Sir? I'm feeling tired and think I'd be better if I went to lie down."

Cole's forehead wrinkled. "Are you sure you're just tired? No more attack?"

"It's long gone. I'm just a little tired now, Sir."

He leaned down and brushed his lips across her cheek. "Go on and nap, little one. I'll check on you soon."

She left the men in the kitchen and went into Cole's bedroom. At his door, she hesitated for a moment and then decided not to close it all the way. She crawled in bed and realized she could hear the men's conversation.

"Next time you break up with your slave of eight years, how

about dropping me an e-mail or sending a text, so I don't shock the hell out of your new one?"

"Sasha's not my slave or my submissive. She's my trainee."

"Horse shit."

"What makes you say that?"

"I have eyes."

"Well, get glasses. She's going back to her apartment and life next week and that's that."

Fritz snorted. "Right."

"She is. I'm not the one for her."

"She know that?"

"Yes, we've been very clear in our expectations."

"She's not like anyone you've ever been with: way too skinny, short dark hair. Nice legs, though. Seems a bit quiet for you. Kate, that one you couldn't get to shut up."

"We are not having this conversation."

"Fine then. How is Kate? Damn, I can't believe you two broke up. I thought if anyone would be together forever, it'd be you two."

"She's fine, living on her own in upstate New York. Probably thrilled to be by herself for once."

Fritz grunted. "I doubt that."

"Doesn't matter to me one way or another what she does. Here." The refrigerator door opened. "Have a bitter and let me show you the house. Then you can tell me what you're doing for Luke and Nathaniel."

Their voices drifted away, and she stared at the ceiling a long time before drifting into an uneasy sleep.

Chapter Eleven

The Friday night following Fritz's visit, Cole took Sasha to Linden, New Jersey, to attend the grand reopening of Luke DeVaan's club. Normally, he didn't go to such events, but Fritz had been the contractor for the project and had invited him, so he felt compelled to go.

Sasha fidgeted the entire drive into the city. She shifted in her seat, picked at her clothes, and drummed her fingers on the armrest. Finally he asked her why she was so nervous.

She looked out of the corner of her eye, but he was pleased she didn't even try to say she wasn't nervous. "A lot of reasons. It's been at least a year since I've been to a club, I've never been to this one, I'm scared I'll mess up, and I fear I'm not cut out to serve you like this."

"That's an awful lot to keep bottled up inside, little one."

"I guess I'm still learning how to better communicate."

"Yes, you need to tell me what you're feeling. For instance, if

I had known that was what you were worried about, I could've told you that I would be by your side the entire night, so it didn't matter how long it's been since you've visited a club. I'd have told you that it's not your place to worry if you're cut out to serve me because I think you're doing an exceptional job. And lastly, I'd tell you that if you messed up, we'd deal with it and move on."

She took a deep breath. "It sounds so trivial when you say it like that."

He reached down and took her hand. "Don't trivialize your feelings, Sasha. I didn't say those things to make you feel badly. I just wanted you to know that if you shared them with me, I could have helped earlier."

"I'll try to do better," she whispered.

He squeezed her hand, and they chatted easily the rest of the way.

They pulled up to the unassuming brick building and parked.

"You said only Abby and Nathaniel will be here from the Partners group?"

"That's my understanding. Yes. Apparently, Nathaniel is considering opening a similar club for the Partners group. That's why they're here."

They made it inside and he watched her eyes dart around, trying to take everything in. He hadn't seen the club before, but it looked phenomenal. There were separate areas for lounging, eating, and playing, and a polished marble bar ran the length of one wall. The whole place had a crisp and contemporary feel. He took Sasha's hand and led her in the direction of the lounge area.

Maybe they would explore the play area next. There were several new pieces of equipment up. He had his toy bag in the car, and he could always go back out to get it. Sasha wore black lingerie under the short skirt and tight shirt she had on. He would really like to see how she handled playing in public.

He looked over the benches and crosses and whipping posts, trying to decide which one he'd pick to tie Sasha to. Definitely not the whipping post. But a cross would be fun. Tie her up and bring her right to the edge and then not let her orgasm. Keep her like that until they got back home? Playing in public sounded better and better with each passing second.

"Sir," she said as they walked past a wall with closed doors. "Can we look at these pictures?"

He hadn't noticed the pictures before, but at her mention, he looked over them. They were black and white and mostly showed a woman in bondage. Several shots showed her profile, though most of them were of her back. He narrowed his eyes. You couldn't see the submissive's face, but she looked familiar.

"They're so engrossing, don't you think?" she asked.

"Yes, they have a very sensual and ethereal quality to them."

They looked them over for a few more minutes, and then Cole indicated they should move on.

The sitting area was well designed with couches and love seats arranged in a way that allowed multiple groups to have conversational areas. At the moment, most guests were doing just that. But the night was early. They'd start drifting to the play areas as the evening wore on.

Cole was also impressed with the number of men walking around with Monitor T-shirts. He'd heard Abby had almost been assaulted in this club before DeVaan bought it. Hopefully nothing similar would happen again.

Nathaniel stood when they approached, but Abby was kneeling on the floor and didn't move. Or at least she didn't move until Nathaniel brushed her shoulder and whispered, "Feel free to talk to our friends. I know you wanted to speak to Sasha. If Master Johnson is okay with that?"

Cole nodded. "Yes, of course. Sasha, if you would like to sit with Abby at that free love seat nearby, go ahead. Nathaniel and I will be here."

Abby stood to her feet with a smile and motioned Sasha to follow her. They'd barely sat down before they were talking with their heads together.

"She's talked about nothing but Sasha all day. She's been anxious to hear how she's doing." Nathaniel gave him a pointed look. "I would have thought you would have checked in with me by now. That was part of the agreement."

"I knew you'd be here tonight, but I'm sorry to have caused Abby stress."

The two women were completely wrapped up in their conversation.

"Since we're both here now, let's have a seat so you can tell me how it's going." They wandered over to an open couch nearby.

"It's going really well. She has a teachable spirit, rarely repeats a mistake, and she's getting her spunk back."

Nathaniel watched the two women. "She does look really good. Not as thin and she has a peace about her." He turned his inquisitive stare to Cole. "How are you doing?"

"Me? I'm great."

"Will Ms. Blake be extending her time at your house?"

It was as if the air was suddenly sucked out of the room. "What? No. I'm not. We're not. It's. Aw, bloody hell. No."

Nathaniel crossed his arms and leaned back with a smug grin on his face. "Like that, is it?"

"I'm too much for her."

"Yet we just agreed she's looking and doing well."

Cole shook his head. "It's too soon for both of us. Besides, that wasn't the plan."

"Funny, I'm learning in my old age that the best plan isn't necessarily the one you first decided on."

It wasn't that Cole hadn't thought about asking Sasha for more, he just feared doing so wouldn't be in the best interest of either of them. The last thing he needed after the ending of an eight-year relationship was to jump into another. Sure it had been over nine months, but didn't he need to be by himself for a while? To be something other than Kate's Master?

And Sasha? Who knew how long it'd be before she was ready for something serious. To ask that of her at this point in her journey would be selfish. She needed to experience other Doms, see that there were other men out there she could trust.

But the very thought of her with another man made him want to slam his fist into something.

He was saved from admitting as much by the arrival of a tall blond woman. She looked mildly shocked at seeing Nathaniel, but then her expression changed and she looked around the room. A large smile covered her face when she saw Abby.

Nathaniel had noticed the newcomer, too, and coughed loudly. At the sound, Abby's head shot up.

"Meagan?" she asked.

"Abby," the blonde said, moving to stand near the women. "I wasn't expecting to see you here."

As Abby and Sasha moved to make room for her to sit with them, Cole turned back to Nathaniel.

"Who is that?"

"That, my friend, is a time bomb waiting to go off." He waved at a man walking toward them. "And here comes the match."

"Trouble, two o'clock," Abby said to the blond woman she'd just introduced to Sasha as her boss.

Sasha looked in that direction and saw a man making a beeline for their love seat. He wasn't familiar to her. He was nearly as tall as Nathaniel and had wavy brown hair in desperate need of a cut.

"Damn." Meagan just saw him, too. "I'd hoped to have a few minutes peace."

"Normally, I'd help you, but I can't talk to Doms in a club without Nathaniel's approval and he just shook his head."

Sasha glanced at Cole. "Same here," she said at his mouthed "no."

"No problem," Meagan said. "I can handle this."

"Who is it?" Sasha asked Abby in a whisper.

"Luke DeVaan. The new club owner. He has a history with Meagan. I just don't know what."

"Meagan, sweetheart." Luke was all smiles standing before the tall blonde. "I thought you made it very clear you weren't coming to opening night. Thought you said you were busy?"

"Shut it, Luke."

"I see by your bracelet that you're here as a submissive tonight. Might want to rethink the way you're addressing me."

"My humblest apologies, oh, Lord and Master."

"There you go. Can you say it again without the sarcasm?"

"Probably not."

"That's okay. I'll be patient." He looked toward Nathaniel and Cole, then at Abby and Sasha. "Here with friends?"

"Not that it's any of your business, but I'm meeting someone. A man. A Dom."

"And he's not here yet? Unworthy of you, sweetheart. Let me introduce you to real Doms."

"Master V is a real Dom."

It wasn't Sasha's imagination that Abby stiffened at Meagan's words.

"Master V?" Luke tilted his head. "Why does that name sound familiar? Oh yes, he did try to get in tonight. He was asked to leave. He's not welcome here."

Meagan shot Luke a glance that would have had a lesser man on his knees. Keeping her eyes on him, she reached into her purse and took out her cell phone. She frowned at the display.

Luke didn't seem interested in what she found or didn't find on her phone. He simply inclined his head. "If you change your mind, I'll be around."

"When pigs fly."

Luke's expression changed in an instant. "That's the second time, Meagan. I've worn out quite a few backsides for less. Next time, your ass is mine."

Meagan wisely didn't say anything, but sank into the love seat between Sasha and Abby. Luke nodded to Nathaniel and Cole and then turned back to the crowd and walked away.

"Seriously, Meagan," Abby said. "What's with you two?"

"Long, boring history no one cares about anymore."

"From the looks of the scene I just witnessed, there are at least two people who still care," Abby said.

Meagan waved her hand. "Nah, I don't. Really." She turned to Sasha. "Tell me all about that fine-looking man sitting with Nathaniel. Is he yours?"

Sasha bit back the *I wish* and simply said, "I'm his trainee. Right now we're doing some twenty-four/seven."

"I've never been interested in full-time service, but for *him?* I could probably be persuaded."

Meagan was probably more like the women Cole normally played with. With just one look, Sasha picked up on her strength. She practically oozed it. Meagan probably never had a panic attack because someone called her the wrong name.

But something else struck Sasha about Meagan's words. She, too, had never been interested in twenty-four/seven service before Cole. In fact, she still couldn't imagine doing it with anyone else. Did that mean she was changing herself for him?

How could she move forward if she didn't know with 100 percent accuracy who she was and what she wanted? She needed to take off the Cole blinders. The truth was that after next week, she'd be going back to her apartment and picking up her life where it left off. She needed to remind herself this time with Cole was only temporary.

"That's an awfully serious expression, slave," Cole said.

Sasha jumped. She hadn't even noticed him moving. "Sorry, Sir. I was thinking about something."

"I came over just in time, then. Time to stop thinking and let me take over." He held out his hand. "We're going to the cross over in the far right corner. I'd have you crawl, but I don't want you to mess up those black hose."

She stood and discovered her knees were wobbly. They were going to play in front of people. She and Cole. She'd played in public numerous times before. She enjoyed it, but how different would it be to play with Cole?

"I'll be at the cross in five minutes. I want you kneeling and waiting for me."

She nodded and went to the empty play station he'd indicated. Because she had a collar on, no one spoke to her, though she did feel the weight of several people watching her.

As she waited on her knees for him, she wondered if he would have her take her shirt off. Surely, he'd remember she didn't like to be topless. Especially in front of all these people. But she knew if she dwelt on it, she could inadvertently bring on a panic attack. To head off any potential fear lurking inside her, she closed her eyes and took several cleansing breaths. She could do this. She was strong. She was whole.

"Very nice, little one," Cole said from behind her. "I don't think I'll ever grow tired of seeing you wait for me like this."

She didn't think she'd ever grow tired of kneeling for him.

"Stand up and strip for me. Your back will be against the cross so no worries about that. And I'll ensure you're covered until you get into position."

"That is very kind of you, Sir. To go through that trouble for me." Even as she said the words, she felt the relief course through her body.

"It's no trouble, little one. It was, however, one of your limits and though you trusted me, I know you don't want to share that part of your body with the club."

She felt forty pounds lighter as she stood and began to take her clothes and lingerie off. She left her shirt and bra for last. Cole stood in front of her, looking around to make sure everything was clear.

"Go ahead and step in front of the cross," he said. "With your back to it. Then you can finish undressing while I keep prying eyes away from your back."

She did as he bid and then watched as he approached her, his eyes filled with evil delight. He took one wrist and bound it above her head.

"Are you ready to play, little one?" he whispered in her ear. "Ready to get all hot and bothered in front of all these people?"

"Yes, Sir."

He bound the other wrist above her head. "I'm going to bind your ankles, too. Spread those legs for me. Give me room to work your body over."

He continued his wicked whispers as he bound her ankles to the wooden frame. He stepped back and looked at her with lust heavy in his eyes and she'd never been more thankful to be restrained. If she wasn't bound, she'd no doubt be a puddle on the floor.

He picked up a heavy flogger and her heart started to race. *He's going to start with that one?* She swallowed.

"No talking unless I ask a question or you need to safeword. No moving. No coming. All clear?"

"Yes, Sir."

"You will take this for me."

It wasn't a question, so she took it as a command. Yes, she would. A movement behind him caught her attention and she looked closer. Nathaniel and Abby. It made sense they would want to watch. Abby said Nathaniel had been worried because he hadn't heard from Cole. Maybe after tonight he wouldn't be so worried.

"Close your eyes," Cole commanded.

She closed them and braced for the first stroke of the flogger to hit. Because he'd picked up a heavy one, she expected it to hurt. But in a move that shouldn't have surprised her, it landed with a pleasant thud on her upper thigh.

"I know what you were thinking, little one." He spoke as the tails struck her other thigh. "And if you remember, I told you to expect to be unbalanced when it came to me. Didn't I?"

"Yes, Sir."

"I'm going to bring you so close to the edge, but you're not allowed to come without permission."

He didn't talk after that, but he must have picked up another flogger, because soon there were two different types of tails landing on her. A light one teased the upper part of her body while he focused the heavier one on her thighs. She never cared for the heavier floggers, but in Cole's hand, it felt like nothing she'd ever experienced.

Then one of them started landing closer and closer to where she ached to be filled. He stayed in that spot for a time, letting her grow accustomed to the feeling and then he moved away, resuming his attention to her upper thighs.

She bit back a whine of frustration. If she could just bring her legs together for a bit of friction . . .

But no. He'd told her she wasn't allowed to come. He'd also told her he was going to take her to the edge. With that in mind, it wasn't a surprise when one of the tails landed on her clit.

Damn, that felt good.

She waited for it to fall again and bit back a moan when it did. *So good.*

"What color, little one?" he asked.

"Green, Sir. So, so, so green."

His chuckles were accompanied by others.

He brought the tails down over and over again and then it disappeared. The loss made her feel so empty and needy. But it wasn't until the heavy thud suddenly struck her clit again that she realized just how needy. The feeling of release rushed up behind her and before she could control it, it pushed her over the edge with the next stroke of the flogger. Her body trembled as her climax overtook her.

The floggers stopped immediately and the entire club grew eerily quiet.

"Did you just come, slave?" Cole's voice was colder than she'd ever heard.

"Yes, Sir." Now her body trembled for a different reason.

"What did I tell you about coming?"

She wondered if she could even get the words out. "That I couldn't without your permission."

"Did I give permission?"

"No, Sir."

He didn't say anything. Her eyes were still closed and she decided she'd like to keep them like that forever. Or at least until his voice wasn't so cold.

She heard him step forward, and one by one, he unbound her limbs.

"I didn't bring a cane, so we're going to improvise your punishment. Look at me."

She slowly opened her eyes. He didn't look pleased, but he was very much in control of himself.

"I'm going to have you move to the empty padded table to my left. I want you on your back. Knees spread. You want to come without permission? I'm going to have you come so many times, you'll be begging to have the orgasms stop."

Oh, fuck.

She'd never experienced forced orgasms, but she'd heard enough subs talk about them. She had a feeling that before the night was over, she was going to wish he'd brought his suit and cane. Someone really needed to invent a way to fast-forward through life's unpleasant moments.

"Go," he said.

She took a step forward and it wasn't until she felt a blanket fall around her shoulders she remembered that in walking to the table, her back would be exposed. That he remembered, even when she'd disobeyed him, brought tears to her eyes.

He was a much better Master than she was a sub. Never before had she felt the enormity between them as she did in that moment.

She climbed onto the table, removing the blanket when she got on her back. With her feet flat on the table, her knees were spread, but her legs shook and she hated that. *Damn it all to hell.* This was supposed to be a fun night and she messed it up.

It wasn't long before Cole was at her side. She'd never done a scene like the one he had in mind, but he was out of his freaking mind if he thought for a second she would be able to come once, much less multiple times. Best if she kept that thought to herself, she decided.

He placed a tube of lube and a vibrator next to her head. "Why are you on the table, slave?"

"I came without permission, Sir."

"Yes, you did, and just to be clear, you are allowed to come whenever you wish whilst you're on the table."

"Thank you, Sir." She'd made the mistake once before of not thanking him for allowing her release. It wasn't going to reoccur tonight.

"Very good, little one." Faint praise, but at the moment she'd take it.

He squirted some lube on his finger and applied it to her clit, and slipped more inside her. "Do I need to bind you to the table?"

Since she'd never done this, she nodded. "Please, Sir. I think you'd better."

"Thank you for being honest."

Minutes later, she was bound so tightly, she couldn't move. She'd noticed while he tied her to the table that the crowd at the cross had remained to watch. Nathaniel, Abby, and Meagan were nearby, and she wasn't sure, but she thought Fritz stood off to the side.

"I'm not going to blindfold you," Cole said. "I want your eyes on me."

She'd rather be blindfolded. Or at least able to close her eyes.

"I know this is hard. It's supposed to be." His voice matched the firm resolve in his eyes. "We'll start slow."

He turned the vibrator on and teased her with it, running it near her clit, but never touching it directly. Though he told her to watch him, his eyes weren't always on her, but she kept her focus on him. If he looked her way, she wanted him to see she was following his instructions.

As he continued teasing her, she came to realize she had vastly underestimated him. He'd obviously been very astute when it came to how to turn her on. She didn't think she'd be able to come at all while she was on the table, but Cole knew her body. And he used every bit of knowledge he had to get her hot and bothered.

Her body tensed as her climax approached.

"The first one's easy," he said. "So easy you can almost forget it's a punishment."

Just as he said, the first one came and went, bringing nothing but pleasure, though the pleasure was tinged with a bit of trepidation. Their first night together, she'd come three times with him. How many would he push her through now? Five? Six? He wouldn't do more than that, would he?

"I reckon the second one isn't that hard, either." His eyes were intent as he repositioned the vibe closer to her clit. He slipped a finger inside her and stroked. "Of course, technically, this is three for you. So it might not be as easy."

She relaxed her body as much as possible and focused on just feeling. If she didn't fight the orgasms, maybe it wouldn't be as bad. He looked her way and his face was unreadable as the familiar feeling of impending release grew.

"Give it to me," he said, and she came with a soft cry and panting after.

That was three in a relatively short period of time. She didn't think it possible for her body to do it again. Cole leaned over her.

"Now's when it gets hard. When you don't think you can have another one. But your body will betray you and you won't be able to stop it. What are your safe words?"

Oh, holy hell, he was asking for safe words? She didn't like the insinuation.

"Green, yellow, and red, Sir."

He nodded. "Use them if you need to."

She took a deep breath and nodded.

"Understand, I'm only stopping if you safeword."

Her fingernails dug into the palm of her hands. "I understand, Sir."

He didn't say anything else, but took the vibe and placed it directly on her clit. The bundle of nerves was already sensitive after her previous climaxes and she cried out as the buzzing instrument tormented it further.

It was the strangest combination of pleasure/pain and heaven/hell she'd ever experienced. Almost as if the wires in her brain were crossed or confused. Part of her thought there was no way she'd ever come, but she felt the sensation between her legs start to do just that. She tensed up because she knew it would fucking hurt.

This orgasm wasn't going to be calm or peaceful or quiet. She closed her eyes as it approached.

"Eyes on me," Cole said.

Her eyes flew open right as the peak of her climax struck and she yelped.

"Who owns your orgasms?" Cole asked.

"You do, Sir." Maybe he'd turn the damn thing off now. Please let him turn it off.

"Very good. You're going to come again."

Fucking hell, he turned the vibe up a notch. She shifted her hips trying to get away. "No, Sir. I can't. I can't."

"Be still or you'll find another one in your arse."

She whimpered. Her lower body tingled in a combination of feelings. The damn vibe was going to drive her crazy. She didn't think she could handle another climax. But Cole was unrelenting and he kept it right on her clit. Sweat beaded on her forehead.

"When do you come?" he asked.

"Oh my God, turn it off."

Her flesh balked at another orgasm, but she knew it would happen anyway. The evil buzzing thing wasn't going to stop until she came.

"Either say the right word to stop it or answer the question."

The word. She could stop it with a word. Red. Red would stop it.

Cole met her eyes and in his gaze she found what she needed.

"I come when you tell me, Sir."

"That's right."

Fucking, fucking, fucking hell. He'd turned it up again. She panted and tried to keep her hips still. The next one was running up on her, and she was certain it'd crush her. She couldn't do it. Couldn't do it. Couldn't do it.

"Come," Cole said.

Her back arched off the table as the climax consumed her. Consumed. Empty. Void. She searched for Cole, but of course he was right there. She had to tell him. Had to.

"Red."

Everything looked hazy. Or maybe that was the buzzing that still continued even though she knew he'd put the vibrator away.

"I've got it," he said to someone. "Look at me, Sasha. Are you okay?" His hands were busy untying her limbs.

Her breath still came in pants. "Yes, Sir. Will it stop?"

He brushed her cheek and his hand was warm. "It will."

"When?" She shook as another wave of sensation swept over her body.

"Pretty soon, I would think." He looked to this right. "Hand me that blanket. No, I need it before she sits up."

She didn't want to sit up. She didn't want to move at all.

He took the blanket and laid it across her. "I'm going to pick you up so your back is covered and carry you to a private room. Are you okay with that?"

"Yes, Sir."

When he picked her up, she was still shaking, but she found comfort in his arms and hoped he didn't let her go anytime soon. She closed her eyes and only knew they made it to the private room when he sat down.

He situated her on his lap and held her close. "Has it stopped yet?"

"Almost, Sir," she said as another tremor hit her body.

"I'm glad you used your safe word, Sasha. That brings me more comfort than you know."

"This sounds crazy, but I'm glad I got the chance to use it. Is that weird?"

He stroked her hair while he talked. There wasn't anything sexual about his touch; rather, it soothed her. And she got the impression it soothed him, too.

"No," he said in answer to her question. "I don't think that's weird. After the scene with Peter, I think you needed to safe-word and see that everything stopped. So, while it wasn't my intent for you to do so, I'm glad you did."

"The other thing is, once I knew I had to, I didn't hesitate to say it."

He kissed her forehead. "Good. And just so you're aware, I was seconds away from ending the scene. You had endured enough."

She sighed deeply and curled closer to him.

"That does not mean, however, that we should play without safe words."

His off-handed reference to how she'd played with Peter chilled her just a bit. "I know, Sir."

"I didn't say it to be a bastard."

"I know that, too, Sir." Though why did it make her feel bad that he'd said it?

"Here." He reached to the table at his side and pressed a bottle to her mouth. "Drink for me, little one."

She sipped the water. "Tastes good."

"I have chocolate, too." He held up a fun-sized bar.

"Even better." She smiled at him as she ate it, but it felt forced. Telling herself it was just her emotions going haywire after the scene, she settled back into his arms, certain things would feel different in the morning.

Chapter Twelve

Something was off with Sasha, Cole thought the next morning as he watched her kneeling and doing her morning meditation. It was so subtle, he didn't think he'd have noticed if he wasn't around her for so much of the day. She said the right things, did the right things, and she wore the smile that always made him feel warm inside.

So what was it?

He'd been honest with her the night before. He had planned to stop after that last orgasm and it did comfort him that she said her safe word when she felt the need.

When they'd made it back to the house, he'd drawn a bath and washed her. After, he'd poured them both some wine and they cuddled some more in bed.

He didn't plan on her doing anything sexual for at least the next twenty-four hours. Her body had been tested last night and it needed to recuperate. More importantly, her mind probably did, too.

Though he normally took her mouth after she meditated, today, he stood in front of her and held out his hand.

"Slip your dressing gown on and come have breakfast with me," he said.

She looked up at him and her eyes were red and wet.

"Sasha?" he dropped down to her side and put his arms around her. This wasn't a panic attack, this was something more. "What's wrong? Why are you crying?"

She sobbed. "I don't know."

"I do," he said. "You're having one hell of a sub drop." Her body's adjustment to the drop in endorphin levels had never been this severe, but it wasn't unexpected due to the night before.

"It's never been so bad before."

"I imagine not, but I'm here and we're going to get through it."

She brought her knees to her chest and hugged them. "Okay."

"First thing you need to do is get some clothes on and eat something. Let me make a quick phone call while you get dressed." He'd had a few calls scheduled for today, but he needed to be with Sasha. The calls could wait.

She looked delicate and fragile when she stepped out of the bathroom. He held out his hand and she hurried to take it. At least she still liked him to touch her.

"Ready to eat?" he asked.

"Yes, Sir."

"I think I'll just do something quick. Oatmeal sound good?"

"Perfect, Sir."

In his mind he updated his plans so he could be with her. They would eat breakfast and go on a walk around the property. Exercise usually helped sub drop, and he'd been wanting to get Sasha's opinion on the landscaping and to see if she had any ideas on improving the yard.

He squeezed her hand as they walked down the stairs. Hopefully, by this afternoon or evening, she'd feel more like her normal self.

While they ate, she brought up something that took him completely by surprise. He'd just finished making a cup of tea when she asked, "You know what I'd like to do?"

"What?"

"I'd like for you to host a tea party and have me serve everyone."

He put his teacup back down. "Indeed? Where did that come from?"

She ducked her head. "I was watching you drink your tea and thought about how much I liked serving it to you. And then I thought I'd like to it do for more than one person. Like you'd talked about once before. I've never served tea for a group. And part of me would like to show people I'm better than I was last night."

Her words were hurried, like she was afraid he'd turn her down or say no.

"Your mind is a delight, Sasha."

She blushed slightly.

"I think a party would be a brilliant idea, but I want you to do it because you want to. There is no need for you to try and make up for an error that's already been corrected."

"I understand."

She didn't appear as though she was going to change her mind, so he simply added, "I'll give it some thought."

The following Wednesday night, ten minutes before people were due to arrive, Sasha stood in the kitchen, mentally running through Cole's plans for the day. The food was all prepared and ready to serve. It wasn't time to boil water for the tea just yet. She'd moved the china into the dining room earlier. Cole had decided to only invite the senior Dominants for tea.

She pressed her palms against the black dress Cole had picked out for her to wear. It felt damn awkward wearing clothes. Made her feel like she was hiding something. A nervous giggle escaped her. Who would have thought she'd ever feel more comfortable walking at home either naked or in skimpy lingerie than fully clothed?

"What's so funny, little one?"

She jumped at the sound of Cole's voice. Damn it. How did she miss him entering the kitchen? He stood in the doorway wearing a suit and tie. His hands were casually shoved in his pockets and a wide grin covered his face.

Her cheeks heated at being caught unaware. "Just thinking about how comfortable I am being naked and how I wouldn't have thought it possible a month ago."

The grin was still in place as he crossed the room to her, though his eyes had grown dark. He lifted her chin with his hand. "I'm immensely pleased to see your growth as a submissive and how you've embraced your training."

"Thank you, Sir."

"And I have no doubt you will be exemplary in your service to me today."

A not so subtle reminder as to where her focus should be. "I truly enjoy serving you, Sir." She nibbled on her lip, debating on whether or not she should say anything else. The thought of leaving him in a few days, of him taking off his collar, kept her quiet. She ran a finger along its edge.

"Sasha?"

But now was the time to show exactly how much she'd grown.

She felt as if she'd accomplished so much in the short period of time they'd been together. Serving him was like nothing she'd ever experienced and he'd been so patient, helping her in her journey. She only had to think back to the tender way he cared for her during the sub drop she experienced to know she wouldn't be in the place she was if it hadn't been for him.

"I just wanted to say thank you for agreeing to these two weeks. I've learned so much and I think when the right Dom asks, I'll be ready."

His hand slipped to cup her cheek and he dropped his head so his lips almost brushed hers. "You *think* or you *know* you'll be ready?"

"I know, Sir."

"Words, little one." His breath was warm on her skin. "They have meanings."

"There's something else I know."

"Yes?"

"I know I don't want to leave in two days."

He froze. She didn't think he breathed. And then he nearly growled, "Bloody hell, Sasha," and took her lips in a deep kiss she felt in her toes.

She whimpered in a combination of bliss and need, pleased that his only reply was to pull her closer. Her fingers tangled in his hair and he moaned when she gave it a tug. Damn it all, she would never get enough of his kisses.

The chime of the doorbell made them both jump.

Not ready to meet his eyes, she buried her head in his chest. But as always, he wouldn't let her hide.

"Look at me, Sasha."

She peeked at him, but couldn't read his expression. "Sir?"

"I'm not finished with this conversation. When everyone

leaves, we're picking right back up where we left off." He kissed her quickly on the forehead and then left.

The exchange left her weak kneed and shaky and she was grateful for the few minutes she had to compose herself. Her focus needed to be on the upcoming tea service. Her talk with Cole would have to wait.

A few of the senior Doms stood in the living room, talking. Daniel and Evan were off to the side talking to Nathaniel. Jeff was sitting down, texting someone. Probably Dena. She didn't see Master Greene. Sasha's role was to be on the lookout for ways to help, but to remain as unobtrusive as possible. And she wasn't to speak to anyone without Cole's permission.

Cole inclined his head slightly at her entrance and the right side of his mouth lifted in a hint of a smile. Sasha gave him one of her own and then glanced around the room to ensure everything was in order. She noticed Kelly Bowman, the female Domme, had watched the exchange between her and Cole.

She turned around to check on the table for the third time and when she turned back to the group, Kelly was at her side.

"Master Johnson," she said, getting his attention. "May I have your permission to speak with Sasha?"

"You may, but keep it short. She's busy." He looked at Sasha. "You may talk for five minutes."

Sasha felt like dragging Kelly down the hall so they could talk in private. Until that moment, she hadn't realized how much she'd missed girly conversation. Talking to Julie or Abby on the phone wasn't the same as being in the room with someone. Besides, with the tea party being a group event, she wasn't at liberty to gossip with the Domme.

Kelly pulled her to a quiet corner. "You look good. Everything going okay?"

"I've rarely felt more content, Ma'am."

"As soon as word gets out I've seen you, Julie and Dena are going to be hounding my ass for details. For the next five minutes, I'm just Kelly." She flipped her hair over her shoulder. "If you feel that's too disrespectful, do it anyway and I'll tell Master Johnson you've been a naughty little slave so he can punish you."

Sasha laughed. "Thanks, Kelly. Seriously though, I really don't want this time to end. It's been eye-opening and insightful and he's, well, he's incredible."

"Dear Lord, Julie will go batshit crazy."

"Most likely."

"Have you talked to Cole? Does he know how you feel?"

"We're talking tonight, when everyone leaves."

"I hope you get everything you want, Sasha. You've been through a lot, but you took a bad situation and you learned from it and grew stronger."

"Thank you. I feel stronger."

Kelly leaned in close. "There's no feel about it. You are stronger. Own it. Own it with pride."

Cole was only half listening to the conversation among Daniel, Nathaniel, and Evan. The majority of his attention was focused on Sasha's conversation with Kelly. The Domme had said something that made Sasha laugh, but the rest of the conversation must have taken a more somber turn; she only laughed that one time. They spoke for a few more minutes until Sasha glanced at a wall clock, hugged Kelly, and made a turn around the room to ensure everyone was content.

Kelly stayed where she was and looked him over as if observing him for the first time. He sort of felt the way he did when meeting a girl's father, back when he was a teenager. He fought the urge to fidget and instead raised an eyebrow in Kelly's direction. She studied him a few seconds longer before turning her attention to her phone.

Assured nothing in the room needed her attention, Sasha shifted her focus to him. Finding him looking, she smiled briefly before dropping her eyes. Still, he watched her as she moved to stand near one of his couches. Out of the way, but available if needed. Watchful, but not overbearing. The dress he'd picked out hugged her in all the right places, and he was pleased to note she'd lost both the gaunt and the lost looks.

All in all, she was transformed from the cowering submissive he'd first met in Daniel's playroom. She was sharp, strong, and sexy as hell. She accepted him for who he was, and took everything he'd thrown at her in the last week and a half.

She'd shocked the hell out of him when she admitted she didn't want to leave, because he didn't want her to leave, either. He could no longer imagine working without her in the room, catching up on the news without her knitting by his feet, or pushing her body to its limit. He loved watching her experience unknown pleasure before he brought her back down. And how could he go to sleep without her snuggled against him, awed by her trust in him?

He couldn't imagine it, and he wouldn't do it. When everyone left, they would talk and somehow work something out so she wouldn't leave. If she didn't want to wear his collar permanently, they would find a middle ground.

She glanced his way with a slight frown and he realized he was late moving everyone to the dining room. Bloody hell, she was probably worried about the food and timing the water.

He'd made her worry, and that had never been his intent. He was supposed to support her, not cause her undue stress.

Sorry, my fault, he mouthed, and the worry lines left her face. He gave her a nod and she hurried to the kitchen while he rounded everyone up and led them to the dining room.

As everyone sat down and Sasha started serving, he let out a relieved breath. Everything was going great. She'd been worried the last few days. He'd done his best to reassure her, but knew deep down that only actually doing the service would erase the doubt.

His eyes followed her around the table with an odd mixture of pride and desire. Bloody hell. What was it about a slave serving tea that turned him on so much? He could watch her forever and fortunately, everyone was talking among themselves so he didn't feel the need to make small talk.

He almost missed Evan's hand shoot out to cover his cup before she could pour him water. "I'll just have ice water, thanks."

Sasha faltered, just for a second, before nodding and continuing around the table. Most likely she was going to finish with the tea before getting Evan's water. Exactly what he would have instructed her to do.

"It's rare to see someone be both an ass and a dick at the same time," Kelly quipped from across the table. She had never gotten along with Evan, but no one knew exactly why.

"I don't see how this is any of your business, K," Evan said. "I just don't like hot tea."

"You're missing the entire point. If that's the case, why did you come today at all?"

"I assumed there would be a discussion at some point about group business. I wanted to be part of it."

"In that case, you let her prepare the tea and you don't drink it. Were you raised in a barn?"

Sasha had made her way to Cole and though she'd appeared calm from across the table, up close he could tell she was trembling. Because of Evan or something else?

Cole reached out and lightly brushed her wrist as she served him. He wanted her to know she was doing great and how proud he was. She relaxed under his touch.

"Excellent job, little one," he whispered, and she slipped into the kitchen, her demeanor calm once again.

He would pull Evan aside after and talk with him. Though from the look and sound of it, Kelly was doing a good job setting him straight. He let them go at each other for a bit, but knew he had to put a stop to it before Sasha returned.

"Kelly, Evan," he said, purposely leaving off their titles. "Sasha will be back any minute, and I strongly suggest you cease the bickering now. I will take it very personally if you stress her out in any way."

"Sorry, Cole," Kelly said, throwing one last glare at her nemesis across the table. "You're right."

Evan huffed but didn't say anything.

"Do we need to step outside?" Cole asked the young Dom. "You *will not* cause her stress."

"I assure you, Master Johnson, I wish her no harm."

Cole gave him a curt nod, but the air still hummed with tension when Sasha reappeared. Daniel took over the conversation, changing the subject by asking for volunteers to work the melanoma fund-raiser.

Minutes later, Sasha was serving everyone smoothly and Daniel had several positions filled. Cole rolled his shoulders and relaxed into his chair. Now, hopefully, he could simply enjoy his tea and the slave who served it.

A strangled cry from the far end of the room made everyone jump. Jeff pushed his chair back from the table and fumbled in his pockets. His hands shook.

Nathaniel reached out to touch him. "You okay? You look like you've seen a ghost."

"Dena," he said in an anguished whisper. "She's bleeding."

Within minutes, Cole was driving Jeff to the hospital. Sasha was in the backseat and Daniel followed behind in Jeff's truck. Nathaniel had left to pick up Abby and Julie. Though it felt like the longest trip he'd ever taken, Cole couldn't imagine what it felt like for Jeff.

Jeff either stared straight ahead or checked his phone for news. The never-ending refreshes confirmed there were no updates. Sasha was just as quiet. She sat huddled in the backseat, blowing her nose occasionally.

Halfway to the hospital, Jeff slammed his fist against the dash. "Damn it. Drive faster. She's by herself." His voice broke. "I have to be there. She can't go through this alone."

He was already going twenty miles over the speed limit, but Cole pushed down on the gas pedal and went even faster. After what seemed like hours, he finally pulled up to the Emergency Department. He wasn't sure the car had come to a complete stop when Jeff unbuckled his seat belt, opened the door, and jumped out.

He took his time parking, not really wanting to face what he knew they would likely find when they made it inside. He remembered all too well the vacant stare Dena had the time she talked about losing their first pregnancy to a miscarriage.

Sasha seemed to share his thoughts. She moved slowly, a deliberate delay on her part. "It's not fair," she said as they approached the main gate. "They just want a child." She sighed. "Look at what happened the last time. They shouldn't have to deal with this again."

Cole slipped his hand around hers. "I know it's easy to look at the negative, but let's not speculate. We'll know what's happening soon enough."

Once inside, a nurse gave them directions to a waiting room. Cole dropped onto a couch, expecting Sasha to do the same, but instead she slid to her knees at his feet. They were the only people waiting at the moment, but that could change any second.

"You can sit next to me if you want," he told her. "I'm not going to insist on any formal protocol in a hospital."

"Let me sit here. Please. I can't explain it, but I feel more peaceful like this."

"As long as you're comfortable and you're aware that you can sit by me any time you want."

"Yes. Thank you, Sir."

She sat cross-legged on the floor at his feet, randomly flipping through magazine pages. He didn't think she was actually reading anything, just trying to keep her mind occupied.

"I should have thought about bringing your knitting," he said. "I was just so focused on getting Jeff here."

She peered up at him with tear-filled eyes. "It's okay. I was working on something for Dena. I don't think I could get any more of it done under the circumstances."

He reached down and wiped her tears away with his thumb. He wished more than anything he could tell her everything was going to be all right, but he was terribly afraid it would be just the opposite.

Daniel and Julie peeked inside the waiting room. Nathaniel and Abby were behind them.

"There you guys are." Daniel sat beside him. "Heard anything yet?"

"Nothing," Cole answered.

Sasha moved closer to his leg so Julie could sit next to her. "I can't decide if it's good or bad that there's no word yet."

"Maybe it won't be much longer." Julie folded her knees up in front of her and wrapped her arms around them. "I think if it was bad, Jeff would have known as soon as he got here."

Which didn't necessarily mean Jeff would have rushed out to tell them bad news, Cole thought. He remembered months ago, Dena talking to him about her miscarriage. The loss of that baby had served as the catalyst in ending her relationship with Jeff. But the couple was stronger now and recently married.

And yet couples split up all the time over much smaller issues.

The room fell into silence, and even when Kelly arrived, there were only nods of acknowledgment exchanged. Sasha's magazine sat discarded on the floor. Abby looked out the window, with Nathaniel by her side. Julie rocked slightly and Kelly paced.

They all nearly jumped when the door opened and a tousled-looking but smiling Jeff stepped inside.

"They're both okay." He wiped a tear away. "Ultrasound showed the baby is perfect."

Everyone started talking at once and Jeff held his hands up. "Hold on. Wait a minute. They're not completely out of the woods. There's an issue with the placenta, so Dena's on bed rest for the foreseeable future. And we're staying overnight, just as a precaution because of our history."

"Can we see her?" Sasha asked.

Jeff nodded. "They'll let two people at a time go back. Why don't you and Julie go see her?"

The two ladies went back to see Dena while Daniel gave Jeff a silent hug. Cole felt strangely out of place. It was an odd and unexpected feeling. He was used to infiltrating and fitting in any number of out-of-the-way or exotic locations. Yet here in a Wilmington, Delaware, hospital, he may as well have been on the moon.

The uneasiness lasted all the way back to his house, even with Sasha chatting away about Dena, how nice it was to see everyone, and pregnancy in general. The pregnancy chatter didn't ease his mind. It only brought back the arguments he'd had with Kate.

She seemed to pick up on his mood not far from the house. Her chatter slowed a little before ceasing completely. By the time they pulled into his driveway, she was silently gazing out the window.

Though it had been afternoon when they left, the sun had long since set at their return. Sasha quietly entered the house, looking back over her shoulder expectantly.

Damn. They were supposed to talk.

He sighed. "All things considered, Sasha, it's been a very trying afternoon and evening. I think it'd be for the best if we postponed our discussion until tomorrow."

"Yes, Sir."

"And I have work to catch up on. You can go on to bed. No need to wait up."

She gave him a resigned nod and simply said, "Good night, Sir," before heading up the stairs.

Cole watched her make her way upstairs and down the hall. Then he turned toward his office, where he knew no work would get done.

Sasha rolled over and peeked at the clock on Cole's nightstand. *Two.* She punched her pillow. And he hadn't made it upstairs yet.

Something had happened at the hospital. The man who drove her home wasn't the same one who had driven her there. It made sense he wanted to wait until the next day to talk. But the part of her that dreaded the conversation wanted to get it over with now.

If they didn't talk soon, she wasn't sure she'd have the determination to say and do what she needed to.

She'd had the realization at tea. When Evan had spoken to her the way he had, she flinched away. Even William with his kind smile hadn't been enough to sway her. She only wanted one man, one Master, one Sir. She only felt safe with Cole. Only Cole could ignite the submissive within her.

In other words, the retraining was an utter failure.

Should she tell him? Or would that lead him to bring in other Doms for her training? She didn't want that. Maybe she wouldn't tell him.

So far in the training, all he'd been able to do was ease her into trusting him. Submitting to him. If she reacted the way she did to Evan and William with Cole right next to her, how much worse would her reactions be without him there?

Today's tea party showed her she still had work to do when it came to submission. Cole had given her the tools to use—she just needed to work with those tools on a practical level. And, though she didn't want to admit it, without Cole nearby.

She didn't want to think about leaving Cole. Everything felt so right when she was with him. The way he cared for her, looked out for her, pleasured her, and, hell, even the way he punished her. She had a nagging suspicion that no Dom would ever live up to the high bar he'd set.

She kicked the sheets off her body. The bed just didn't feel right without him in it. Taking his pillow and hugging it tightly to her chest, she inhaled the comforting scent of him and fell into a listless sleep.

Though it felt like mere minutes, when she cracked an eye open, the clock read seven thirty. She stretched her arms above her head and decided she liked the soreness that followed an intense night of play over the achy stiffness insomnia brought. She also liked waking up next to Cole, but considering the untouched appearance of his side of the bed, he'd never made it upstairs.

He didn't come to her while she was meditating. When he first gave her instructions on meditating, he'd told her to kneel for fifteen minutes or until he came for her. Every morning before this one, he'd come for her. She stayed in place for twenty minutes just to be sure. By then she could no longer pretend she just needed to wait a bit longer. He wasn't coming this morning.

She rose slowly and saw he hadn't laid any clothes out for her, so after a quick shower, she walked down the stairs, naked, and found him out on the patio, reading.

She knelt at his feet. "Good morning, Sir."

Her chest ached, knowing there probably weren't going to be many more times she greeted him in such a manner. She closed her eyes and waited for him to stroke her head, but the touch never came.

"We need to talk, Sasha. But you need to get dressed and eat first."

His words didn't surprise her. Over the last two weeks, she'd quickly learned that their emotions and thoughts ran in parallel. From all appearances, he was experiencing the same doubts she had.

Five minutes later, she was dressed and back on the patio with him. He'd cooked her a bowl of oatmeal and topped it with the dried cranberries and walnuts she loved so much. Tears filled her eyes. He always thought of everything and missed nothing.

She wasn't hungry and played with her oatmeal instead of eating. Did she tell him she now realized the retraining hadn't done any good? She put the spoon down with a sigh.

"Are you okay?" he asked. "Sasha?"

She couldn't hold her turmoil inside anymore. She shoved her hands into her lap so he couldn't see her shake. "Yesterday at the tea party I realized something, and it scared me."

He waited patiently.

"I'm only strong enough to submit to you." She shook her head. "So, I don't think I should stay here any longer. I need to use the information and methods you gave me to prepare myself to serve others."

Because that had been the intent of the retraining—to prepare her to serve other Doms. Besides, Cole had said multiple times, he wasn't looking for anything serious.

His hands fisted on the table. "That's not what you were going to say before the tea party, was it?"

"No, Sir."

He swore under his breath. "Sasha, if I've deterred you from serving other Doms, you have to know that was never my intent."

"I know it wasn't. I think—I think the problem is you set the bar so high, no one else can come close to reaching it."

"Maybe you bring out the best in me."

She laughed, but it sounded strangled to her ears. "You did say once it would take a certain kind of Dom to handle me."

"I remember."

"You wanted to talk about something last night, too."

He waved his hand. "Not important." But his expression belied his words. "Do you want to finish out our two weeks, or would you prefer to go back home now?"

It took all her strength to look him in the eyes when she spoke the words that ripped her apart inside. "I want to go home."

"Are you sure? I could bring in some other Doms. Allow you to get a feel for someone else."

God, no. Anything but that. It was bad enough to think about submitting to someone else, but to do it in front him?

"Please. Let me go home."

Her apartment felt odd.

Not in the sense that someone had broken in or was in her apartment, but rather it was the *absence* of a particular person. She felt the difference as soon as she crossed the threshold, and it only intensified as the day went on.

Almost all of her time over the past week and a half had focused on him: his needs, his wants, and his preferences. Without that, she felt a bit incomplete. Her fingers itched with the need to write her thoughts down and after she'd scribbled out a page and a half of her feelings, she laughed.

He'd told her before that he wanted to weave his way into his submissive's mind and that's exactly what he'd done with her. Hell, look at her, she was writing!

She shook her head at the absurdity and picked up her knitting. Now that everything looked good for Jeff and Dena, she could finish her gift without hesitation.

She worked so intently that she accidentally dropped everything when her phone rang. Muttering a few choice words, she checked the display.

Cole.

Her heart pounded and her finger trembled as she answered. "Hello," she said.

"Hi, Sasha. It's me. Just wanted to make sure you made it home and got settled."

She fought the urge to tell him everything. If she was still at his house, she would have. But she wasn't, and she told herself not to act like she was.

"I'm home and trying to get settled." It was close enough to the truth. "Just different now."

"I imagine so. I'm here if you want to talk. Or maybe you should chat with Abby."

"That's a good idea. Or maybe Dena. I'd have a captive audience that way. It's not like she can get away, being on bed rest and all."

He chuckled. "True."

It was too strange talking to him on the phone. They should be in the same room. She should be kneeling at his feet and his hands should be in her hair.

Footsteps sounded outside, alerting her that someone was coming to see her. She sighed. Probably Julie.

"I think Julie's outside, I better go."

"I'll call you tomorrow, before the meeting?" he said and she felt she should tell him there was no need. He wasn't her Dom or even her trainer. But she wanted to hear his voice, especially before the meeting, so she agreed before they said their good-byes.

She opened the door before Julie could knock. "Hey, honey. I'm home," she said to her surprised friend.

"I thought I saw your car," Julie said, stepping inside. "Everything okay?"

Damn, she was tired of everyone asking that. "My goal is to one day have someone look at me and say, 'I don't even have to ask how you're doing, it's written all over your face.'"

"I only asked because you're back sooner than I thought you would be."

They sat down on the couch. Sasha took a pillow and hugged it to her body. "We covered everything we needed to."

Thankfully, Julie didn't comment on her vague reply, but she raised an eyebrow. "You're still wearing your training collar."

Sasha didn't want to think about that just yet. It would be hard enough to deal with tomorrow. "There's a brief meeting before the party. Cole's going to take it off then."

"What's it like, being a slave?"

"It's wild and decadent and raw. It's intense and scary and sensual. It's the hardest thing I've ever done, yet I'd do it again in a minute." She closed her eyes and allowed herself just a moment to remember how it'd felt.

She looked up to find Julie sitting absolutely still. "That good?"

"That great."

Julie started to talk, but stopped and stood. "I better get back downstairs. I just wanted to see you real quick."

Sasha dreaded the play party, but not nearly as much as she dreaded her meeting with Cole, where only a handful of members would be present. He called her an hour before, but she once again kept it short. He no longer had a need to know everything she was thinking and feeling. She was allowed to keep some things to herself. But she soon discovered keeping things to herself only made her stomach hurt.

Though she really didn't fathom what a stomachache was until she found herself kneeling once again before Cole in front of the other senior group members.

She bowed her head and tried not to think about how it would be the last time she'd do so. He stroked her hair, bringing his fingers down to lightly graze her cheek, and her heart hurt so much she almost couldn't breathe.

"You have done well, little one." His thumb caressed her cheekbone. "I therefore release you from training." The hand at her face dipped lower and undid the collar at her neck.

She felt its loss immediately, and had to force herself not to throw her hands up to put it back on. She heard Dena say once that when Jeff took his collar back, it was as if he sent her to prison. She hadn't understood at the time. Now she understood all too well.

"Stand up for me."

She slowly rose to her feet, wondering if he could sense her inner turmoil. But when she met his gaze, she only saw his.

"I hope I've served you as well as you've served me." He slipped the red plastic band marking her as a submissive onto her wrist and then dropped his head to whisper, "You are strong and sweet and sexy as hell. My fervent hope is that you find the one you're looking for and that he is worthy of you."

She swayed on her feet.

"Easy now," he said, holding out his hands to steady her.

"Thank you, Sir." She really didn't want to go to the party. She thought about going back home, but she wanted to be there even less. At least at the party she wouldn't be alone.

"I'm DM tonight. If you need anything, come see me."

"Thank you, Sir."

At least as DM he wouldn't be playing with anyone at the party. She wasn't sure she could stand to watch that. Of course, it was only a matter of time until she saw him with someone else. Maybe it would be better to get it out of the way now. Sort of like ripping off a Band-Aid. Make the break complete.

Cole looked over her shoulder and nodded. Seconds later, Daniel dismissed the meeting. And just like that, her time with Cole ended.

He gave her one long, last look and then left to attend to his duties. Sasha hugged herself and secretly hoped no one asked her to play. Tonight it would just be enough that she was here. She glanced around the room and made her way to Julie.

As she walked, she felt the weight of numerous stares, but she didn't even care. Not one of them was from *him*.

"You know," Julie said when she'd made it to her side, "I don't even have to ask how you're doing. It's written all over your face."

Sasha choked at hearing her words from the day before. "I meant for you to say that when I'm blissfully happy."

"There's one thing that would make that happen, and you just let him go."

"I had to. I was becoming more and more dependent on him."

"Dependency is one of the best things about a committed relationship."

Sasha crossed her arms. "*This* from the woman who has said nothing positive about me and Cole?"

Julie sucked in a breath like she'd been punched. "I deserved that. It's only, you didn't see him. It was written all over his face, too."

"What was?"

"How much it cost him to let you go."

Most of the time, Cole hated being DM at a party. Usually, he'd prefer to find a willing partner and spend a few hours indulging in hedonistic pleasure. Tonight, though, he didn't want just any willing partner, he wanted Sasha. Short of that, he'd gladly be DM.

The downside being, he found himself checking in on her every so often. And though he tried to tell himself he was only looking out for her best interest, he knew that wasn't the truth.

He walked back into the living room. Across the room, he saw Evan push back from the back wall and walk his way.

"Master Johnson," he said. "Can I talk with you for a minute?"

Cole nodded.

"Thought you'd be interested in knowing I asked Sasha to play."

Cole was unprepared for the possessive rage that shook his body. He actually had to hold on to the chair beside him so he didn't punch Evan in the face.

"Oh?" he managed to get out.

"I invited her to go with me to the garage. I thought she might be more comfortable there, since we wouldn't be alone."

Either it had been a short scene or she'd turned him down. Cole hoped for the latter. "What happened?"

"She thanked me for the offer, but said she had to turn me down." A mischievous grin covered his face. "She went on to say she couldn't play with anyone who didn't like hot tea. Said it was a hard limit."

Cole's laughter drew the attention of several people. Evan chuckled. "Yeah, I thought you'd get a kick out of that."

"She's a handful," Cole admitted.

Evan nodded toward Cole's right side. "William drank tea. Maybe he'll have a better chance."

Cole didn't want to, but glanced over his shoulder to where Master Greene talked with Sasha. "I'll go check it out," he told Evan.

The younger Dom slapped his back. "Have fun with that."

Cole crossed the room. William stood with his arms crossed, looking down at Sasha. She had a determined look on her face. *Uh oh.*

"Master Greene, Sasha, everything okay?" he asked.

"I came over to see if she'd be interested in playing," William said. "I'll let her tell you her reply."

Cole looked down at her and raised an eyebrow. "Sasha?"

She sighed. "I told him he could give me his checklist, I'd take it into consideration, and get back in touch with him sometime later this week. But that I knew he had a long-distance relationship and I didn't much feel like being number two on anyone's list."

Cole swallowed his laugh. "Even for someone who drinks hot tea?"

"Heard about that already, Sir?"

"Word travels fast."

"Yes, even for someone who drinks hot tea."

He looked up to find William had left. "You're chasing potential Doms away, Sasha."

"If they were worth my time, they wouldn't run."

Her words still rang in his ears over a week later as he drove to upstate New York, where he had a speaking engagement. He didn't feel that he was in the proper mind-set to speak, much less to the group of women he'd be addressing—Kate's hoity-toity women's club. He'd agreed to speak to the club over a year ago, when he and Kate were still together, about fifteenth-century England. It didn't seem right to cancel just because he wasn't with her anymore. Damn, he wished he'd canceled.

At least he could make the trip there and back in a day. If he left early enough and didn't mind getting back home in the dark. Of course, the long drive gave him too much time to think.

He second-guessed everything he had done with Sasha. Was he wrong to have given her a taste of a slave's life? Had that been what made her feel like she couldn't submit to anyone else?

He wanted to hate that she didn't feel comfortable being with someone else. He just couldn't bring himself to do it. Deep inside, he was secretly pleased. He didn't want to imagine her serving another Dom, much less witness it.

He kept repeating her words at the party. She was usually very direct, but did she mean *he* shouldn't have been chased away? Should he have insisted she stay?

After driving over four hours thinking about little else, he pulled into the driveway of the historical house with no answers. Kate saw him pull up and opened the door to meet him. It was just after ten and the meeting didn't start until eleven thirty, so now he got to spend over an hour with his ex. Great, just great.

"Kate," he said, shutting the car door.

"Hello, Cole, thanks for coming today."

She looked beautiful, as always. Perfectly put together, with nothing out of place. She would turn the head of any man with a heartbeat, but she did nothing for him. His fantasy involved a feisty brunette with short hair just the right length for his fingers to run through.

"Think nothing of it," he said.

She glanced behind him. "You're alone?"

"Yes."

"I thought Sasha would be with you."

Bloody hell, even hearing her name hurt. "Sasha is no longer my trainee."

"I didn't expect her to be here as your trainee."

It was bad enough he had to spend time alone with Kate, but he'd be damned if he was going to spend it talking to her about Sasha.

"We aren't going to have this conversation," he said.

In a move he recognized from seeing it for years, she tilted her head and studied him. Though they hadn't been together for months, they had years of shared history. She probably only had to look at him to see the truth.

"I have something I need to work on. Is there somewhere I can sit? Outside maybe?"

She waved toward the house. "There's a patio off the back with a table and chairs."

"Thanks," he said. "I'll be out there if you need me."

He carried his briefcase to the back patio and even took out some papers, but he didn't get anything accomplished. He read the same paragraph four times before giving up and standing to his feet.

The backyard of the house had been meticulously landscaped. He imagined the property booked for weddings and the like years in advance. Had it been a private residence, he could easily see the owners spending a lot of time outside. He took a deep breath, inhaling the scent of freshly cut grass. It brought to mind the afternoon she'd gotten him wet and he'd taken her against the tree.

It seemed like eons ago when it'd been so easy to picture her with him. What had changed? Their relationship had done nothing but grow stronger as they spent more time together. Fuck. He *had* allowed her to chase him off. He'd run away when he should have stayed and fought.

"Cole?" Kate's voice broke through his thoughts.

"Yes," he said, ready to think and talk about something else.

"I know you don't want to talk about it, but I have to know." Kate's eyes were curious. "It was different with Sasha, wasn't it?"

"What do you mean?" Of course it was different. Everything about him and Sasha had been different. He just didn't know it was that obvious to everyone else.

"Let me ask you this, when we were together and you did something for me, was it out of obligation or devotion?"

"What are you saying, Kate? Are you implying I wasn't devoted to you?"

"I'm saying I think you were more devoted to being a good Master than you were to me." She held up a hand to stop his protest. "It's not a bad thing, and it worked for us for a long time. But now looking back, I think I could have been anyone."

She stood up and walked to the edge of the patio. The light breeze ruffled her hair, blowing it away from her face, and he found no sadness in her expression. Even after the revelation she just made.

"When I was serving you, did you ever look at me and want to know more? Long to learn everything about me, breathe me in as if I was the air you needed to survive, please me because it brought you joy? Or did you learn what you needed to know as my Master, but no more? Please me because it was your duty?" She turned to face him fully. "I was never your air, Cole. You wanted a slave and I wanted a Master, but in the end it wasn't enough for me. The baby situation was the final nail."

He felt like he'd been punched in the gut because he knew, *he knew* she was right. "Kate, I'm sorry."

She waved her hand, dismissing his apology. "It's okay. You weren't my air, either. I wanted you to be, I tried to make you, but I finally realized you can't force it. That's the real reason I left. I want to need someone as much as they need me. And that's why she was different for you."

She held his gaze for several beats of his heart, and when she started to speak, he knew exactly what she would say. Knew it because he felt the truth threatening to choke him.

"Sasha's your air, Cole."

Sasha frowned at the ringing of the doorbell. It was Sunday, so the shop was closed. Julie would have called. She didn't want to talk to anyone, she was working tomorrow and that would be soon enough. If she ignored it, maybe whoever it was would go away. Or maybe it was Cole? Her heart raced and with a trembling hand, she flung the door open.

It was Abby.

"Oh, Abby." She couldn't keep the disappointment out of her voice. "Come on in."

"I'm sorry. I know I'm not who you wanted to see. But since I wasn't at the play party, I wanted to make sure we talked."

Sasha led her inside and they sat on her couch. She really didn't feel like talking about Cole, because she knew once she did, it'd be expected for her to find another Dom to play with. And that wasn't happening anytime soon. If ever.

But Abby didn't ask her anything. She leaned forward. "Nathaniel and I were together as Dominant and submissive when we first met. It was sex only. No feelings. Nothing."

Sasha's eyes widened. She hadn't heard of their courtship. They didn't date first. That was surprising. Especially considering how crazy in love they were now.

"I'm not going to sugarcoat anything. He was an ass. I won't go into details about how, because that's in the past. All you need to know is he was an ass. He hurt me emotionally, and I left him. Took his collar off in front of him, put it on the table, and walked out."

"Wow."

"We didn't speak after that for months. In fact, I'm not sure we would have ever spoken again except my best friend married his cousin." Abby shook her head, remembering. "But they got married and Nathaniel was best man and I was maid of honor."

"I'm guessing you two worked it out?"

"We did. The thing I want you to know is men can be assholes. Even the best of men. Even the Dominant men. Maybe especially the Dominant ones. Because they think they're protecting us or doing what's best for us. And all they're doing is breaking our hearts."

Sasha raised an eyebrow. "Has Cole spoken to Nathaniel?"

"No." Abby shook her head. "At least, not that I know of. I heard Cole had a speech to give at some women's club, but that's all. I just know how men are and I know Cole. If he thought it'd be in your best interest to be without him, he'd let you go even if it killed him."

"Even if it made him look like an ass?"

"I'm not saying he's acted like one. Just that men don't always think clearly when emotions are involved."

"I don't get it, though. He was with Kate for years."

"Don't assume you know how that relationship went. Just because they were together for years, even in a twenty-four/seven relationship, doesn't mean they were the loves of each other's lives."

"But eight *years*."

Abby shook her head again. "Doesn't mean anything. It might have been they thought it easier to stay together than to find someone new. Although in this case, I know children came into the picture."

"Cole has a child?" Hell, she didn't know him at all.

"No, that was the problem. He didn't tell you? Kate wanted kids and he didn't. Or doesn't."

"Oh." That was interesting. She wondered why it never came up that he didn't want kids. Especially with her knitting on the floor by his feet. He'd never said anything.

"I guess the fact that he didn't tell me speaks volumes."

Abby wrinkled her forehead. "What do you mean?"

"If the kid thing meant so much to him and I meant so much to him, he would have told me. The fact that he didn't tell me leads me to believe he didn't care so much for me."

"Now, that's where you'd be wrong, little one."

She thought she'd imagined it, but just in case, she looked to the door and gasped.

He stood in her doorway with a huge grin on his face. "You really should lock your door. It's not safe to leave it otherwise." He nodded toward Abby. "Abby."

"Hey, Cole," Abby said.

Sasha was still staring at him like he'd descended from a UFO. Cole was here. In her apartment. "Cole," she said. "What are you . . . why?"

He walked farther into the room. "Abby, if you don't mind, I'd like to speak to Sasha privately. Matter of fact, I'll make you a deal. If you let us talk privately, I won't tell Nathaniel about the asshole speech."

"Please." She waved her hand. "Nathaniel *wrote* the asshole speech."

Cole lifted an eyebrow.

"Okay, okay." Abby stood up. "I'm out of here. Call me, Sasha. And you." She pointed to Cole. "You were picked for a reason. Live up to it."

"I will," Cole said. "Now out."

Sasha couldn't keep her eyes off him, afraid if she looked away that he'd disappear. But he wasn't saying anything.

"Why are you here?" she whispered.

"The short answer is, I'm not letting you chase me away."

Her breath caught. "What?"

"I'm a Dom worthy of your time." He took three steps in her direction. "So I'm not letting you chase me away. I don't care how long it takes or what I have to do. I'm going to prove I'm the man able to Master you."

She got up and stopped when she stood in front of him. Not quite close enough to touch. "What made you change your mind?"

"I thought it wouldn't be right for me to ask you to only be with me. That I'd be somehow cheating you out of something if you didn't experience more than what I offered." His expression grew serious and he looked unsure for the first time. "But I love you, Sasha, and if you might perhaps feel the same about me, I think maybe it doesn't matter that you experience other Dominants."

He loved her?

She couldn't contain her silly grin. He loved her.

"I love you, too," she whispered. "And no, it doesn't. It doesn't mean I'm not strong if I only want to be with you. It just means I only want to be with you. I'm sorry I didn't understand sooner, and I'm sorry if I made you feel like you failed me."

"And I'm sorry I let my fears and doubts get the best of me." He closed the distance between them and cupped her face. "You are more than just strong, you're strong enough for both of us."

She entwined her fingers in his. "I can't imagine you're afraid of anything. What do you fear?"

"Abby was right. I don't want kids. Ever. It was one of the things that ended my relationship with Kate. I should have told you sooner, but since I wouldn't allow myself to think of a future with you, I didn't see why I should."

"Cole, I—"

"Wait," he said. "Let me finish. You're my air, I need you, and if you want kids, well, we'll somehow work it out. But I'm not going to let that keep us apart." His smile eased the hurt in her heart. "You're more than my air, you're my sun, and my moon, and when I'm weary and tired, you're my shelter." He lowered his head so their foreheads touched. "Let me be the same to you."

She lifted her head and her wet cheeks brushed his chin. "I love you, Cole. I want to live with you and for you and by your side and at your feet. And not having kids doesn't bother me."

"You may change your mind one day."

"And purple aliens may invade Earth, but I'm not going to let the possibility of something that might happen in the future take away my happiness in the present."

"You humble me. How you accept so much of me. Everyone else has always tried to change me." He ran his knuckles across her cheekbone. "You're amazing. Has anyone ever told you?"

"No, Sir."

He nearly growled at the *Sir*. "Bloody hell, Sasha."

She couldn't reply because he pulled her into his arms and settled his mouth over hers in a kiss that had her entire body begging for more. His mouth was hungry and urgent and she parted her lips to taste him. He trailed his fingers down her spine. She brought her hands to his waist. She wanted to feel him.

He pulled back. "Wait."

"Why?" She could have groaned in frustration.

"Trust me."

"Always."

"Before I take you again, I want to show you something I found on my way back from my speaking engagement."

She tried to think of what he could want to show her that would take precedence over where she thought the kiss was leading.

"You wrinkle your nose when you're trying to understand something. Did you know that?"

"I do?"

"Yes." He kissed the tip of her nose. "It makes me smile."

She brought her hands up to his chest and started unbuttoning his shirt. "I'm glad it makes you smile. Now will you show me the thing you found so we can get back to the kissing part?"

"So impatient, little one."

He was being an awful tease. "You're in my apartment. We're alone. And my bedroom is right down the hall. Give me one reason not to be impatient."

"You underestimate me. I'll give you five: One, because I said so. Two, I love you. Three, I want you. Four, I want everyone to know you're mine. And five," He slipped his hand into his pocket and withdrew a slender box. "I want you in my collar. And not a training one this time."

She stared at the box as tears filled her eyes. "Oh, my God."

"Sasha?"

It was too much. Him coming to her apartment and saying he loved her and then offering her his collar. It was all her best days wrapped up together in one. Emotion welled up in her throat and she buried her face in her hands right as a sob escaped her throat.

"Don't weep, little one."

"I just, it's only . . ." She looked up. "I never imagined."

"And I can't imagine anything else. Will you wear it?"

She bit her bottom lip. She wanted so badly to say yes, but knew better than to let excitement overrule her common sense. "If I agree to wear it, will I be your submissive or your slave?"

"As long as you're mine, I'm flexible as to how we work." His fingertip traced her collarbone. "Which would you prefer?"

His response was everything she wanted it to be. "I enjoyed being your submissive, but it was being your slave that made me complete."

He tilted his head. "I'm hesitant to collar you as a slave right now, but I think we could start out in a structured, daily Dominant/submissive role and work toward Master/slave."

"I'd like that." She put her arms around his neck. "Will I live here or at your place?"

"I want you at my place as often as possible, but there's no reason for you not to keep the apartment. I doubt you want a stranger living above your shop."

Suddenly she didn't see herself living in the apartment for much longer. She wanted to be with him every night, every morning, for always.

"Yes, Sir, I'll wear your collar with pride. Please."

He opened the box and took out a necklace that left her breathless. The collar was made of interlocking links of white gold, black ceramic, and diamonds. "I knew the moment I saw it. It carries a unique sensuality that reminds me of you."

"I've never seen anything more beautiful."

There were no words spoken as she caught his eye and slid gracefully to the ground. Only when she felt the floor beneath her knees did she drop her gaze.

He ran his fingers through her hair and whispered, "I have."

The collar carried the warmth of his skin as he put it around her neck. Her eyes closed against the swelling rush of emotion gathering within her. His fingers lingered around her collarbone.

"I vow to always be worthy of you," he said as the collar clicked into place. "Stand up for me, Sasha."

She rose on shaky legs, feeling the heaviness of his collar around her neck while at the same time feeling weightless and light. "I hope I always please you."

He took her hand and pulled her close. "Never doubt for a minute how much you please me." He smiled as he looked in her eyes. "Your eyes sparkle and no longer look lost and uncertain. Your smile is sincere and makes me smile in response. And the way you carry yourself shows an inner strength that is sexy as fucking hell. There isn't a part of you that doesn't please me."

She could truly get used to this—but somehow, she didn't think she ever would.

"Except," he said and her breath caught. There was something that didn't please him?

"Your clothes," he continued. "You're wearing them and they'd please me more on the floor."

She laughed, remembering how he told her to expect to be off balance with him. And as she slipped her shirt over her head, she knew there was no other way she'd want it.

Epilogue

Abby
One week later

I pulled up to Cole's house and found the new couple holding hands while looking over the expansive front yard. I couldn't help but smile. If Cole thought he'd turned a few heads in the group by agreeing to train Sasha in twenty-four/seven service, he didn't want to hear the phone calls Nathaniel had fielded when he collared her.

Fortunately, Nathaniel knew exactly how to put people in their place without them even knowing he'd done it. "I'm not sure what they think I'm going to say or do," he said after one such call. "I mean, I collared you not over a week after we officially met. And we hadn't even slept together."

"You probably shouldn't hold that up as preferred practice," I teased.

He laughed and pulled me into his lap, mumbling about how he preferred to practice a little something different at the moment.

The memory left me all smiles as I hopped out of the car and waved. From all appearances and based on my talks with Sasha, she was doing and living exactly the way she should. She rose up on her toes, kissed Cole, and then jogged over to me.

"Hey, Abby. Cole and I were just going over what we wanted to do with the yard in the spring." She didn't wait for a response, but motioned me to follow her into the house. "I asked you to come over to look at something. We were in the attic a few days ago. We were supposed to be cleaning it out, but Cole got inspired by the exposed beams and then he found some rope and, well . . ."

"I've cleaned out an attic or two in my day," I assured her.

"The previous owner's left so much stuff up there." She led me to the living room. "Anyway, once we stopped fooling around, we went through some old trunks we found. I opened one that had a ton of books in it and, of course, I thought of you."

An old trunk sat in the middle of the living room. My fingers itched to open it and look inside.

"Is that it?" I asked.

"Yes, and Cole said he'd put it in your car, but first I wanted to show you these."

I looked at the items spread out on the table. "Magazines?"

"Yes."

I picked one up. "Why?" It was a fashion magazine from over fifteen years ago. The cover model was pretty, but her look was dated. *Wait.* I squinted my eyes. "Is that who I think it is?"

"Your boss, Meagan," Sasha confirmed. "And get this. Check out the photo credit."

My eyes drifted to the tiny print at the bottom of the cover. "Holy fucking shit."

"That's him, isn't it? I remember Cole saying he did photography on the side."

"Luke DeVaan. That's him all right."

"So, now we know part of the story," Sasha said. "And I'm willing to bet this is just the tip of the iceberg."

Also available from
New York Times bestselling author

TARA SUE ME

TARA SUE ME

THE
SUBMISSIVE

THE WORLDWIDE PHENOMENON
Before there was **Fifty Shades of Grey**...

Abby King yearns to experience a world of pleasure
beyond her simple life as a librarian—and the brilliant and
handsome CEO Nathaniel West is the key to making her
dark desires a reality. But as Abby falls deep into
Nathaniel's tantalizing world of power and passion, she
fears his heart may be beyond her reach—and that her
own might be beyond saving...

headline
ETERNAL

TARA SUE ME

THE
DOMINANT

THE WORLDWIDE PHENOMENON
Before there was **Fifty Shades of Grey**...

Nathaniel West doesn't lose control. But then he meets
Abby King. Her innocence and willingness is intoxicating,
and he's determined to make Abby his. But when
Nathaniel begins falling for Abby on a deeper level, he
realizes that trust must go both ways—and he has secrets
which could bring the foundations of their relationship
crashing down...

headline
ETERNAL

TARA SUE ME

THE
TRAINING

THE WORLDWIDE PHENOMENON
Before there was **Fifty Shades of Grey**...

It started with desire. Now a weekend arrangement
of pleasure has become a passionate romance.
Still, there remains a wall between Nathaniel West and
Abby King. Abby knows the only way to lead Nathaniel
on a path to greater intimacy is to let him deeper into
her world than anyone has ever gone before...

headline
ETERNAL

TARA
SUE ME
The Chalet

From the *New York Times* bestseller
A SUBMISSIVE NOVELLA

Submitting her body was only the beginning.
Abby King didn't know true passion until she gave herself to
Nathaniel West, one of New York City's most eligible
bachelors and desired Dominants. Now, on the eve of her
marriage, she realizes all her dreams are coming true.
And with a romantic honeymoon getaway planned at a
secluded Swiss chalet, she's sure Nathaniel will find
even more fantasies to fulfill...

headline
ETERNAL

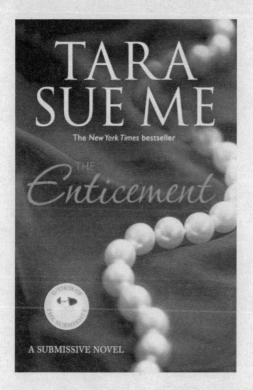

TARA SUE ME

The *New York Times* bestseller

THE

Enticement

AUTHOR OF THE SUBMISSIVE

A SUBMISSIVE NOVEL

Abby West has everything she wanted: a family,
a skyrocketing new career, and a sexy, Dominant husband
who fulfills her every need. Only, as her life outside the
bedroom becomes hectic, her Master's sexual requirements
inside become more extreme. As the underlying tension
and desire between them heats up, so does the struggle
to keep everything they value from falling apart...

headline
ETERNAL

Desperate to escape the pressures of her carefully controlled life, Dena Jenkins joined a BDSM club as a submissive. There she met brooding Dominant, Jeff, and they couldn't stay away from each other. But their blazing connection has proven difficult to maintain and resulted in a history they'd rather forget. To save their passion, Dena and Jeff will have to rediscover what it means to trust—and give themselves to each other completely...

headline
ETERNAL

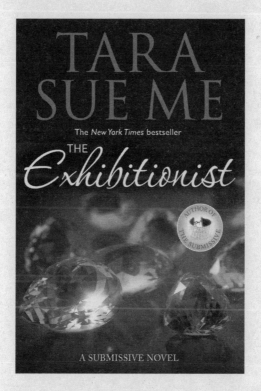

TARA SUE ME

The *New York Times* bestseller

THE Exhibitionist

AUTHOR OF THE SUBMISSIVE

A SUBMISSIVE NOVEL

She's ready for even more... When Abby West discovered her submissive desires, she felt like she was born anew. But lately, her Dominant husband hasn't been the demanding Master who once fulfilled her every passion. Their new BDSM group has invited Nathaniel to guide them to a new level, and he's promised to show them the way. Only this time, uncovering their sexual limits may also expose their relationship to more conflict than it can withstand...

headline
ETERNAL

TARA SUE ME

FROM THE
NEW YORK TIMES
BESTSELLING AUTHOR
OF THE SUBMISSIVE
TRILOGY

SEDUCED
BY FIRE

Julie Masterson craves a taste of danger. And once she meets the seductive Senior VP of Weston Bank Daniel Covington, she's drawn into a titillating new world of passion. As their sizzling connection heats up, the dangerous side of their liaison rears its ugly head, and Julie must decide if she trusts Daniel enough to surrender completely—or if she should escape before she gets burned...

headline
ETERNAL

headline
ETERNAL

FIND YOUR HEART'S DESIRE...

VISIT OUR WEBSITE: www.headlineeternal.com
FIND US ON FACEBOOK: facebook.com/eternalromance
FOLLOW US ON TWITTER: @eternal_books
EMAIL US: eternalromance@headline.co.uk